Melissa K. Roehrich is a dark fantasy romance author who loves coffee, dragons, and constantly rearranging her bookshelves. She spends her time writing, reading, and homeschooling her three boys in the Middle-of-Nowhere, North Dakota, where she lives with her boys, husband, three dogs, multiple barn cats, and chickens on a small farmstead. She is constantly trying to convince her husband they need to add goats and ducks to the mix, and one day, she'll succeed.

LADY OF DARKNESS SERIES
Lady of Darkness
Lady of Shadows
Lady of Ashes
Lady of Embers
Lady of Starfire
Winds of Darkness

THE LEGACY SERIES
Rain of Shadows and Endings
Storm of Secrets and Sorrow
Tempest of Wrath and Vengeance
Dawn of Chaos and Fury

Winds of Darkness

Melissa K. Roehrich

ONE PLACE. MANY STORIES

HQ
An imprint of HarperCollins*Publishers* Ltd
1 London Bridge Street
London SE1 9GF

www.harpercollins.co.uk

HarperCollins*Publishers*
Macken House, 39/40 Mayor Street Upper
Dublin 1, D01 C9W8, Ireland
This edition 2025

1
The Reaper first published in Great Britain
by Melissa K. Roehrich 2022
Unrelenting Winds first published in Great Britain
by Melissa K. Roehrich 2024

Copyright © Melissa K. Roehrich 2022 and 2024

Melissa K. Roehrich asserts the moral right to be identified as the author of this work.
A catalogue record for this book is available from the British Library.

ISBN: 9780008743475

Set in Goudy Oldstyle Std by HarperCollins*Publishers* India

This novel is entirely a work of fiction. The names, characters and incidents portrayed in it are the work of the author's imagination. Any resemblance to actual persons, living or dead, events or localities is entirely coincidental.

All rights reserved. No part of this publication may be reproduced, stored in a retrieval system, or transmitted, in any form or by any means, electronic, mechanical, photocopying, recording or otherwise, without the prior permission of the publishers.

Without limiting the exclusive rights of any author, contributor or the publisher of this publication, any unauthorized use of this publication to train generative artificial intelligence (AI) technologies is expressly prohibited. HarperCollins also exercise their rights under Article 4(3) of the Digital Single Market Directive 2019/790 and expressly reserve this publication from the text and data mining exception.

Printed and bound in the UK using 100% Renewable
Electricity by CPI Group (UK) Ltd

For more information visit: www.harpercollins.co.uk/green

A COUPLE THINGS

Before you dive into Rayner's story, *The Reaper*, please know that his novella is dark. It is darker than any of the other *Darkness* books have been. Please make sure you check the trigger warnings. If you're okay with that, I hope you love learning how Rayner became the Fire Court Third.

While Briar and Ashtine's story, *Unrelenting Winds*, takes place before the events of the Lady of Darkness Series, it is recommended you read it after reading *Lady of Starfire* to avoid series spoilers. If you choose to read it before the Lady of Darkness series, please understand that Briar and Ashtine are side characters in the Darkness series. You will see them again in the Darkness Series.

Trigger Warnings
Your mental health matters. This book contains descriptive violence and references to SA and resulting trauma. For a full list of possible triggers, please visit my website at https://www.melissakroehrich.com under Book Extras.

For those who are slowly going mad trying to meet the expectations of the world of around them, it's okay to find joy in something just for you.

THE REAPER

PROLOGUE

He waited until Moranna was sleeping. He always did. They had been doing this dance for nearly three years now, ever since he had learned he had sisters.

Two of them.

One full-blooded. One half.

She was pretending she didn't know what he had found out. He was pretending he didn't know she knew.

Rayner slid from the bed. Moranna's naked form didn't move. The white sheet was draped low, exposing her olive skin. Black hair with vibrant red streaks throughout fanned across the pillow. He hadn't been asked to fuck her tonight, but he would have. Anything to keep her focus on him rather than his sisters. She never forced him, as if she were some benevolent master over all of them. As if they were given such a choice.

Wise choices.

That's what she always encouraged them to make.

He'd declined the first few times she'd asked him to come to her bed, finding the idea . . . awkward to say the least.

He had just been assigned as one of her personal guards after over two decades of training. Two decades of learning to wield ashes as weapons. Two decades of learning to move among the smallest amount of smoke. Two decades of violence and brutality and helping to keep those beneath him in check. It was the natural order of things. He was one of the most powerful Fae on the Southern Islands. Power dictated status. There were few above him, which is why he had been promoted to one of the Baroness's personal guards. He hadn't realized that included serving her in *every* way.

But the first time he'd declined her invitation to her bed, he'd spent the night in a cold sweat. He hadn't slept at all. Anxiety and fear had clawed at him throughout the darkest hours of the day. There wasn't anything in particular that had him pacing around his windowless quarters. He was one of the few Fae who had more than a small bedchamber, but none of the spaces had windows. Not when they were housed inside enchanted cliffs. A colony hidden away from the world for their own protection. If others discovered what kind of power they had, they would want it for themselves. The Baroness kept them protected and safe.

That's what he had been taught to believe.

The second time he had declined her invitation, he'd spent the entire night paranoid that someone had found them. He'd wandered around the various levels of the cliffs like a madman. Not wanting to tell anyone about what was going on and appear weak, he had performed his daily duties without any reprieve the next day.

A few days later, the Baroness had requested he accompany her into one of the producing rooms. He'd never been in one. One of the few rooms he did not have unlimited access to. He'd followed the Baroness up her private endless staircase, her red gown swishing around her ankles. She'd looked back over her shoulder at him, a coy smile he wasn't sure what to do with on her lips, before she held her palm to the door. He'd felt the wards fall, recognizing her touch, and she'd beckoned him to follow her in. When he did, he'd fallen still. There was a young Fae cowering in a corner, tears streaming down her face. She could scarcely be past her first bleeding. She certainly hadn't entered her Staying yet. Her golden hair was a mess, and she was in a nightgown, not the usual white linen shirts and pants everyone wore in the cliffs. Her icy blue eyes were wide and full of terror. A male stood off to the side, arms at his sides, wearing only loose-fitting pants.

"I've tried, your Grace," he'd said, his eyes fixed on the ground.

"I know you have, Tyrion," the Baroness had replied sympathetically. "Unfortunately, we need her wind magic, or she would be assigned elsewhere."

The male had said nothing in response, just stood waiting, his eyes never leaving the floor.

The Baroness had moved forward, crouching down before the female. The young Fae had scrambled back, pressing into the corner. "Please, your Grace. Please do not make me do this."

"But you *want* to do this, my dear," she'd coaxed softly, reaching out and brushing back a strand of hair from the girl's face. Her red-painted nail slid along her jaw until she pressed it beneath her chin, tilting her head up. "My sweet child, I need that wind magic to be shared with Tyrion. You desire that too, don't you?"

"I . . ." She'd faltered, her brow furrowing. She'd shaken her head as if coming out of a trance. "No. I do not want this."

Rayner had watched as the Baroness's lips tipped up into a pleased smile. "You are strong as well. Good," she'd purred. Faster than Rayner could track, the Baroness was gripping the female's jaw, and the girl let out a whimper. He'd forced himself to stay rooted to the spot. "You will do this, Catelyn. And for your insolence, you will not enjoy it, even though Tyrion would have made sure you did. But now you have lost such a privilege. Perhaps next time, you will make wiser choices."

Rayner felt fear and torment and . . . *lust* ripple in the room. He shouldn't feel any power in this room. The walls were made of shirastone to stop Fae from using their power.

Then again, it never stopped him from riding among the ashes.

But the power ripple was not what shocked him. It was that it came from the Baroness. He had always known she was powerful, despite never knowing what her actual gifts were. How else would she maintain control over the hundreds of Fae on these islands? He knew now. The Baroness could manipulate emotions.

She'd stood, staring down at the young female. "But Catelyn?"

"Y-yes, your Grace?" she'd stammered, her gaze fixed on the floor.

"If there is a next time, you will face punishment at the hands of my Ash Rider."

The young female had paled even more, her eyes darting to Rayner, who could only stand there. Just as rumors swirled of the Baroness's power and how you did not wish to be on the receiving end of it, rumors swirled of his own abilities. Some true. Some false. All manipulated by the female who ruled over them.

As Rayner had followed the Baroness out of the room, he'd glimpsed Tyrion moving towards the girl. He'd quickly pulled the door shut behind them. As it clicked into place, the wards reconnecting, the Baroness had turned to face him.

"Will you come to my bed tonight, Rayner?"

He'd known then that she had been the one to torment him for refusing her. He knew if he refused again, next time would be even worse. "Of course, your Grace," he'd said gruffly.

She'd reached up, patting his cheek. "It is good to see you making wiser choices."

That was the first time he'd questioned if the Baroness truly desired to keep them safe. He'd never had any reason to believe otherwise until that moment. Why would he? Not when it had been ingrained in him as a youngling that they were only safe because of her. They were blessed by the gods to live away from the rest of the wretched world.

But even on the nights he was not *asked* to fuck her, he slept in her bed. Her "personal guard." That's what she called him anyway. Always by her side.

Her Ash Rider.

He still had his own quarters where his clothing and few personal items were kept, but he only went there to bathe these days. It had only been a year later that he'd discovered he had kin in these cliffs. Then his submission became more about keeping them safe rather than about trying to maintain his own comfort. Ever since that day Moranna had taken him to that producing room, he'd started noticing more and more things. Things that never seemed odd before but now made him uncomfortable. How some younglings seemed to simply disappear. They'd always been told their gifts had emerged and that they'd been assigned to their posts as was custom. But he'd started watching, consciously looking. They were never seen again. Then there were some males and females who looked at the world with dead, vacant eyes. They seemed to see through everyone and rarely spoke. He'd discovered they were all assigned to the producing rooms. He'd dug and dug and learned what happened in those rooms. Eventually he'd learned exactly what the Baroness was trying to do, why they were all here. It was during all this digging he'd come across his own records and learned he had siblings.

Breya and Aravis. Five and seven years of age when he learned of them. Aravis was his full-blooded sister. His mother had apparently died giving birth to her. According to the records, their father had also been a powerful fire Fae. It was his mother who had carried the Ash Rider blood though. There had been other notes written beside his mother's history, but it had been written in a language he could not read. His father had sired Breya with another powerful fire Fae, the female required to drink a tonic of some sort for the duration of her pregnancy. All of this forced in the hopes of his sisters emerging with the Ash Rider gift.

It had taken him two weeks to figure out where they were being held. He'd finally found them in a small room tucked down a side hall on one of the mid-levels. They had been huddled together on a pallet of straw, no fire in the empty hearth. Aravis had black hair like his own and grey eyes. They did not swirl like his did, but his had not started doing that until his gifts had emerged. Breya also had grey eyes, but she had vibrant red hair and freckles smattered across her nose and cheeks. Both girls had shrunk back from him when he'd entered the room.

It took three days before they came near him. It took another few weeks before they began to trust him. Breya was more curious and took to him faster than Aravis did. In time, he'd learned that they were kept in such a dismal state in the hopes that their power would emerge sooner in a bid for survival.

He'd decided then and there he was going to get them out. The simple fact that they had Ash Rider blood meant they were likely destined for the producing rooms. He had often wondered why he had never been sent to one of those rooms yet. It wasn't as if he could ask Moranna. Then she would know what he'd learned.

Moranna.

That was the Baroness's true name. Not that he ever called her that. He had found it written in a letter addressed to her when he'd been searching among her things while she'd bathed one day. The letter had been from someone named Alaric. He'd never learned who that was, but the letter had been written in that same language he had not been taught.

For nearly three years he had bowed to her every whim, had followed orders and carried out her wishes. And for nearly three years, when she slept deeply, he'd slip from her bed. He'd find his sisters, who had been moved to more comfortable accommodations when they had been unable to force their magic to surface. After he'd check on them, he'd disappear among his smoke and ashes beyond the cliff walls and plan how to get them out. He'd visited the main continent, mapped out places they could hide. He'd prepared every last detail all for this night. The night he would take his sisters and leave these godsforsaken islands forever.

Rayner moved silently through the passageways and down the three flights of white stone stairwells to the level where his rooms were located. He'd had small packs ready for weeks so that when the time came, it was one less thing for him to worry about. The packs held a change of clothing for each of them, dried fruit and nuts, small waterskins, and light blankets. Just enough to get them to a location across the island where more supplies were stored. He'd collected funds over the years, enough to pay one of the merchant ships to smuggle the three of them off the islands.

He hadn't told his sisters they were close to being able to leave, not wanting to get their hopes up in case something went wrong and he had to delay things. Their powers still lying dormant was a blessing from the gods, to be honest. The wards around the cliffs picked up magical signatures. They wouldn't have any, and he'd been working his way around them for years. No, the hardest part of this would be getting them out of the cliffs themselves because he could not carry others in his ashes and smoke. They would have to walk out the main entrance that was always monitored by no less than five sentries.

He already knew who was on guard duty tonight. Five sentries who liked to visit the mid-level rooms where the "power vessels" were held. The most powerful Fae who were forced to mate in the hopes of producing even more powerful offspring. "Practice for the producing rooms" the sentries would always chuckle crudely, winking at Rayner on their way by.

He would have no issues sacrificing them tonight. He wouldn't carry guilt for them, unlike some of the other lives he'd been forced to take by Moranna. It didn't matter that he'd had to follow orders to keep others safe, to keep his sisters safe. Those kills still left their marks deep on his soul.

He fished out the packs where he had them stashed into the sleeves of a heavy tunic in the back of his closet. Smoke and ashes swirled around them, taking them to a pocket realm so they wouldn't need to worry about carrying them. He strapped extra daggers to his belt, sliding two more down his boots. A sword was strapped across his back. He swung a cloak around his shoulders, grabbing two smaller ones he'd stashed in the closet as well, before he silently stepped from the room, closing the door softly behind him.

No one would question seeing him in the halls. They wouldn't dare. Not the Baroness's personal guard. No one would say anything as he escorted two younglings throughout the levels. No one would likely bat an eye until he had the girls on the main level, heading for the passageway that would lead out to the beach.

They were older now. Breya was seven, and Aravis was nearly

ten, but not nearly old enough to fully understand what was going on. He would get them out, and they could have normal childhoods for what remained of them. Their power could emerge naturally. They would never know hunger or discomfort again. He had shelter secured in the Water Court until he could find a way to obtain a portal to the Fire Court. The girls would both emerge with fire gifts when it came time, so the Fire Court was the obvious choice to make a home. He'd only managed to get to the Fire Court a handful of times in his scouting, but he could already picture their faces when they saw the Twilight Fires on the Tana River for the first time. Breya would giggle in delight. And Aravis? She would smile. A real one. One he had never seen on her face before.

He would tell them of his travels, of the things he had seen beyond the cliff walls. Breya would grow bored rather quickly at her young age. He would let ashes drift through the air for her to chase and play with. But Aravis? She would always ask him to describe the world. The sea. The night sky. Birds and fish and deer. But mostly, she wanted to hear about the sun. About how it gilded the world in light. How it warmed your face. How it rose and set every day, telling the realm when it was day and night.

At dawn, she would see the sun crest the horizon for the first time.

A small smile graced his lips at the thought. He rarely smiled here. Never had a reason to. Perhaps that would change too.

He came to the door of the small room that they had been sharing for the past three months, the wards recognizing his touch as most rooms beneath the cliffs did. He pushed it open, anticipating Breya's excited squeal that came from her every night when he showed up, but what he found made his blood run cold.

Moranna sat cross-legged on one of the small beds. She wore a red gown with deep slits up the sides, the dress dipping just as low in the front. Her black hair flowed down around her shoulders, the red streaks glinting in the candles lit throughout the small space.

"Rayner," she said with a pout on her red-tinted lips. "I am so disappointed in your poor choices."

"Your Grace," he said, immediately bowing.

The Baroness braced her hands behind her, leaning back on them as her dark eyes surveyed him. "There is no need for pretending, Rayner. Not anymore." He stiffened, standing upright once more. Her lips were curved up in a pointed, malicious smile. "The young ones' gifts emerged today." Her smile morphed into a pout. "So incredibly disappointing. Basic fire gifts. Both of them. One would think with your blood in her veins, the oldest would have at least had a drop of Ash Rider magic. And the younger one? Scarcely magic at all. Mere sparks."

"Where are they?" Rayner demanded, his voice a deadly growl that had Moranna sitting up straighter.

Her eyes narrowed on him. "I would advise you to make wise choices in this moment, Rayner."

"Where are they?" he repeated.

"They have been assigned to their duties, as all Fae in the colony are when they emerge."

"Where are they?" he bellowed, ashes falling from his hands. Hands that were shaking so violently, he couldn't control it.

A faint smile reappeared on Moranna's mouth. "The oldest will be assigned as a power vessel in the hopes that something can still come of that Ash Rider blood. The youngest, however, has been assigned to board the ferries, as she will not be able to contribute anything to the colony."

Rayner was spinning on his heel before the Baroness had finished speaking. He didn't bother with the stairs, moving among the smoke of the sconces that lined the various levels , feeling the grey wisps brush along his being as he went. His boots landed on the stone ground of the main level a minute later, and he was running. There was a door at the back of this chamber. A door he only entered when Moranna required him to end life, usually of those who had committed crimes against the colony. The bodies were loaded onto boats that followed the small stream that ran through the cliffs out to the beach where others were assigned to dispose of them, usually those with fire or earth gifts. But to kill a child?

Simply because she would not be powerful? She could do *something* when she was older. But death?

Icy horror washed through him as realization sank into him. The Fae—the *children*—who would disappear, assigned to duties outside the cliffs. They had all been killed for simply not being powerful enough. For not being born with the gifts the Baroness desired. Who would carry out those types of orders?

But he would have a few years ago. No questions asked if the Baroness had told him it was required to keep them safe. Fuck, maybe he had, and she just hadn't told him the truth about those he had killed. She had never ordered him to kill a child, but would he have questioned her?

He had to believe he would have said no because if not . . .

But he hadn't said no to any of the orders he'd been given to hand out death. The sword strapped down his back had innocent blood on it. His gifts had been used to maim and destroy and kill those who had never deserved it. Who had simply been born in the wrong place at the wrong moment in time. They had been taught the gods had blessed them to be born away from the world in the safety of the cliffs, when in reality they had been abandoned by the gods and cursed by the Fates.

He skidded to a halt outside the iron door. He couldn't cross the wards to this chamber of his own volition. One of the few rooms he did not have free access to.

Now he knew why.

Two guards came rushing up behind him, confusion etched along their features. "Do either of you have access to this chamber?" Rayner demanded.

"No, Ash Rider," one answered, his confusion shifting to trepidation as he watched Rayner. "Only the Baroness and the Marshals can enter at will."

The Marshals. He'd known they could enter at will, but that was because there were cells in that chamber to hold criminals while they served time for their crimes. Not because . . .

But the more he thought about it, that fit too. The Marshals not only oversaw the cells, but were in charge of the overseers who monitored the Fae and one Marshal, Feris, was the Captain of them all. He was a mean fucker that Rayner was grateful he'd rarely had to deal with, let alone answer to, but gods. Would he have put everything together sooner if he had been around the male more? Could he have stopped or changed any of this?

The iron door creaked, and one of the Marshals stuck his head out, a flickering torch in his hand. "What the fuck is going on out here? Don't you lot know it's the middle of the godsdamn night?" he grunted.

But that door opening was all Rayner needed. He moved among the smoke wafting up from the flames, appearing behind the Marshal, a dagger already pulled and slicing across the male's throat. He'd snatched the torch from his hand and was racing down the passageway before the Marshal's body had hit the ground.

He could hear them, the sounds of frightened people. He could smell the fear in the air. Moving again among the smoke, he left the torch behind and appeared in the large chamber where the stream filled a large pool. He materialized in the middle of a group of Marshals, two daggers leaving his hands and flying in opposite directions. Ducking when a sword came for him, he pulled a knife from his boot. He threw it, and the knife disappeared among ashes that swirled in his palm. He followed in another wisp of smoke, reappearing behind the swordsman. Rayner spun towards a large hearth along one wall of the chamber where the knife appeared in the ashes, still airborne from the force of his throw, lodging itself in the male's gut.

He heard more boots thundering down the passageway, and he moved to meet the guards, drawing his sword as he did. Arrows flew for him, but ashes were pouring out of one palm, creating a shield around him that the arrows bounced off of, clattering harmlessly to the ground. He lost track of how many guards he killed, the screams of frightened children and Fae echoing in the chamber. He couldn't stop. He couldn't stop until they were all dead, and Breya would be safe and—

"Rayner."

The sound of her voice had him spinning around to find her. How had she gotten down here so fast? But when his eyes landed on Moranna, his magic guttered. His shield fell away, bits of white ashes floating to the ground. She held a dagger in her hand, blood dripping off the end onto . . .

Onto the still form of a child with bright red hair lying in a growing pool of blood at her feet.

He'd dropped to his knees at some point, because suddenly Moranna's red painted nail was tipping up his chin, and he was staring into depthless dark eyes. She clicked her tongue at him, and a pitying pout formed on her lips. "Such poor choices, my Ash Rider."

"She was a child," he rasped, his eyes dropping back to the unmoving body.

"She was no longer of any use to me. Why would I feed and house something that is unable to offer me anything in return?" she replied, finger sliding along his jaw. "You've created quite the mess down here, Rayner. I cannot let this go unpunished."

He dragged his eyes back to her, but before he could reply, something was clamped onto his wrist. "Shirastone does not work on me," he snarled, jerking away from her touch.

"I know," she said soothingly. Then she leaned in closer to whisper into his ear, "That's why it is not shirastone."

He felt it then. The smothering of his magic. It was like shirastone but magnified by thousands. And the draining. Gods, he could feel his magic draining away. More than that, he could feel his very *life-force* draining away.

"What is the final count?" Moranna asked, straightening and taking a step back from him.

"Fifty-two," came the gruff voice of Feris.

She clicked her tongue again. "Fifty-two of my sentries and Marshals, Rayner. I am so disappointed."

His lip curled back, baring his elongated canines at her. "I am going to kill you. I am going to kill you and everyone who knew what was going on here and did nothing. I am to kill every Fae that followed your orders without questioning a fucking thing."

"And you, my pious Ash Rider?" Moranna asked, her arms folding and her chin resting on a thumb and forefinger. "You have killed on my orders. Did you question me?"

"You told me they deserved their deaths," he snapped.

"And they did. They would have drained valuable resources from the colony. Everything I do is to keep those in my charge well taken care of. You know this," she replied placatingly.

"Where is Aravis?"

"Who?" she asked, her brow furrowing in feigned puzzlement. At his snarl, she continued, "Oh! The other child? She has been assigned as a power vessel. I already told you this." She stepped closer once more, bending down to speak softly to him again. Her fingers sank into his hair, her lips brushing the shell of his ear. "As soon as she has her first bleeding, she will be used until she is with child. She will bear many young for me. Surely one of them will be born as strong as you, no? I shall need *someone* to replace you in my bed one day." Her fingers tightened, tugging at his scalp. "But now, my Ash Rider, it is time to come back to bed."

"I will never bow to you again."

There were muffled gasps from the sentries still alive, and a low whistle came from Feris.

"Want him in a cell, your Grace?" the Captain asked, stepping to her side. He sneered down at him.

Moranna stood. "As much as it will hurt my heart to do so, perhaps that would be best for the remainder of the night," she agreed. "Give him one with a proper view of what you will finish carrying out tonight." She patted Rayner's cheek twice before moving to the opposite end of the chamber. Her palm pressed to the rocky wall, and an archway appeared, a set of stairs that wound up appearing. A hidden passageway. That's how she had made her way here so quickly.

Feris pulled him roughly to his feet, dragging him to a cell directly across from the pool and the boats tied to the wooden docks. A perfect view indeed.

The door clanged shut after he was shoved inside. Rayner felt wards sealing it up.

"The Baroness's favorite. Locked up. Can't say I haven't dreamed of this day, Ash Rider."

"I am sure it will be your favorite memory of me."

Feris snickered.

Rayner smiled back. A dark, wicked thing. The smile of a monster that had been awoken at the sight of Breya's lifeless body on the ground. "My favorite memory of you will be when I watch the life drain from your eyes while I hold your heart in the palm of my hand."

Feris stared back at him, blinking once, clearly unsure of how to respond to such a statement. Then he huffed a laugh. "I knew those swirling eyes meant you weren't all there, Ash Rider."

"You have no idea how true that statement is."

Feris didn't bother to reply, turning away and striding back to the remaining Marshals. There was a group of Fae, young and grown, huddled in the center of the chamber. Rayner counted them. Sixteen. Sixteen remained alive, while twelve were already dead.

Then he watched.

He watched as they drew daggers across throats. He watched every Fae fall to the ground, listened to every plea for mercy, and heard every cry of fear from a child. He watched as they filled the boats, and the Marshals boarded to ferry them outside the cliffs.

He watched as Breya was tossed thoughtlessly into the last boat. She would not be given a Farewell. None of them would. Her body might be burned, but she would not receive the rites of the Fire Court like she deserved.

He watched it all, taking in every detail, marking every face that would meet death at his hand. He let all of it feed the monster inside, let it all feed the growing appetite for vengeance. Not vengeance for him. Never for him. He should have done more long before tonight. He'd live with that guilt the rest of his life, however long or short that may be.

But as the chamber emptied and he was left in the silent dark, he made a vow that he would see Moranna dead before he left this world. He would see the entirety of the Southern Islands become a place that only the spirits visited, and even they would not want to linger after he was done with this place.

The sound of the iron door opening drew him from his thoughts. A Marshal appeared in front of his cell, his features shadowed in the flickering flames of the torch he held. He was one of the Marshals who had slaughtered Fae tonight. Rayner said nothing, staring back at him unblinkingly, contemplating which manner of death would suit him best.

"We do not have much time," the Fae said, his voice raspy, as though he rarely used it. When Rayner didn't move, he waved him over impatiently. "Come on, Ash Rider. That deathstone won't remove itself."

His eyes fell to the dark stone encircling his wrist. His wrist was bleeding where the stone was digging in. He hadn't felt a thing. He was numb. Numb to all of it except the rage coursing through him.

"You expect me to believe you are going to take it off of me?" Rayner asked. "I am not a fool."

"No, you are not," the Fae agreed. "You are the only one who can liberate those trapped here. I have waited decades for someone like you to show up."

Rayner's head tilted to the side. "I watched you butcher innocent Fae tonight."

The Fae swallowed audibly, nodding once.

Rayner smiled at him. "If you take this off, I will end you."

Even in the sparse torchlight, he could see the male pale. "It— It will be nothing less than I deserve."

Rayner pushed to his feet, drifting towards the shirastone bars. He gripped them in his hands, leaning down to peer into the male's face. The male took a small step back. "Explain what you mean when you say you have been waiting for someone like me to show up."

The male nodded. "There are few powerful enough to take on the Baroness. The ones who are do not wish to. They like the power they have here, but you . . . You are different. You will do what I would never be able to."

"You could have stopped killing at any moment," Rayner sneered.

"Only to meet my own death. And then what? I would just be replaced."

"But you would not have so much blood on your hands."

The male hung his head. "I am prepared for you to take my life when I free you, Ash Rider. I will face Arius's judgment and spend my eternity in the Pits of Torment knowing I deserve every moment."

Rayner looked the male up and down before meeting his eyes once more. Then he shoved his arm through the bars. With a shaking hand, the Marshal slipped the stone from his wrist. In the next breath, Rayner had moved through the smoke of the torch. The male didn't have a chance to scream as a blade went through his back and pierced his heart.

"Consider a quick death a mercy," Rayner said, his tone low and dark. "For surely Arius will not grant you any."

He let the male fall to the ground, the torch hissing as it went out, rolling across the stone. Rayner didn't need it. He had excellent eyesight in the dark. The minute he was past the iron door, he was moving among the smoke again. He would leave the cliffs, regroup, and then come back for Aravis once his power had fully replenished.

He made his way to the front entry hall, still planning to kill those five sentries before he left, but he drew up short when he found Moranna standing in the archway that would lead outside.

"More unwise choices, Rayner," she chided, her hand clasped around something he could not see. He reached over his shoulder for his sword, but she tutted at him. "Now, now, before you make another unwise choice, let me speak. Should you attempt to take my life, Aravis will be thrown from the top levels."

Rayner spun to find she was not bluffing. He could make out two figures at the railing of one of the top levels. "What are your terms?" he demanded, turning back to Moranna.

"I thought you would see things my way," she simpered, moving towards him. "Give me some of your blood, and I will let you leave these islands. I will not stop you."

"What else?"

She shrugged. "That is it."

"And Aravis?"

"Oh, she must stay."

"I will come back for her."

"I am sure you will," she purred. "Should you make the choice to stay now, I am afraid both of your lives will be forfeit. Which would be . . . unfortunate."

Knowing this was surely a trap, but not seeing any way around it, he nodded. Moranna jerked her chin, and a sentry hurried from the shadows. Rayner's eyes never left hers as the sentry filled five vials with his blood. When he was done, he dropped his arm to his side, the wound already healing.

Moranna stepped to the side, gesturing towards the exit. "As agreed."

Rayner moved forward, waiting for the catch. He turned so he could keep her in his sight, refusing to turn his back on her. He paused as the archway began to shimmer, the beach appearing on the other side. "Your death is mine, Moranna. I am coming for you and everyone here."

"I await your return home," she said with a small smile. "But know that when you cross those wards this night, you shall not remember how to get back here. You will lose all your memories of your time here. I wonder, how will you find your way to someplace you do not even know exists?"

"I have never had such a problem before," he snarled.

"But you always came back to me, Rayner," she replied. "You

had reason to return, and I had reason to want you to. Now I have reason to keep you away for a time, to make you pay for what you have done here this night. How dreadful to not remember anything about your past. To not know where you come from. You will not even remember you had kin, let alone remember to return for one."

"I swear to you, I will be your end."

"We shall see, my Ash Rider."

"I am not your Ash Rider, Moranna, but I will your end."

And with that, he stepped through the archway, breathing in the sea air before everything went black.

CHAPTER 1

They had gotten smarter since the last time he had visited the islands. The last time he was here, nearly four decades ago, the guards outside the cliff's entrance had a fire burning to ward off the night chill from the sea. Rayner had appeared among the smoke and had all five of them lying in pools of blood before they had realized what had happened.

This time he'd had to move among the thick vegetation. He'd assumed they wouldn't make that mistake again, and when he returned this time, he'd come in on merchant ships. It had been two weeks at sea departing from the Water Court. He could have traveled among ashes, but he knew better than to underestimate Moranna, even after all these years.

But she would always wait for him to come to her.

After coming to the islands every few years when he'd finally regained his lost memories, he'd purposefully waited decades this round. He let them relax, lulled them into a false sense of safety. But he'd been just as busy on the continent. It had happened by chance the first time. He'd recognized an overseer in a market in the Shifter territory. A good hour in an abandoned building and a few calculated stab wounds had the male telling Rayner all he needed to know. Moranna's superiors were moving people out because of the destruction he was causing. Many of the guards and overseers had been spread to various positions throughout the continent. The male hadn't known what exactly everyone was doing, but some had been assigned as spies in various territories. He had been one of those spies. The male had eventually died of suffocation.

From smoke inhalation.

And Rayner had found himself with a new purpose while planning his missions to the Southern Islands. He'd promised he would kill every single one of the people who had helped to keep the innocent people trapped in the cliffs, and he had suddenly found his hunting grounds expanded. He knew he'd become a rumor, a being as mythical as the Oracle. But people did not refer to him as the Ash Rider. No, he was whispered about as The Reaper, as if saying the name too loudly would summon him.

The last time he'd come to the Southern Islands, he'd nearly been caught. Arrows with shirastone tips. It didn't stop his gifts, but they still hurt like hell when lodged in one's kidney and caused sloppy movements. He'd managed to get a group of twenty-five out, half of them children. It was the most he'd ever moved out at one time. When he'd left, he'd estimated there were still at least two hundred innocents left in the colony, but that number would be higher now. Lots of younglings could be born in forty years, and he would guess the Baroness was a little more *tolerant* of those with lower power levels, considering her dwindling pool of subjects.

It was helping, he supposed, in one way. She allowed more to live, thus keeping them safe until he could come back for them. Although, safe probably wasn't the best word to use. It kept them alive, which was better than dead . . . for most of them.

Despite that upside, there was the issue that Moranna had moved her most prized and most powerful. They were kept locked away and hidden, and he knew that would include Aravis if she was still alive. He'd had yet to figure out where exactly Moranna had stowed them away though. Which is why he had waited all these years. He wanted the sentries to have their guard down. He had no intention of making his presence known this time. There was only one Fae he had his sights set on for this visit.

The Captain of the Marshals.

Fortunately for the guards outside the cliffs, that meant they would get to keep their lives this visit if all went according to plan. He crept from the thick expanse of trees and plants, smoke drifting from a small torch he kept smoldering. He was several hundred feet away from the entrance into the city beneath the cliffs. It was the only place a person could walk in and out, the brand that was given beneath their skin when they were born their key to enter. He lifted a hand, ashes pouring from his palm and seeking the wards surrounding the place. He'd once thought he could only move among existing smoke and ashes. It wasn't until he had remembered his training from this cursed place that he learned he could create his own. It drained his reserves far too fast to do it regularly though.

But he'd learned even more about his gifts since his time spent inside the cliff walls. Things he had been more than happy to share with those who kept the innocents trapped here like slaves. Like how he could control which parts of him shifted to ash. How he could send those ashes into a body, wrap them around hearts or lungs or bones.

Ashes swirled halfway up the cliff side, and Rayner's lips kicked up in a wicked grin. One of her failsafes. Moranna always left one small weak spot in her wards to make her own escape if necessary. She'd gotten clever with them since he'd left, but not clever enough. In the next breath, he was hovering above the ground in his ashes. The next blink, he was inside.

He immediately disappeared among the smoke of the sconces lining the wall. Nothing had changed. Everything was still pristine and white, spelled to always look that way. She still made Fae clean every day, saying they needed to earn their keep, as if being bred like prized livestock wasn't enough.

Rage coursed through his veins at the thought, the monster she'd created lifting its head. His ashes trembled beneath his skin, as hungry for violence as he was. He breathed deep, the scent of smoke and fire filling his senses, fueling the surging anticipation inside.

Staying hidden, he flitted among the braziers, taking in everything happening. With the ward breech halfway up, he was on the mid-levels. Everything was quiet, Fae hurrying along when they passed, eyes fixed to the floor. The white clothing everyone was issued blended in with the walls, the floor, everything. The only color in the place had been Moranna in her bright red attire.

Until he'd returned and added a little color of his own with blood splatters on the walls and pools of it on the floor, corpses left in his wake. He'd glimpsed Moranna once in all the times he'd come back to these cursed cliffs. She'd appeared on the highest level the third time he'd come back, staring down at him, a faint smile on her red painted lips. He'd only been a few levels below her, so he'd heard the words when she'd said, "Welcome home, my Ash Rider."

By the time he'd moved through the smoke to reach her, she'd disappeared. He'd had to choose between going after her or getting the group of Fae he'd already gathered out. If he went after Moranna, those Fae were surely dead, so he'd left her for another time.

He maneuvered up through the levels. Feris had been housed on the same level his own rooms had been on when Rayner had resided here. It would be easy enough to see if that was still the case. He was nearing the top when a scream made him stop mid-leap between ashes. Smoke swirled when he stepped from it, his boots silent on the pristine floor. Calculating what level he was on, he realized this was either on a floor of producing rooms or a level where some of the more powerful used to be housed.

Keeping to the walls to avoid being seen along the railings, Rayner moved quickly, straining to pick up any other sounds. The walls were thick rock, and the doors were solid wood. To be heard through them, the scream had to have been roaring. He sent his ashes from his palm as he went, seeping under the cracks of the doors and seeking any sign of sentience. His ashes, usually associated with death, always reacted differently to life. They would vibrate, strain to get closer; whether curious or seeking to destroy, he was never quite sure. But when they trembled and pulled him closer to one of the last rooms, he knew they'd found something.

Pulling them back into himself, Rayner pushed the door open, feeling the wards crackle over his skin. Just as shirastone did not affect him, he was able to pass through most wards without issue. But when he stepped across the threshold, he stilled, taking in the scene before him. This was a producing room all right, but this was not one of Moranna's assignments.

This was sentries and overseers taking what they wanted.

His lip curled back, his ashes vibrating beneath his skin for an entirely different reason now. But he still didn't move. Because one overseer, the one closest to the female, was on the ground.

An arrow shoved into his eye.

Where the arrow had come from, Rayner didn't know. There was no bow in sight and no other arrows. Just the one protruding from the man's face.

He lay there, moaning and cursing, yelling at the other two males in the room to get the arrow out. But they stood frozen against the wall, and Rayner was fairly certain it wasn't because of him.

The female was young. He was certain she hadn't gone through her Staying yet. Her long, black hair was braided into a plait over her shoulder, and she wore a black gown, not the usual white attire. She was on the shorter side and barefoot, and when his gaze connected with hers, amber eyes stared back at him. Not that she could see him beneath his hood, but her wide eyes told him she knew exactly who he was.

"You . . . are the Reaper," she whispered. Rayner said nothing. "I did not think you were real. I thought . . ." She trailed off, but Rayner was already focusing on the males in the room.

"Did you do this?" Rayner asked.

She hesitated before answering. ". . . yes."

"Are you hurt?"

"No."

Rayner nodded, advancing farther into the room. "Get out of

here. All the way out if you can. There is a merchant ship leaving in an hour that will take you to the continent if you can make it to the ship in time. Take others with you if you can. The guards are about to be preoccupied."

He hadn't looked at her again, his attention fixed on the still-whimpering overseer, but he felt her make her way across the room, felt her pause beside him.

"They have made preparations for your return," she said softly.

"Close the door behind you."

When it thudded shut, he moved to stand next to the overseer. His attention shifted to the other two sentries. "Do not try to run."

They both nodded, and he heard one audibly gulp as he lowered to a crouch beside the overseer. His hands were still on his face, smearing blood across his brow and cheeks.

Rayner reached for the arrow, but the male shrieked, "No!"

He paused, fingers an inch from the arrow shaft. "Were you not just screaming at your companions to remove it?"

The male blubbered, incoherent mumblings coming from his lips, and before he could sense the movement, Rayner snatched the arrow, tugging it from the man's eye socket. The organ itself was attached to the arrowhead, and the sound of it popping free had one of the sentries behind him retching.

And the other one running.

Moving through the smoke from the lit torches on either side of the doorway, Rayner materialized in front of the sentry. He tried to backtrack, his boots slipping across the floor. Before the male could beg, Rayner's hand was nothing but ashes, reaching into the man's leg. Fingers of ash closed around bone, and the male's screams filled the room when Rayner tore it from his limb. He tossed it to the side. It clattered on the stone, blood and sinew splattering. The male was already on the floor, and Rayner lowered down in front of him to peer at his face. Tears were tracking down pale cheeks, spittle dripping from his chin as he clutched at his leg.

"I told you not to run," Rayner said, his tone low and icy. "If you try to drag yourself out of this room, I will remove every bone from your body and make sure you feel it all."

The male nodded emphatically, trying and failing to quiet himself. Still holding the arrow in his other hand, Rayner moved back to the overseer, crouching beside him once more.

"Were you going to be the first to rape her?" Rayner asked, twirling the arrow between his thumb and forefinger after he removed the now useless organ from the end of it. The man only whimpered. "Tell you what. You answer a riddle; I let you keep your other eye."

A puddle slowly formed beneath the male, the smell of piss mingling with the raw terror in the air.

"What is a dreamer's lie?" he asked casually, placing the tip of the arrow over the male's heart. He could hear it beating too rapidly. The male whimpered again, trembling violently now. "Quickly. I have others to tend to."

The male's mouth opened and closed, gaping like a fish out of water. "I— I don't . . . I don't know," he gasped as Rayner slid the arrow up his chest and along his throat.

Rayner leaned in close, whispering into his ear as the arrow pressed along his cheekbone just enough to draw a thin line of blood. "A dreamer's lie is that all nightmares have an end." Another strangled cry. "The truth is, some nightmares go on forever, and yours is just beginning."

The sound of more retching mingled with the screams when he brought the arrow down again, taking the male's other eye. Rayner was doing him a favor really. He wouldn't be able to see all the ways he was about to make him bleed. Then again, without his sight, the sensations would be intensified. Maybe it wasn't a favor after all.

By the time his attention shifted to the one sentry who wasn't bleeding, the two other males were no longer breathing. He stood from dealing with the one now missing not only a leg bone, but a couple ribs, and a few vital organs. The remaining sentry had sunk to the floor, piles of vomit off to one side. He was pale and trembling, staring up at Rayner when he moved to stand in front of him. The male closed his eyes, seeming to brace for the agony he'd witnessed his companions go through.

"I have some questions for you," Rayner said.

"I will answer them," he gasped out. "I will do whatever you ask in order to live."

"Who said anything about you living?" Rayner asked, pulling a dagger from beneath his cloak. "Answer my questions, and I will give you a quicker death than your companions received. But keeping your life is not on the table." Rayner thought the male might be sick yet again judging by the way he somehow paled even more. "Feris. Are his rooms still on the upper level?"

"The Captain? Yes. Two levels below the Baroness."

"These preparations the female mentioned. What are they?"

"I don't know."

Rayner struck, snapping one of the male's fingers back. The male howled, clutching his hand to his chest. "That was not the answer I was looking for," Rayner growled.

Tears were leaking from the male's eyes, beads of sweat forming on his brow. "I don't know," he sobbed. "I am not high-ranking enough to know such details."

"But high-ranking enough to take from the females? Somehow I doubt that."

"I swear it," he cried, trying to press back from him more.

"Lie to me again, and I take a kneecap," Rayner snarled, lifting a hand and letting it fade into ashes.

"I don't know!" the male cried again. "I don't know what they have planned for you! I oversee the younglings! That's my job!"

Rayner paused. "Explain."

"The Baroness is moving them. Taking them off the islands. My job is to ready the young on transport days," the sentry said.

"Transport them were?"

"I'm not told that. I take them to a transporting room on the main level."

Transporting room? That was new. There had never been such a thing when Rayner had resided here.

"Aravis. Do you know who she is?" Rayner demanded.

"I do not know that name," the sentry said, shaking his head.

"She has been here for over a century. Black hair. Grey eyes. Fire gifts," Rayner said. "The Baroness would keep her close by."

"Her most guarded are hidden away. Only a few know where," the sentry replied, his trembling seeming to have lessened as they spoke.

"Who else would know besides Feris?"

Dread filled the male's pale blue eyes. "I don't know," he whispered.

"Then you are no longer of use to me."

Rayner's dagger slashed across the male's throat. He left him there, choking on his own blood. A quicker death than his companions had received, as promised.

He stepped from the room, moving up a few more levels to the housing block where Feris's quarters would be. Ashes flitted from his fingertips, drifting along the floor, seeking life or death. He passed what was once his quarters, continuing on to the other end of the level.

And when his ashes started buzzing in anticipation, a cold smile formed on Rayner's lips.

He had a favorite memory to make.

CHAPTER 2

The fire burning in Feris's hearth was more than enough for Rayner to materialize inside his rooms. He took in the space. Dirty uniforms crumpled in a heap in the corner. Unmade bed. Weapons discarded haphazardly across a desk.

He could hear him moving around in the bathing room, and Rayner swiped up one of his daggers, examining it. Shirastone. The upper-level guards were each issued one. The other weapons were of standard make. Steel and practical.

He leaned back against the desk, lifting a palm. Smoke swirled, the arrow from the producing room appearing in his hand. He held it up, studying the arrowhead. That was not shirastone. It was darker, seeming to absorb light. Memories of the same material digging into his skin when he was in a cell flashed in his mind. The Marshal who had let him out had called it deathstone, but Rayner had never seen it on weapons when he was here. Unless this was one way they had prepared for his return.

The sound of shuffling feet told him Feris was coming. Rayner didn't even bother to look up. When he heard the muffled curse though, he slowly raised his head, peering out from beneath his hood.

Feris stared back at him, hatred shining in his eyes. "The favorite returns," he spat.

"Am I still the favorite?" Rayner questioned, reaching up and pulling back the hood. He wanted Feris to see his face. Wanted him to know he had come to collect the memory he had promised to make. "That doesn't say much about you. I have been gone for decades, and you still haven't managed to take my place."

"The Baroness has plans for you," Feris snarled, but it sounded more like he was reminding himself. Rayner had no doubt Moranna had issued orders about what to do with him if he showed up, and those orders did not include Feris killing him.

"I have plans for her as well, but first I need some information," Rayner said.

"Fuck off, Ash Rider. If you think I'm going to tell you shit, think again."

Rayner only smiled. Holding his stare, he tossed the arrow up. Ashes swirled around it, and when it reappeared, it went through the back of Feris's shoulder.

He bellowed out a curse, trying to grab the thing, but it was lodged just out of his reach.

"That is quite the weapon," Rayner said casually. "Are there more?"

"It is deathstone, you fucking prick. We do not have weapons with it." His face was turning a mottled red from pain and anger.

Rayner sent him a frank look. "Do not lie to me, Feris."

"I'm not." His lip curled back, but it quickly morphed from a sneer to a grimace. "She only has a few items of deathstone. Arrows are not one of them."

"Then where did it come from?"

"You tell me. You are the one who possesses such a thing."

Rayner studied him as he continued to struggle to reach the arrow. He was almost inclined to believe that he did not know where the arrow had come from, which opened up a whole new set of questions. It couldn't have simply appeared out of nowhere.

"What preparations have been made?" Rayner asked in a low voice.

"Fuck. Off," Feris ground out again from between his teeth.

Rayner sighed, pushing off the desk and prowling forward. The male's lip peeled back, elongated canines bared, but the arrow was suppressing his earth magic. He was also weaponless, having clearly just come from bathing. Sloppy. Rayner always had a dagger or knife within reach, even in the bath. Feris was just as arrogant as ever, his next words only solidifying that fact.

"Go ahead and kill me, Ash Rider. I'm not going to tell you a godsdamn thing."

Rayner lifted a hand, flesh becoming ashes. "You won't be meeting death until I say so, Feris, and that will not happen until I have the information I need."

His hand snapped out, sinking deep into his throat where fingers of ash wrapped around his windpipe, squeezing. Feris's eyes bulged, Rayner's favorite look of panic settling into his cold eyes. He abandoned his attempt to reach the arrow, now clawing at his neck, mouth gaping.

"When I allow you to take a breath, I expect to hear what preparations have been made for me. If that is not what I hear from your mouth, you will learn a few more of my new talents."

He eased his grip, pulling his hand back and wiping it on his cloak. Feris sucked in breaths, gasping, "You twisted fuck."

And Rayner's ashes sang as they sank into the length of Feris's arm. They expanded, layering along the bones, muscles, veins . . . and then they sank in even further, turning it all to ash. Feris screamed, feeling every bit of desecration.

He pulled his magic back, keeping a grimace from his face. His magic reserves were starting to deplete. He needed to make sure he had enough magic left to get back to the continent, so he really needed Feris to start sharing some secrets.

The male opened his mouth, but before he could speak, Rayner said, "The words you are about to say had better be how she has prepared for me."

"She has an enchantment on the islands. The entirety of them," Feris rasped, beads of sweat running down his brow. He was staring at his boneless arm, and Rayner snapped his fingers in his face to keep him from going into any type of shock.

"How?"

"I don't know, but she knows when you come. Every time. She knows you are here now."

"Then why hasn't she come for me?"

"She's not ready for you yet."

Whatever the fuck that meant.

Rayner didn't have time to waste on this now. He had other things he needed to know, then he needed to get the fuck out of here while he still had the power to do so.

"The most powerful. Where does she keep them?"

Something hardened on Feris's face as though he were going to decline to answer, but Rayner merely needed to lift his hand again, ashes drifting from his fingers, and Feris was blurting, "In one of her secret chambers. I haven't seen them since she moved them there."

Interesting.

"Aravis. Where is she being kept?"

At that, something sinister crept across Feris's face. "When she's not fulfilling her assignments, she warms my bed, Ash Rider."

A snarl of rage left Rayner as his hand plunged into Feris's chest. This time, he didn't leave it as ashes. He let his flesh reform, solid fingers wrapping around Feris's heart.

The male gasped, face contorted in agony, but he still managed to say, "She let me take her for the first time. Let me teach her how to prepare for her duties. And she will use her to claim you once more."

He bellowed a roar of pain when Rayner sank a dagger deep into his side, twisting sharply. "Arius will welcome you into the Pits of Torment," Rayner snarled.

"You will be in the Pits with the rest of us," Feris rasped between ragged breaths as Rayner's fingers tightened around his heart.

"I'm counting on it," Rayner replied. "I will find you there and finish what I started here."

He ripped his hand back, Feris's heart in his palm. Blood bubbled from the male's lips as he sank to the floor, and Rayner watched the life drain from his eyes before he tossed his heart atop the body and disappeared among the smoke.

He'd been right. That would forever be one of his fondest memories.

CHAPTER 3

He took a drink from his mug of ale. This was one of the more rundown taverns in Solembra. It was tucked into a back alley on the edges of the capital city, and it was frequented by some rather questionable patrons. But they had the best ale in the Fire Court, and he was one of those questionable patrons, so Rayner found it rather suitable. He had to hand it to the prince of this Court. While this might be one of the more shady establishments in the city, he'd seen much worse throughout the continent. But even the Fire Prince couldn't keep every corner of his lands neat and tidy and perfect. It was a far cry from the legends of the Black Syndicate, but thieves and cheats and hirelings still found their way in.

He was a prime example.

He had a small house located farther into the city, closer to the markets and businesses. The Fire Court seemed the natural place to have a home, if he could even call it that. When he spent too much of his magic, it was where he recovered. Like he had been doing for the last two seasons. It's where he planned and plotted when he wasn't off wandering to the farthest reaches of the continent trying to track down answers. He'd had a house on the outside of the city at one point. A small estate with room to run.

He'd sold it as soon as he'd remembered he owned it.

Decades. It had taken him decades to overcome the enchantment Moranna had put on him when he'd left the cliffs on the Southern Islands. He'd wasted so much godsdamn coin on false seers and Witches who swore they could brew up a tonic to bring back his memories. He'd found it a better use of his time to live among the smoke and ashes and pick up on rumors throughout the various kingdoms, then follow the rumors to see if they were true. Even that had been largely a waste of his time.

Until the day he found his way to the Oracle.

* * *

He paused to catch his breath. This was stupid. Foolish and idiotic and stupid to try to get through the Witch Kingdoms without alerting any of the Covens. The High Witch had eyes and ears everywhere. He was running out of ashes and smoke too. Once he cleared this small town, he would be hiking to the cliff cave.

And hopefully avoiding any run-ins with the Witches.

He took another few moments to breathe deep and let his heart rate settle before he set off again, flitting between the smoke billowing from the houses of the village. The ashes of a fire pit a few miles out let him get a little farther than anticipated, but here was where his magic wouldn't be of much use for traveling.

He fingered a few of the small medallions in his pocket. He'd wasted a lot of coin on false Witches, but these had actually come in handy. They had been created by magic, so he was able to imbue them with some of his own. He stored ashes in them, allowing him to throw them and move among the ashes released if there were no smoke or ashes around to move through. If he ran into a Witch, he'd need all the advantages he could get.

He pulled a map from a pocket realm, looking it over before folding it up and tucking into the pocket of his cloak. Detailed maps of the Witch Kingdoms were nearly impossible to find. Another thing he'd paid an obscene amount of coin for, and it wasn't even a decent one. It had simply been better than any other map he'd ever come across.

Knowing it was foolish to linger too long in one spot when he did not have permission to be in these lands, Rayner set off at a brisk pace. The grey skies only added to the chill of the territory. There wasn't snow on the ground, but frost still clung to everything.

There were various rumors about where to find the mythical Oracle. Too many rumors to ever try and substantiate them all. Some were ridiculous, but some he'd looked into. Most had led to dead ends, but a few had paid off. Bits and pieces of a few rumors woven together over the last few decades were how he'd finally figured out where she was.

Or where he hoped she was (if it was a she), because if this turned out to be a complete waste of his fucking time and he had to start over from scratch, he wasn't entirely sure what he would do.

He stepped from a copse of ancient trees at the base of the cliffs when he heard it. The screech of an eagle.

Except it wasn't an eagle.

It was a griffin.

Fuck.

He slipped a medallion from his pocket, clenching it in his fist while he kept moving. He didn't make it very far. The griffin dove, hard and fast. If he tried to make a run for it, Rayner knew he'd find more than one arrow in his back. His only real option was to stop and pray to Anala that the Witch would escort him to the border.

The ground beneath his boots shook when the beast landed fifteen feet away from him, its rider slipping from its back. And as she stalked towards him, drawing her sword from her back, he knew he was well and truly fucked.

Hazel Hecate. The High Witch.

She stopped in front of him, her blade leveled at his throat. "Lower your hood," *she ordered in an icy tone, violet eyes burning into him.*

"I would rather not," *he replied, fingers itching to reach for his own weapons.*

"It was not a request."

Keeping the medallion in hand, he slowly lifted his arms, pushing back the hood of his cloak. If the High Witch was surprised by the swirling smoke in his eyes, she did not show it.

"I have heard rumors one of you had been spotted on the continent."

"I have heard rumors the Oracle resides in your kingdom," Rayner countered.

The High Witch's lip curled slightly in disgust. "Do you know what we do to males in my lands, Ash Rider?"

"I do."

"And yet here you stand."

Rayner did not answer. Just held her gaze, waiting to see what she did next.

She slowly lowered her sword, holding it at her side. "There has not been an Ash Rider born in centuries."

"That you were aware of."

"What business do you have with the Oracle?"

"None of yours."

Her head tilted. A predator assessing prey. "Tell me, Ash Rider, do you value your tongue?"

"I find it useful," he conceded.

"Then I suggest you mind how you speak to me." She took a step towards him. "I do not care if you are the last Ash Rider that will ever walk this realm. I will not hesitate to take you from this world for male arrogance."

"I meant no disrespect, Lady," Rayner replied. "Truly."

"What is in your hand?"

"A trinket."

"Show me."

He opened his fist, showing her the medallion. She held out her own hand, and he begrudgingly dumped the medallion into it. She held it up between two fingers, studying it intensely, before she slipped it into a pocket of her witchsuit. "I will take you to the Oracle."

It took everything in him to not show the shock that rippled through him. "Why?"

"The Oracle told me one would come with such a trinket. When he did, I was to show him the way." She turned, sheathing her sword down her back as she added, "It is the only reason you are not dead." Rayner watched her walk back to her griffin, the beast lowering to the ground at her approach so she could hoist herself onto its back. When its large wings flared wide, preparing to take to the sky, the High Witch said, "Meet me where you see him land."

Rayner stood on the edge of the copse and watched the creature soar up, climbing higher and higher. It was several minutes before it banked to land somewhere well over halfway up the side of the cliffs. Which was . . . fucking great.

Gritting his teeth, he pulled the cloak hood back into place. Even though no one was around and the High Witch knew who he was, he felt far too exposed when his hood wasn't hiding him from the rest of the world.

It took hours to climb up the cliff side. If it weren't for the healing capabilities of the Fae, he would have arrived there with bloodied palms and numerous bruises. The rocks were covered with the same frost that glistened on the purple and turquoise leaves of the ancient trees, making them difficult to climb even with the extra grips on the soles of his boots.

The High Witch was standing next to an entrance to a cave when he finally pulled himself over the lip of a ledge, her griffin perched on rocks a little higher up. His golden eyes were fixed on Rayner, lion's tail swishing back and forth. The feathers on his wings ruffled slightly, and he clicked his beak when Rayner moved towards his master. Beside the High Witch sat a small stone table, a vial atop it.

"You are not permitted to take weapons in with you," the High Witch said. "You can retrieve them when the Oracle releases you."

Releases him? That sounded . . . promising. But he'd come this far, and he needed answers, so he again found himself without much of a choice.

After removing the various weapons strapped to his body and setting them aside, the High Witch gestured towards the vial. "This will temporarily nullify your gifts. The Oracle will give them back when you have heard what you need to."

Without letting himself think about it, Rayner swiped up the vial and downed the contents. He instantly felt empty, void of the ashes that drifted in his veins. He knew if he could see his eyes, they would be an unmoving grey. No swirling with the telltale sign of what he was.

"See what awaits," the High Witch said, motioning to the cave mouth. He took a step, but she called out, *"And Ash Rider?"*

Looking back over his shoulder, he said, *"Yes?"*

"You would do well to be out of my lands by dawn."

"Understood, my Lady."

The High Witch nodded once to him, and he turned back to the cave. He knew she'd be long gone whenever he emerged, but someone would be watching him to make sure he was indeed across their borders when the sun next rose.

He entered the cave, navigating the pitch-black interior. Even with his Fae sight, he could not see a thing. His gifts had always given him an extra advantage due to his need to move through smoke. Without that gift, he felt blind. Fingers gliding along the rocky wall, he moved down the passageway. It only took a few minutes before a glow appeared up ahead, and when he stepped through, he blinked in surprise at what he found.

No one knew the Oracle's true form. It was said she appeared differently to each person who came to her. But why he was staring at a child, he had no idea.

The girl had to be no older than seven with bright red hair and freckles across her nose and cheeks, but her violet eyes held a depth and knowing to them that told Rayner she was far, far older than she appeared. The girl wore a simple dress, feet bare where she stood on the dirt-covered cave floor, and Rayner had the strangest feeling that he knew this child. He could not place her though, no matter how hard he tried.

"And so the one with many names has finally found his way to me," the little girl said, watching him carefully, hands clasped behind her back.

"You are a child?" Rayner asked without thinking, still trying to figure out how he knew her face.

"I am many things to many people. I am whatever you need me to be," she answered, her voice small and innocent.

"And I need you to be . . . a child? Why?"

"Why indeed."

Rayner reached up, pushing back his hood, suddenly unconcerned with being too exposed in the Oracle's presence. "The High Witch said you have been waiting for me," he said hoarsely, not liking how much the sight of a child was throwing him off balance.

"I have been," she agreed, her head tilting slightly. "But I did not know if it would be the Ash Rider who found their way to me or one of the many other titles you go by or will go by."

"You are the Oracle. How could you not know?"

A faint smile appeared on her lips. "Fate is constantly changing. Every choice one makes alters what is to come, which means every future I glimpse is only one possibility." She began to move, leaving small footprints in the dirt as she circled him. "What do you seek from me?"

"My memories," he answered. "My past. I do not . . . My earliest memory is from nearly six decades ago. I know nothing of my life before that."

"No," the girl said, shaking her head. "That is not what you seek."

Unsure of what to say to that, he watched for a few silent moments before he said, "That is all I have sought since I found myself on a beach in the Water Court, unaware of how I arrived there."

"That is what you think you have been seeking," she corrected, disappearing into the shadows of the cave where he could no longer see her.

Rayner spun, her voice coming from behind him now. "Then what is it you think I have been seeking?"

"Why do you seek these lost memories?"

"Who wouldn't want to know where they came from?"

"What does it matter?" the voice countered, coming from his left this time. "Will your past decide your future?"

"Maybe."

"Why?" The question was full of a child's curiosity.

"Why? Why wouldn't it?"

"Will it define who you are?"

"I already know I am an Ash Rider."

"That is what you are. Not who you are. And even then . . ." Rayner whirled, the voice coming from another spot in the cave now. "Even then, that is not entirely what you are. You are more than ash and smoke. You are more than Fae. But none of that is who you are. So many names in your past. So many names in your future." She stepped from the shadows, a slightly terrifying smile on her small face. "Ash Rider. Wanderer. Favorite." She slipped back into the dark, stepping from somewhere new that had Rayner spinning around yet again. "Reaper."

"Reaper?"

Her smile tipped up even more, her head tilting. "Brother."

"Brother?" he repeated in a slightly horrified whisper.

"Would you like to know some other names that could be yours?"

"I . . ." He paused. Did he want to know? "No, I just want to know what lies in my past."

"Why?"

Frustration coursed through him. "Because how can I know who I am if I do not know where I came from?"

Her smile widened, and she stepped right up to him, her bare toes touching his boots. Her head was tipped back, and she spoke softly when she said, "That is what you seek, Ash Rider. Not your memories. Not your past. You wish to know who you are, who you are supposed to be."

Rayner flinched back when several torches burst to light, flames flickering and casting shadows along the cave walls. The child moved to a stone table that appeared in the center of the room, a basin atop it. She climbed upon the table, stirring the contents with her fingers.

"One not of this world took from you. Took more than your memories." She looked up, violet eyes connecting with his where he still stood across the chamber. "Understand that if I give these memories back to you, there is no undoing it. Consider that sometimes it is better to not know than to live with memories you cannot change. Consider that maybe losing these memories was a blessing rather than a curse. And consider that learning such secrets of your past still may not tell you who you are."

"Do you know what these memories are?" he asked.

"No," she answered. She reached into the basin, and when she pulled her hand back out, a vial was held between her fingers. "Make your choice, descendant of Anala and those who hunt."

"What does that mean?"

"There is so much more to your gifts than you know. So many futures," the child mused. *"I wonder which will come to pass."*

* * *

He'd taken the vial, and the moment he'd swallowed down the elixir, the entirety of his first three decades came flooding back to him. The Southern Islands. The cliffs. Moranna. Feris. Aravis. Breya.

He'd sunk to his knees when he realized the Oracle's form was that of his youngest sister who he'd been unable to save.

But he'd left the cave with a new title.

The Reaper.

That's what he had become. His sole purpose had become freeing the innocents still trapped in the cliffs, hoping he was not too late to save Aravis.

Rayner signaled the barkeep to bring him another mug of ale as he watched the Fae around him. A shady game of cards was happening in a dark corner. One deck of playing cards had already gone up in flames. He would bet this deck would go up within the next hour. A few females were off to one side, scoping out their options. Some for pleasure, some for coin. He knew if he lowered the hood of his cloak, one would approach within minutes. It was why he kept the hood up.

Well, one of the reasons.

The other was as soon as people saw his eyes swirling with the ashes and smoke, they quickly realized what he was, and that always brought about a gambit of reactions. Some wanted to employ him. Some wanted to fuck him. Some wanted to fight him. All of them annoyed him.

Which is why he snarled a warning when the barkeep brought his mug of ale over and someone else dropped some coin onto his table to cover his tab.

"Do not accept that," Rayner growled, reaching for his own

coin. He didn't even bother to look at whoever was attempting to buy him a drink. He didn't incur debts, and he didn't accept favors or kind gestures. Such things always ended up turning into debts in the end.

The barkeep glanced from him to whoever was standing at the table, wiping his hands nervously on his apron. "Sorry, sire," he finally answered. "I must accept it," he added, quickly swiping up the coin and bowing before he scurried away.

The bowing was perplexing.

Until someone slid into the chair across from him. Then it made perfect sense.

Bright amber eyes stared back at him, soot-black hair falling over his brow. He wore a dark red short-sleeved tunic, gold and copper threads embroidered along the collar. The male braced his forearms on the table, a faint arrogant smirk tilting on his lips.

The Prince of the Fire Court.

CHAPTER 4

Rayner wasn't sure what he had done to garner the attention of the Fire Prince, but he knew better than to speak first in these types of situations. If he was going to be accused of something, he didn't want to implicate himself for the wrong thing. If he was going to be asked something, he didn't want to give any illusion that he was the type of male who took part in friendly conversation.

"You are an incredibly difficult Fae to track down," the Fire Prince said, that arrogant smirk kicking up even more.

Rayner didn't say anything in reply. Just continued to stare at him from beneath his hood. He twisted in his seat at the sound of another chair being dragged over before a female plopped unceremoniously into it. She huffed loudly, crossing her arms, a red-gold braid hanging over her shoulder.

"How do you even know it is him?" the female drawled, signaling the barkeep for a mug of ale.

"I have eyes in my city," the prince answered, golden eyes still fixed on Rayner.

He held in his scoff of amusement. *Eyes in his city*. Fae were naturally stealthy. Light on their feet. Keen senses. But few could move as he did. Few could hide in the ashes and hear things not meant to be overheard. Only the Wind Walkers were comparable, the winds carrying secrets to them. But the only known Wind

Walker had recently been killed in a war he didn't care about. It was yet to be seen if her daughter would be blessed with the gift.

"Lower your hood," the prince said.

"I'd rather not," Rayner returned, and the prince's brow arched.

"Do you know who I am?"

"Of course I know who you are."

The smirk became a full grin now. "Good. Then a formal introduction on my end is unnecessary." When Rayner said nothing, he pressed, "Am I to simply call you what you are then, or will you deign to share your name?"

"What do you think I am?"

The Fire Prince leaned in closer, his voice dropping low. "I think you are someone who sees and hears everything, yet is never seen himself," he answered, echoing Rayner's thoughts from moments ago. "I have been trying to find you for over a decade."

"I think you have mistaken me for someone else, your Highness."

"Sorin," he said. "Call me Sorin, and I am certain I have not mistaken anything. I rarely make such errors."

Arrogant prick.

Silence fell among them as the barkeep arrived again, placing a mug down in front of the female. He also placed a glass of amber liquor in front of Sorin. When Sorin held out more coin to the male to cover the drinks, the barkeep tried to decline. He said the drinks were on the house, but Sorin insisted, shoving far more coin than required into the male's hand.

Rayner watched the exchange curiously. The female's grey eyes flicked to the prince for a moment before she picked up her mug and took a deep drink without a word of gratitude. The prince didn't seem to care. His attention already settled back on Rayner. He seemed to sense Rayner's question despite not being able to see his face.

"I would introduce her to you, but it seems unfair for you to know both our names when we do not know yours," Sorin said.

"She is your consort then?" Rayner asked.

The female spluttered, choking on the drink she'd just taken.

Sorin looked at her with amusement as she continued to cough around the ale she'd undoubtedly swallowed wrong. "No. She is not my consort. She is a sentry in my armies with a foul temper who gets into all sorts of trouble if she is not watched over."

Red splotches appeared on the female's cheeks. Not embarrassment, but fury. Rayner would recognize that type of rage on anyone. Honestly, he had to commend her for holding her tongue. He had a feeling it was only because she didn't wish to disrespect the prince in a public setting. She didn't strike him as someone who would care about offending him otherwise. But he'd watched enough people from the ashes over the decades to recognize that something was fractured in the female. That she may be harsh and ill-tempered, but she was also barely hanging on. Somehow the prince was helping her keep it all together, not as a consort as he stated, but as . . . something.

Something he'd never had before. What would it be like to simply have people in your life who didn't want something from you?

Didn't matter. He didn't need others. They got in the way of what he needed to do.

"I have a problem," Sorin said.

There it was. Back to being sought out because someone wanted something from him. The prince probably desired help in this war that had been playing out for centuries. Rayner knew the prince's parents had been killed by Queen Esmeray a few years ago, but Rayner had been unconcerned with the war. He had his own war to wage. The people of this continent could fight and kill each other all they wanted. He had other things to hunt down and kill.

"You are the Fire Prince with multiple resources at your disposal," Rayner answered.

"Yes, but they are all proving to be ineffective."

"I do not care about this war."

Sorin waved a dismissive hand. "We are all breathing easier since Queen Eliné and Queen Henna put up the wards to keep out those who wish our people harm. Plus, I have other people at my disposal for that, as you said. They are quite effective at their jobs. My people wish to return to their normal lives after decades of war."

Rayner still didn't care, but he was rather intrigued at this point. When he didn't respond, Sorin took it as a sign to continue with his request.

"There is a thief in my Court. One that has proven even harder to track down than you. I have been receiving complaints of large amounts of coin and other valuables mysteriously going missing."

Rayner scoffed. "I am sure the wealthy will survive the loss of a little coin."

"Yes, but while the thief does seem to target the elite, they do not appear to discriminate either. Only the poorest of my Court seem to be left alone from what we can tell over the decades."

"*Decades?*" Rayner repeated.

Sorin nodded, face going serious. Gone was the slight smirk and arrogance. In its place was what one would expect the Fire Prince to look like. Embers flickered in his golden irises at the fury he felt on behalf of his people. This was a prince who did whatever was required of him to fight for those in his charge.

"Yes," Sorin answered. "As I said, our efforts have proven fruitless. The thief does not seem to have any pattern. One report comes in from Threlarion, the next from a village nestled in the Fiera Mountains. Then one comes in from Solembra, with the next near the mortal border."

"The port city as well, I am assuming?" Rayner asked.

"Oddly, no. Aelyndee is the one place no one has reported any theft. There is theft there, of course, but from what we can tell, it is not this particular thief."

That was odd. One would think the docks full of goods would be a prime location for such thieving.

"I would pay you for your time and expertise, of course," Sorin continued. "Whatever resources I have would be at your disposal."

"I appreciate the offer, but I have my own matters to tend to," Rayner said, reaching for his mug.

"Anything I can offer assistance with?"

Rayner blinked at the prince, not that he could see him with his hood still in place. "What?"

"These tasks you have. Can I be of assistance in any way?"

"I do not exchange favors or work."

"Understood. I am not offering under such assumptions. I would offer my assistance even if I was not seeking your help," Sorin answered, sipping at his liquor.

That . . . didn't seem right. No one simply offered services without expecting something in return. Not that the prince could help anyway. No one could help him with this task. You had to carry the brand to find the entrance to the cliffs, and then there was navigating the various levels.

"Again, I appreciate the offer, but I do not think there is much you can do to assist me."

The prince's brows rose. "You understand I am the sitting Royal? I have numerous resources at my disposal. Relations with other Courts. Relations with other territories, including the Shifters."

"As I said, I do not think there is much you can do to assist me."

Sorin sat back in his chair, his golden stare intense as he tried to peer beneath the hood. "What will it take to convince you to aid me in this matter?"

"Respectfully, I decline any and all offers."

The female huffed a snort of amusement, and Sorin sent her a look that said he was not impressed. He sat in silence for a few moments, appearing to be debating something internally, before he said, "Whenever you complete your tasks, find me. I trust you will be able to track me down. And if you find you could use my assistance after all with those tasks . . . Well, again, you know how to find me." Sorin stood, tossing a purse of coin onto the table. "Consider it an advance if you decide to take me up on my offer, and if not . . ." He shrugged. "Consider it compensation for your time today."

"I don't need it," Rayner said, trying to shove the coin purse back at him, but Sorin was already stepping away from the table, the female moving with him.

Sorin shrugged again, looking back over his shoulder. "Then give it to someone who does, Ash Rider."

"Rayner," he called after him when he'd taken a few more steps, unsure why he was suddenly offering up his name. "My name is Rayner."

Sorin looked back again and nodded, the arrogant smirk ghosting over his lips once more. He turned back to the female, and Rayner heard him say, "I will get you a portal back to the palace. I have to meet with Eliné."

The Fae Queen.

How had Rayner forgotten that the Fire Prince was also the Fae Queen's Second?

The Fae Queen was powerful, and rumor had it, she had access to some ancient magic. Power that had long ago disappeared from this world.

Rayner lurched to his feet as he called, "Fire Prince."

Sorin turned once more, a brow raised in question.

"Perhaps there is something you can assist me with after all."

CHAPTER 5

"Sorin!"

A youngling's voice pierced the silence as Sorin escorted Rayner through the Black Halls. His hood was down. The guards of the Halls had refused him entry unless he revealed his face, and Rayner needed the help of the Fae Queen more than he needed to remain unseen, so he'd complied.

He paused when Sorin stopped outside of what appeared to be a sitting room, and a child of no more than three was making her way as fast as she could on little legs to the prince. Tangled mahogany hair surrounded her small face, and her jade green eyes were full of delight and fixed entirely on Sorin.

The Fire Prince crouched down, catching her gently. "Talwyn, what are you doing awake?" He glanced up at the harried nursemaid, who was making her way over. "Should she not be napping?"

"Tell her that," the nursemaid replied, blowing stray hair from her face.

The child just giggled.

Talwyn Semiria. Orphaned daughter of the late Queen Henna, Queen Eliné's sister. The child would be the Fae Queen of the Eastern Courts when she was of age. Until then, it appeared her aunt was raising her.

"I will watch her for a bit, Rosemary. Take a break," Sorin said, still crouched before the Fae Princess who was peering up at Rayner. She watched him, eyes narrowed in suspicion as she pressed into Sorin.

The nursemaid wrung her fingers together. "Are you sure, your Highness? I do not wish to impose."

"It is fine, Rosemary," Sorin answered, a warm smile filling his face. "Do whatever you need to do."

The nursemaid bowed, excusing herself, and Rayner's attention was drawn back to the prince when Talwyn said, "Fire, Sorin!"

The prince chuckled, flames springing up and moving around the room while the princess chased them about. Sorin pushed back to his feet, lifting a hand, and a fire message disappeared among some flames. "I will have Eliné meet us here."

Rayner merely nodded, unable to tear his eyes away from the little girl. Memories of another child with bright red hair giggling while his ashes had drifted around her and she tried to catch them in her small hands.

"Rayner?"

He blinked, finding the Fire Prince studying him. Rayner cleared his throat, forcing himself to look away from Talwyn. "Yes?"

The prince appeared to hesitate before he said, "I want to make it clear that I do not expect any form of repayment for arranging this audience. You are not indebted to me in any way."

Rayner stared back at him. "You want nothing?"

"I still hope you will reconsider and aid me, but I am not requiring such a thing."

"Sorin?"

They both turned at the sound of the feminine voice, and Rayner took in the Fae Queen. She was ethereal. Dark brown hair was swept into a knot at her nape, icy blue eyes surveying them all. A silver circlet sat atop her brow, and she smiled when her gaze landed on her niece.

"Eliné," Sorin said, striding towards her. "This is Rayner."

"Your Majesty," Rayner greeted, bowing at the waist.

"A pleasure, Rayner," she replied. Her head tilted as he straightened. "Sorin has been searching for you for quite some time."

"This has nothing to do with that," Sorin cut in quickly, catching Talwyn by the arm when she tripped over the rug and nearly landed on her face. The child giggled as he swung her up, settling her on his shoulders. "I will leave you two to visit while I take this one to nap."

"No!" Talwyn cried, squirming atop his shoulders, but then she was giggling again as tiny flames danced along her arms and feet.

Eliné watched them leave. She waited a bit before she said to the two sentries standing guard. "Leave us." The pair hesitated, but when the queen sent them another look, they bowed their heads before doing as they'd been ordered. When the doors to the room were shut, she motioned to a set of armchairs near the hearth. "Please sit."

"After you, your Majesty," Rayner replied, stepping back for her to pass.

When they were both seated, Eliné's hands folded and resting in her lap, she said, "What can I do for you, Rayner?"

It was strange to hear his name. So few knew it, and even fewer used it. It was always Ash Rider. Known for what he could do, not for who he was.

"I am in need of your knowledge."

A brow arched. "I am intrigued."

"Do you know of a way to kill a being who can manipulate and control emotion?"

Eliné went utterly still. "There are no such beings in this world."

"But if there were, how would you defeat one? Shirastone does not seem to affect—"

"You speak as if there is one in this world, Rayner," the queen interrupted, the temperature in the room dropping noticeably.

"There is," he confirmed. "She is powerful, and I do not believe her to be Fae, but something . . . else."

The Fae Queen stood abruptly. "Where? Where is this being?"

"The Southern Islands," Rayner answered, watching her begin to pace in front of the hearth.

"There is nothing on those islands."

"There is an entire colony hidden among some cliffs. There are powerful enchantments around them."

"Who? Tell me her name," Eliné demanded.

"Those forced to live there call her the Baroness, but her name is Moranna."

Eliné hissed a soft curse at the name. She was muttering, speaking to herself, and the only thing Rayner could catch was, "She must have come through with . . ." She cut herself off, turning and offering Rayner an apologetic smile. "Forgive me. It has been a very long time since I have heard that name."

"You know her?"

"I know of her. I know . . ." Eliné grimaced, her icy blue eyes holding pity when she met Rayner's gaze. "I know what she does. I know how you likely came into this world. I did not know she was here though, or I swear to Saylah, I would have done something. I will take care of this."

But Rayner was already shaking his head. "Her death is mine."

He proceeded to tell the Fae Queen what he knew, how he had been Moranna's personal guard, how he had learned what she was doing, the curse that took his memories, and what he had been doing since the Oracle had helped him recover them. He left out the parts about Breya and Aravis. She might be willing to help him, but he didn't trust anyone with information like that. Not when it could easily be used against him. Not when Aravis was still being used against him.

The queen clasped her hands behind her back. "You are correct in your belief that she is not Fae. She was created to serve a different purpose. Shirastone does not affect her because she is not Fae."

"She has bands of deathstone. Not much, but she has these bands for the wrists that stifle my gifts. Do you know of a way to combat that?"

Eliné shook her head. "There is no way to combat deathstone, and such a thing would suppress her gifts, but then you are still with the problem of actually ending her."

"There are also wards around the islands," Rayner continued. "They used to just be around the cliffs themselves, but I was informed on my last visit that she has somehow warded the entirety of the islands. She knows the moment I step onto them, so taking her by surprise will not be an option."

The queen smoothed her hands down her dress. "If you have some time, I may have a few things that can be of assistance. I can have food prepared for you?"

"I am fine, thank you."

She nodded. "Would you like a room to rest?"

"I am fine here if that is all right with you."

She nodded again. "I will send some refreshments."

Rayner could have told her it wasn't necessary, but he knew she'd do so anyway. Royal propriety and all that.

It was perhaps ten minutes later when the doors to the small sitting room opened again. It wasn't the help with refreshments though, and it wasn't the Fae Queen. It was the Fire Prince, a sleeping princess in his arms, head resting on his shoulder. There was some sort of chocolate smeared on her cheek.

"Eliné said you were staying for a bit," Sorin said by way of greeting. Rayner only nodded, eyes fixed on the sleeping child. "I would take her to her room, but I promised to be here when she woke up. I don't break my promises to her."

Rayner nodded again. He'd made promises too.

And then broken them.

"But I can keep you company," Sorin added after a stint of silence.

"That's not necessary."

"I know," Sorin replied, gently laying the sleeping princess on a sofa and covering her with a blanket. "Not necessary, but I also told Eliné I would deliver these."

There was a burst of flame along a small table and a tray of sandwiches, nuts, cheese, and drinks appeared.

"Also not necessary," Rayner said.

Sorin shrugged, moving towards the food. "Eat or don't. I will keep you company either way."

Rayner watched him fill a plate. Then watched him float that plate over to him on a flame along with a glass of liquor before he started fixing another plate for himself. But Rayner could just stand there, holding the plate and glass. When Sorin turned back to him, he stopped mid-step, a brow lifting in question.

"You are serving me?" Rayner asked.

"Do you need to get your own food?"

"You are a prince."

"Whose job is to serve those in his care. Do you not have a residence in Solembra?"

"Yes, but—"

Sorin grinned, jerking his chin toward an armchair. "Just take a seat and eat, Rayner."

He waited until Sorin had taken a seat in the armchair the queen had sat in before he lowered into the one opposite him. Sorin already had half a sandwich gone when Rayner said, "Thank you again for arranging an audience with the queen."

Sorin waved him off. "What do you plan to do when you have accomplished these tasks of yours?"

Rayner blinked at him, the plate forgotten in his lap. "I've never thought about it."

"You have family?" He glanced at the sleeping princess. "Children?"

"No," Rayner answered. "No children."

"Family then." Rayner stared back at him. "I am not trying to pry," Sorin said, setting his plate off to the side. "My parents were killed a few years ago. This war is finally dying down with the wards up to keep my people safe. We are . . . rebuilding."

As terrible as it was, Rayner felt himself relax at the prince speaking of his own loss and keeping the focus on himself. He picked up a sandwich, listening to the Fire Prince speak of his Court, plans he had for the future, relations with the other Courts and territories, and Rayner found himself asking follow-up questions. Not because he cared per se, but because . . .

Because he'd never actually had casual conversation with

someone like this. His gifts had emerged when he was twelve, and he'd immediately been sequestered away. He'd been trained by private tutors in all areas—his studies, combat, magic—and once he'd mastered them all, he'd been assigned as Moranna's personal guard. No one wanted to be associated with the Baroness's personal guard. He had been hers, just as she'd always wanted.

He'd always been alone. He'd never considered the idea that he didn't have to be. That once Moranna was dead and those islands were nothing but a graveyard, it didn't have to be just him and Aravis.

So when the Fae Queen returned, requesting to speak with Rayner privately, he stood while Sorin gathered the still-slumbering Talwyn. "I have connections across the continent and throughout your Court. I will have them start looking for this thief, and when my tasks are complete, I will find you."

"That is not necessary," Sorin replied. "As I said, you are under no obligation to repay me for anything."

"I understand, but I will still have them look into it. They might already know something the way it is."

Sorin nodded. "I appreciate it."

When he had left, the doors being closed behind him, he found himself once again alone with the Fae Queen. She lifted a hand, and a dagger appeared amidst a flurry of snow. It wasn't anything special. The blade wasn't even shirastone. It was just . . . a dagger. Fiera steel maybe? But Rayner knew that would not be enough for Moranna.

He was trying to figure out a way to word his refusal of the weapon without sounding like a complete ass, when the ghost of a smile flitted across the queen's lips. "I know it does not appear to be anything special, but since your gifts will most likely be inaccessible when you face her, you shall need something to fight with." She held the dagger out to him, and he took it, turning it over in his hands, trying to see if he'd missed something. "It is imbued with magic not found on this continent," she continued.

"Then how will I access it?" Rayner asked. It wasn't uncommon for weapons to be imbued, but the bearer needed to possess that same power to access the magic.

"With ancient magic that has long been lost to this land," the Fae Queen answered. Another flurry of snowflakes, and a book appeared in her hand. It was an old book, leather and worn, and when she opened the cover, it was a language he could not read. She flipped to a particular page before turning the book around and holding it out to show him. On the page was a Mark, but nothing like the Fae Marks that were given by the Artists. This one was sharper, harsher somehow.

"This is Blood Magic," Rayner finally said.

The queen smiled softly. "That is one name for it, yes."

"I cannot perform Blood Magic."

"The Ash Rider gifts are rare gifts from Anala, Rayner," she answered gently. "I think you will find there are still secrets to be discovered about what those gifts can offer you."

"You speak like an Oracle," he mumbled before silently chastising himself for the insolence.

She just laughed softly. "While I do possess Witch gifts as my sister possessed Shifter gifts, my gifts of prophecy are quite lacking, I am afraid." The humor slipped from her features a moment later. "Moranna, however, was in service to a very powerful being who taught her many things. Moranna may not be a Witch, but many of their spells and ways can be learned without such gifts. It simply takes more effort and sacrifice. This Mark will activate the magic imbued in the dagger. The first Water Prince imbued it at the Eternal Springs when Fae first came to these lands. Study the Mark. Memorize it. I cannot let you take this book, but beware, Rayner. If that Mark is not done perfectly, things will not end well for you."

"What is the cost?"

He wasn't a fool. All magic had a cost, and Blood Magic required the greatest sacrifices of all.

"The magic contained in that dagger could very well take your life when it takes hers," Eliné answered.

That was fine. As long as Aravis got out, he would gladly give his own life if it meant taking Moranna from this world. He could speak with the Fire Prince. After spending only a few hours with the male, Rayner could tell the prince would do whatever he could to help him, including helping Aravis get settled into his home. Rayner would leave everything to her. He already had. A will was secured at the bank with instructions for all his assets to go to her upon his death.

But if he did survive this . . .

He met the queen's stare. "There is one other thing I was hoping you would aid me with."

CHAPTER 6

"Fuck," Rayner muttered when his boot slipped on the cliff side. The spray from the waves crashing on the rocks below made the surface extra slick, and the grips on his boots were doing absolutely nothing to help. He already had a particularly nasty gash along his brow from an earlier slide down the rocky side.

Gritting his teeth, he regained his footing and pulled himself up, his fingertips digging into the ledge he was holding onto. He'd always used his gifts to find his way into the cliffs, to find that weakness in the wards, but he was conserving every drop of his magic tonight. Moranna knew he was here with that enchantment she had around the islands, but she never seemed to tell anyone when he would come to wreak havoc. The guards were never on high alert. He'd surprised Feris in his godsdamn rooms. He was banking on her not telling them he was here this time either, and he didn't want to run into any of them. Which was nearly impossible without his magic since he'd need to go through the hidden entrance.

Which was why he was climbing the fucking cliffs.

Because near the top, there was a ledge that served as a balcony for Moranna's rooms. The ledge was small. Just enough room for a small table and two chairs. The ledge itself was sunk into the cliff side and not visible from the outside. It was her other failsafe. When he had resided here, he was fairly certain he was the only one who knew about it. He didn't know if that was still the case or not, but it was his only way in without using any magic.

He was hoping once he made it up there, he would have some time to try to figure out where the entrance was to this secret passageway she'd used the night she'd killed Breya in front of him. From what he could piece together, she had more secret rooms where she was keeping Aravis and the most powerful. If she was in her rooms, he'd deal with it, but he was hoping it was early enough in the night she wouldn't have retired yet. If her habits hadn't changed over the decades though, she wouldn't come to bed until well after midnight.

The dagger the Fae Queen had given him was strapped to his belt beneath his cloak. He had shirastone knives down his boots, and twin short swords strapped to his back with Fiera steel. He still had that arrow with a deathstone tip stored in a pocket realm too, but if his magic was inaccessible, he wouldn't be able to get to it.

He heaved himself up onto the ledge, staying in a crouch as he surveyed the space. The moonlight couldn't even reach into the dark space of the alcove. There was no railing, nothing that would make a passing ship think something was up here.

Rayner moved silently into the shadows, stepping around the table and chairs and pushing open the glass doors. He felt the wards ripple around him. He didn't know if Moranna was able to tell exactly where he was, but either way, he didn't want to waste time. Pulling his hood down, he took in the rooms. Nothing had really changed. A sofa in front of the hearth. A large walk-in dressing room and attached bathing room. A small dining set. A large bed off to one side.

The male in it though.

That was new, considering that had once been him.

If he was her new personal guard, he was shit at it. The male hadn't even stirred when he'd entered. Rayner didn't have time to play tonight though. He gathered smoke from the fire in the hearth and sent it straight into the male's lungs, overwhelming him before his Fae instincts could try to counteract it and heal him.

When he could no longer hear the male's heart beating, he shifted his attention back to the rest of the room. He took in the walls, how furniture was arranged, where decor was placed. Anything that would give him some type of clue as to where the entrance to this secret passageway was. When he came up with nothing, he released his ashes, letting them feel along the cracks and divots in the stone.

He was about to give up when the ashes called him into her dressing room. He followed their path, black and white dust fluttering to the floor, guiding him behind a section of red gowns that he shoved to the side. There was nothing remarkable behind them. The wall was pristine white stone. No grooves or cracks or indents.

He swiped his hand down his face in frustration before he ran his palm along the smooth expanse, searching for a trigger of some sort, startled when he left a smear of blood in his wake. The wound above his brow, he realized. He was keeping a tight leash on his magic, which included his ability to heal himself. But the smeared blood was flaring slightly, appearing to glow, and then an archway was appearing. Just like the main entrance that appeared in the presence of the brand beneath his skin.

Stone steps descended, torches lining the walls every few feet. These walls were not the white of the colony though. They were brown and weathered, like the outside of the cliffs. Pulling his hood back up over his head, he stepped inside, making his way down. It was nearly five minutes before he reached a passageway that branched off from the still-descending stairs, and Rayner took it, not wanting to overlook anything.

There were wooden doors lining the passageway, all of them containing small windows with shirastone bars across them. When he peered in a few, he found basic living quarters. Beds, sofas, hearths. They appeared to have bathing rooms attached as well. Some were empty while some rooms also contained sleeping Fae who all appeared healthy and well nourished. He wondered if their eyes would look as haunted and dead as so many of the others in the colony looked if they were awake.

He kept going, checking each room for signs of Aravis, but when he reached the end, he hadn't found her. So he trudged back, descending the stairs once more. It was ten minutes before he reached another passageway. There were wooden doors down this one too, but they were far more interspersed. There were no windows on these doors either. He checked every one of them. One appeared to be a records room. Rows and rows of shelves stacked with papers. Another was a small library with books lining the walls. He continued along, finding more of the same, until he came to a room at the end of the passageway.

This one had double doors, and they weren't wood like the rest of them had been. These doors were heavy stone, intricate carvings etched into them. He traced his finger along one of them, realizing they weren't symbols at all but a language. The wards were stronger around this room, and he loosed some ashes to find their way in, seeking out the weak spots. It took longer than he expected, and it took far more of his magic than he liked to work out a point past them. But he found it. A hairline crack near the center, just enough for him to get through in his smoke.

He materialized on the other side of the doors, finding himself inside a large room. There were various tables throughout. Some had cauldrons smoking atop them. Others had papers and books strewn about. There were some with herbs and plants. There were five different hearths, all lit.

An apothecary room, Rayner realized. This was a large apothecary room like the Witches had. Eliné had said Moranna had been extensively trained by a powerful being who had taught her the way around spells and blood magic. He was looking at the proof of that.

He took a few careful steps into the room, not wanting to upset any of the potions brewing or elixirs cooling. Activating even one of them could alter all of his plans. He made his way over to some of the notes, muttering a curse when he again found them all written in a language he could not read. The books were the same.

His gifts were buzzing beneath his skin, and he let his ashes out, if only to release some tension. They speared across the room to a bookcase, and Rayner followed. A few of the shelves held books. A couple of them held various instruments and scales, but on the middle shelf was something else. On one side sat a replica of what he could only assume were various worlds that were thought to exist. Which one was their own, he couldn't say, but beside the replica sat another sphere off by itself. This one had symbols too, but they differed from anything he had ever seen. The symbols seemed to move, fading in and out in a way that held him captive. He didn't realize what he was doing when he lifted a hand, reaching for the thing, too mesmerized by it to note his own actions.

The tip of his finger skimmed over it, all the symbols fading away so it was nothing but a light grey orb. He called some ashes forth, letting them drift around it, but the symbols did not return. Nothing happened at all.

He let his hand fall to his side at the same time a female voice said from behind him, "How incredibly disappointing."

He spun, finding Moranna standing in the doorway. Red dress. Black hair with red streaks pinned back. Dark eyes. Red-painted lips. Exactly as she had looked the day she'd sent him from these very walls.

"Moranna," Rayner said, his tone dark and cold.

She stepped into the room, graceful and fluid as ever, moving to a table. She stirred a cauldron, sprinkling crushed herbs into it. "I see you have finally returned home with purpose."

"I have had purpose every time I have returned to these wretched islands," Rayner spat, calculating her every movement.

"I have let you come back here. Let you get this vengeance you seem to need. I have not interfered once, but last time, my Ash Rider . . ." She trailed off, moving to another table. "Last time you made a very unwise choice in regards to whom you took from me."

"Feris was always going to die. Just as the rest of them will. It was only a matter of time," Rayner retorted.

"Feris is not of whom I speak," Moranna scoffed, bracing her hands atop a worktable and leveling him with a cold glare. "One of my most powerful vessels disappeared that day. I can only assume it was you."

"I took no one out with me that day," he countered. He still hadn't moved, still trying to figure out his best course of action. He'd scarcely killed anyone the last time he had come here. Three overseers and Feris. That had been it.

"I let you go out into the world," Moranna continued. "I let you wander the continent, learn what you thought you needed, and waited for you to come back with all that knowledge. And you repay me in this way?"

"I was always coming back to kill you, Moranna."

She laughed. "You cannot kill me, Rayner. You know if you do, your beloved sister dies."

"Where is Aravis?"

Moranna held up her hand, a band of deathstone held between her fingers. "Put this on, and I will take you to her. Then we will discuss what must be done in regards to your poor choices."

"And if I refuse?"

She smiled at him, the kind that told him she was humoring him. "You will never find her."

Rayner stalked forward, snatching the band and sliding it onto his wrist. His ashes thrashed beneath his skin, unable to break through, before they eventually quieted into nothing. Moranna reached up, patting his cheek. "Wise choice, my Ash Rider."

"I will kill you before the sun rises," Rayner gritted out.

"You are powerful, Rayner, but not that powerful. Come."

He fell into step beside her, grimacing internally at how natural this felt. How he had done this thousands of times. Escorted her all over the cliffs, but never here. Never to this secret place within the secret colony. How many did she keep here? And if he was one of the most powerful, why hadn't she kept *him* here?

Moranna led him back down the passageway to the stairs where they descended to the next passageway. The Baroness stopped outside a room, her hand on the handle. "Remember that her survival depends on you."

It always had. That's why he was here.

And tonight he would ensure her survival was no longer in the hands of Moranna.

Moranna pushed the door open, stepping aside so Rayner could enter, and there she was. Sitting near a hearth, doing needlework. Healthy and whole. Raven-black hair braided into a plait hung over her shoulder as she focused on her task.

And then she looked up.

Rayner sucked in a breath when grey eyes that matched his own without the swirling landed on him. They were haunted and broken like so many others he had seen, but there was also something in them he never glimpsed in the others.

Hope. There was a glimmer of hope there.

She dropped her needlework, lurching to her feet, a hand coming to her chest. Rayner reached up, pulling back his hood so she could see his face.

"Rayner?" she whispered, but he could only nod. Her eyes flicked over his shoulder before settling back on him. "What have you done?"

"Now you have seen her. Alive and well. Let's discuss the terms for keeping her that way," Moranna said softly from behind him.

The sound of her voice—the way she spoke to him about Aravis—had the monster she'd created waking deep in his soul. Rayner descended to that place where the Reaper dwelled inside him. Aravis must have noticed the shift because her eyes widened slightly, and she took a step back from him as he turned to face the Baroness.

"What are your terms?"

"You remain here, where you belong," Moranna said. "I have let you roam long enough, and you have taken much from me. Too much. I was hoping when you returned you would have learned more about your gifts, but it appears even that was a waste."

"You wish for me to return to being your personal guard?" Rayner asked. "Just go back to how things were?"

"Oh no," Moranna purred, stepping up to him. Her hand came

up, brushing back hair from his brow. "You see, your sister has been unable to produce any offspring of quality. But I suspect you might, with all that ash and smoke running through your veins. There are a few bloodlines I wish to cross with yours. I was hoping the blood you supplied me when you left would be enough, but it has not been. None of it has been enough." She trailed off, muttering more to herself by the end.

"If I agree to this, no one touches Aravis again. *No one*," Rayner said. "I am given free access to her and her to me."

"You will return to my bed, like before," Moranna countered. "But I agree to allow you to visit her whenever your duties allow you to do so."

"And no one else will touch her," Rayner repeated. "I want a Blood Vow, Moranna."

Aravis sucked in a breath, at the demand for a Blood Vow or the use of Moranna's name, he wasn't sure. Moranna's lips tilted up in a victorious grin. "Of course."

He pulled a dagger from his belt. An unremarkable blade of Fiera steel. He sliced it across his palm, the deathstone stifling his healing abilities. Moranna held out her own hand, her smile growing when he sliced along her palm next.

"I agree to your terms of aiding you in producing powerful offspring."

"Rayner, no!" Aravis cried, lurching forward, but Moranna held up a hand. Aravis immediately stilled, her features filling with horror as she watched.

"I will resume my role as your personal guard, in whatever capacity you require of me," Rayner continued. "All these things I vow to uphold for as long as you remain on this side of the Veil. I vow and swear this with my blood."

"I agree to your terms that no one touches Aravis again. She will remain here and be given free access to you, but she will not be required to perform her duties any longer," Moranna said. "I vow and swear this with my blood."

Their palms met, and when Rayner glanced at Aravis, he saw

silent tears tracking down her face. She was shaking her head in disbelief, but Rayner had sworn long ago he would do whatever was necessary to keep her safe. To keep them both safe. He'd failed Breya. He would not fail Aravis.

"Welcome home, my Ash Rider," Moranna said, intertwining the fingers of their still-joined palms. "Let's go celebrate your return." She tugged on his hand, leading him to the door. He only had a moment to look back over his shoulder at Aravis.

The hope he'd glimpsed in her eyes was gone.

CHAPTER 7

He let Moranna lead him back up the stones of the secret passageways to her quarters at the top of the cliffs. The archway dissolved back into the wall in her dressing room when they emerged.

"I'm going to clean up," she said, finally releasing his hand. Her palm had already healed. His was still steadily bleeding. She frowned slightly, fingers brushing over the band on his wrist. "You understand why I cannot remove this yet, yes?"

"Of course, your Grace," he replied, stepping aside to let her pass.

Her frown morphed into a smile, and she sighed wistfully. "How I have missed you. Your replacements have been . . . inadequate."

He smiled faintly, nodding his head, and she moved out to the bathing room. He followed, slipping beyond into the bedroom where he removed his cloak, boots, and various weapons.

For Aravis. This was all for her. He didn't matter as long as she was safe.

He was pulling his tunic over his head when Moranna stepped from the bathing room wearing nothing but a sheer red robe. Her dark hair spilled over her shoulders, hunger shining in her eyes as they raked over him. She held out a hand to him, and when he took it, she tugged him over to the bed. She shoved at his chest, pushing him down onto the mattress, and he went willingly. Anything required of him to keep Aravis from being touched like this again.

Moranna climbed into his lap, fingers sinking into his hair while she straddled his waist, her breasts pressing against his chest. "So many travels," she murmured. "Yet you keep coming back." She brushed her lips across his. "You have always been mine. No matter how far you strayed."

He gripped her hips, tugging her closer, and she gasped lightly at the movement. He slid a hand up her spine before grasping the back of her neck.

"When you have proven yourself loyal to me once more, I can remove that band," she said. "Then I can see all that power swirling in your eyes."

"Whatever you desire, your Grace," he replied, bringing her mouth to his. She deepened the kiss instantly, hunger and lust and want driving her. He opened when she nipped at his bottom lip, meeting each stroke of her tongue with his own. Her hands were roaming over him, down his arms, across her chest. Fingers skated along his torso, and when they reached for the ties on his pants, he flipped them.

Another gasp came from her when he settled between her thighs, her robe falling open. He broke their kiss, bracing himself on one hand while he trailed his fingertips up her abdomen, between the valley of her breasts. She squirmed beneath him, and he could sense her growing impatience.

"I learned some fascinating tricks on my travels," he murmured, fingers moving along her collarbone.

"Do tell," she said breathlessly, hips pressing up against him. "Or better yet, show me."

The corner of his lips tipped up. "I plan to, your Grace." His fingers trailed downwards again, stopping over her heart. He pressed his palm flat, leaving a smear of blood from his still-bleeding palm. "This reunion is all about you," he went on, fingers trailing around one breast, then the other. "It has always been about you." They trailed back up the valley of her breasts, into the blood smear. "But now that I am bound irrevocably to you, tell me, your Grace. What are we working so hard to achieve?"

She smiled up at him, eyes brightening with a different kind of hunger. "Power, my Ash Rider," she breathed, her back arching as his finger kept moving. The lightest of touches to keep her seeking more, keep her on the edge of anticipation. "The more power I can breed for my king, the more power he will bestow upon me. And now that you are back where you belong, I can finally make progress. I am hoping that one of your offspring will be able to activate the—"

But her words got stuck in her throat, her eyes flying wide.

A wicked smile filled Rayner's face as he leaned in close, the dagger piercing her chest sliding in a little further. "I do not give a single fuck," he whispered.

"You cannot kill me," she rasped, fingers clawing at his hand that was holding the blade in place. "You are not powerful enough. No one here is."

"I am aware," he replied. "Which is why I sought help. From a Fae Queen. She seemed to know of you."

Moranna's lip curled up into a sneer despite the agony. "Eliné," she hissed. "In service to the daughter of the traitorous ones. I told Alaric to take care of her." She grimaced when Rayner twisted the dagger. "But even she is not powerful enough. Fae magic cannot take my life. As much as this hurts, it is nothing compared to what your punishment will be for this poor choice," she gasped. She coughed then, blood trickling from the corner of her mouth.

"I know that too," Rayner answered, reaching with his other hand to swipe up the blood with his fingertip. He began drawing a Mark on her chest.

Right above the Blood Mark he'd stabbed the dagger into. In a moment, he would place the final line of that Mark and trigger whatever magic was in the dagger. It might take his life, it might not. But in the off chance he survived . . .

"What are you doing?" Moranna gasped, struggling even more beneath him.

"I want this enchantment you have around these islands," he replied, continuing the Mark. "When you are gone from this world, living your eternity in the Pits of Torment, I want these islands to die with you. No one will inhabit them ever again. I want to know if someone sets foot on them."

She laughed, and it turned into another cough, more blood sliding down her chin. "My sweet, naïve, Ash Rider. Not only is your sister bound here by these wards, you can only transfer this enchantment with Blood Magic, and there is only one being who has created such a Mark."

"Then this one shouldn't affect you," Rayner said, his manic grin growing when Moranna went still beneath him. "I think you already know I can use the Marks though, and once I control the enchantments, I can let Aravis leave them."

"Rayner, wait," she gasped. "Wait, you don't know everything. Let me explain—"

But she was arching off the bed again when he completed the Mark, the dagger sinking deeper into her chest. He felt it. The shift. Something settling over him, and then he could *feel* the islands themselves. Every soul moving among them. Those in the cliffs. The merchants at the docks. All of them.

"You are going to regret that," Moranna snarled.

Rayner said nothing. Just lifted his hand, showing her his still-bleeding palm. "The Fae Queen also gave me this dagger. Said it was imbued by the first Water Prince at the Eternal Springs."

Her thrashing turned frantic, hands clawing at him. "Please, Rayner. Whatever you like, it is yours. You want to leave? Go! You want to take Aravis with you? It is done!"

He bent over her once more, the dagger sliding in to the hilt. "The only thing I want, *your Grace*, is for your death to be as painful as possible. The Fae Queen assured me that would be the case."

He moved to bring his hand down, but her nails raked down his arm, drawing more blood. He tried to brush her hand aside, but she dug her nails in further. With a final yank, he pulled free, grasping the dagger with his bleeding hand.

But not before her fingers hooked on the deathstone band in her desperate attempts to stop him. The band slid off, being flung through the air at the same time that black flames flared out from the dagger. Rayner was thrown off of her, flying across the room by the blast of the flames. Flames that were so hot he should have been incinerated on the spot, but his ashes were pouring out of him, a tight shield forming and growing thicker as it strained to guard him from the onslaught of dark fire.

Moranna was screaming, and Rayner flipped onto his hands and knees to watch as the black flames consumed her. Eliné had promised she would suffer, and she hadn't been lying. His magic was being pushed to its limits as it held back the flames from reaching him. He knew he wouldn't be able to hold out much longer. And that was fine. He would go to his death willingly as soon as he was sure Moranna had gone there first.

Her screams died moments before his magic gave out, and when silence settled, he felt a ripple of power rush from the room. He didn't know what it was or what it meant, and he frankly didn't give a fuck.

Rayner stumbled to his feet, going to the bed to find nothing. Not even ashes. The black flames had consumed every last bit of her. The dagger was gone. Nothing left but scorched sheets and memories.

He turned back to the dressing room, getting dressed and strapping his weapons back into place before looping his cloak over his arm. He had arranged for merchant ships to be waiting offshore, waiting for his signal. All the innocents would come with him today. Any overseers and guards remaining would meet their deaths. When he left the islands today, they would be nothing but the graveyard he'd once said they would be.

But Aravis was first. He would get her to the merchant ships, then come back for the rest.

He raced down the stairs as fast as he could without tripping over his own feet. He was exhausted. He hadn't planned to use all of his magic reserves so quickly. It would take months to replenish any of it, and he felt hollow and empty without the comfort of his ashes.

He threw open the door to Aravis's room to find her curled in a ball on her bed, tears still streaming. She looked up at him, eyes rimmed in red.

"It's over." That was all he could say. He couldn't get anything else past the lump in his throat. But he took a step closer to her, and she was up and off the bed, throwing her arms around his neck. She clung to him, and he embraced her just as hard. "I am sorry it took so long," he murmured.

She just cried, her tears soaking into his tunic.

After several minutes, he gently eased her back, wrapping his cloak around her shoulders. "Are you ready to see the sun?"

She smiled—a real one—through her tears. "Yes," she whispered. "Yes, Rayner, I am ready to see the sun."

Her hand gripped tightly in his, he led her out of the secret passageway and back up to Moranna's rooms. He took her straight through, not letting her take in the space. He didn't want any more of her memories to be made here. They took a side stairwell that was only used by Moranna and her personal guard. It was so tight, they could only move single file down the stairs, designed that way for the Baroness's protection he'd once been told.

When they reached the bottom, they came out right next to the hall that would lead to the exit. He had Aravis wait while he took care of the guards at the archway. She didn't need to see that. She'd seen enough death to last lifetimes.

He could feel her trembling when they approached the archway, and he glanced down at her while they waited for it to form completely. She was decades old and had never seen the sun or the sky. She had never seen the sea or felt the breeze on her face. The entirety of her life had been lived inside these cliffs.

He wanted to watch every moment as she took this all in.

Her breath caught at the first glimpse of blue from the archway. She went to take a step forward, but he stopped her.

"Take off your shoes," he said, nodding at her feet. "Feel the sand between your toes."

She smiled up at him, the smile that hadn't left her face since he'd mentioned the sun. The smile he'd sworn he would see when he had set out to take her from here all those years ago.

Her shoes in one hand, he took her hand in the other and led her outside. He felt her suck in a deep breath as they stepped out onto the sand, and when they had moved down the beach, away from the cliffs, she stopped and tipped her face to the sky. The sun had just moved above the horizon, bathing everything in a morning glow.

He slipped one of his medallions from his pocket. He still carried them with him out of habit, and he was glad he had them today. They would give him just enough ashes to send a message to the merchant ships. He turned back to Aravis after he had sent the message off, intending to tell her what the plan was now, but—

He dropped to his knees where she was lying in the sand, staring up at the blue sky. She was pale, which was to be expected after living inside cliffs for decades, but the blood running from her ears, her nose, her mouth . . .

"What is wrong? What's happening?" Rayner demanded, not knowing what he was looking for to be able to help her.

She stared up at him, the smile still on her face. "I am bound here by the wards," she rasped softly, reaching for his hand.

"No," he said fiercely, squeezing her fingers. "I took the wards from her. I control them now. I say you can be free of them."

Her smile turned soft, and she lifted her other arm. A Mark stood out starkly on her forearm, just below the crook of her elbow. "When you left, she gave me this. Should you ever try to take me from here, it would kill me. It is separate from the other wards, Rayner."

"No," he growled again, gathering her into his arms. "I will take you back inside. I will find a way to break the Mark, and then—"

Her fingertips were pressing to his lips. "I knew what would happen when I stepped onto this beach, Rayner."

"You didn't say anything. You didn't—" He swallowed thickly, realizing his face was wet. Tears were coursing down his face. "Why didn't you say anything?" he rasped, wiping the blood from beneath her nose with the corner of his cloak still wrapped around her.

"Because I am tired, Rayner," she answered, eyes going back up to the sky. "I do not wish to live another day inside those cliffs."

"Just until I can find a way to counteract the Mark," he insisted. "Please, Aravis. Please don't do this. All of this has been for you. You and Breya. I couldn't save Breya. Let me save you. Please."

She cupped his cheek, grey eyes settling back on him. "I do not wish to live with these memories another day. You did save me, Rayner. You got me out. Now let me be free. Please."

Two tears slid down her cheeks, her thumb brushing along his jaw. He gathered her against his chest, pressing his face into her hair. "I'm sorry, Aravis. I'm sorry I took so long."

"You did not fail me, Rayner," she murmured. "You have saved hundreds of innocent people from terrible things. You have taken horrible people from this world. You killed the Baroness so no one else will suffer. You have not failed, Rayner."

He could hear her heart slowing, feel her breaths getting shallower.

"Please let me try, Aravis," he begged. "Let me take you back—"

But she was shaking her head. "I wish to cross the Veil where I can see the sun, Rayner. Please."

He stared down at her for the longest moment, and when he finally nodded, he felt her relax with relief. He shifted them so he could still hold her and she could still see the sky.

"Promise me something, Rayner," she said softly, squeezing his fingers.

"Anything," he answered hoarsely.

"You have done what you set out to do. You have liberated those beneath the cliffs. You have ended Moranna. You have saved me. When you have finished with those inside, let the Reaper die here with me. Only let him rise again to save your family."

"*You* are my family," Rayner answered, resting his cheek against the top of her head.

"Then promise me you will find another family. People to love as fiercely as you have loved me and Breya. Promise me that—" She paused, her entire body shuddering. He knew she only had a few breaths left. "Promise me you will move on from this nightmare."

"Some nightmares never end," he murmured through his tears.

"Yours will," she countered gently. "If you let it. Promise me you won't be alone anymore, Rayner."

"I promise, Aravis," he whispered. "I promise."

And he held his sister while she took her last breath, staring at the sunny sky with a smile on her face.

THE FIRE COURT THIRD

Six Years Later

"I don't even get the courtesy of being seen in his Highness's throne room?" the thief griped as Rayner led him down a hall at the Fiera Palace in Solembra. The thief craned his neck to peer into the formal dining room, then looked back at the door they'd stopped in front of. "Really? A fucking pantry?"

Rayner didn't say anything, letting his ashes push open the door as he shoved the thief through.

The Fire Prince was seated at a table, dealing two hands of cards. He looked up when the door opened, that arrogant grin Rayner saw so often these days appearing. "I was beginning to worry," Sorin said, dealing the last few cards. He nodded at the one empty seat. "Sit."

The thief looked over his shoulder at Rayner. "I'm to watch you two play cards?"

Rayner rolled his eyes. "He's talking to you, you dick. Just sit down." He stepped around the thief, moving to the bar that ran along the back of the room.

"That one's for you," Sorin said, pointing at a full liquor glass beside the cards he'd dealt.

The thief's golden eyes bounced back and forth between the Fire Prince and the Ash Rider. Rayner just sent him a taunting smile.

"I am not going to bite," Sorin drawled, taking a sip of his own liquor.

"No. You'll just toss me in your cells for a time," the thief bit back.

Sorin sighed. "Sit down, Cyrus. I have a proposition for you."

Cyrus's eyes narrowed. "How do you know my name?"

The prince sat back in his chair, swirling his glass, the ice clinking. "I know a lot about you. I know you grew up in my port city of Aelyndee, but have not been back there in decades. I know you have been a thief since you could walk. I know you have swindled more people than I can count. I know you have been robbing some of the wealthier of my subjects."

Cyrus opened his mouth to speak, but Sorin held up his hand. Rayner took a sip from his glass to hide his smirk.

He'd been working for Sorin since he came back from the islands six years ago. The prince and Eliné had helped find homes for all the innocent people he'd freed from the colony. In fact, the Water and Fire Princes had been waiting for them when they docked in the Water Court. Once they had all been settled, Rayner had taken the time he'd needed to refill his magic reserves, but he'd kept his word. He'd had people looking into this thief Sorin was having troubles with. They had quite a few leads for him to follow, and as soon as his reserves were full several months later, he'd started looking into all of them. They'd eventually led him to Cyrus, where he'd watched him single-handedly pickpocket an entire tavern in minutes and then walk into a wealthy district and do the same thing at a theater.

Rayner could have brought him in that very day, but Sorin had asked him to watch the male. Learn about him. Figure out why it had taken them so long to catch up with him. Figure out what made him so godsdamn good at what he did. Rayner could admit he was looking forward to seeing the male's reaction to Sorin's proposition.

"I also know you are an excellent thief because you can read people," Sorin was saying. "You have learned to watch others and figure out what makes them tick. You know how to find weaknesses and exploit them. You know how to do this without the other person realizing they have been swindled until it is done and you are long gone. That is talent, my friend." He tipped his glass in salute at Cyrus before taking another drink.

"I know I'm good at what I do," Cyrus drawled, swiping up his cards and putting them in order. "If you dragged me all the way here to congratulate me on effectively robbing your subjects, you could have just asked me to come. You didn't need to send the Ash Rider after me."

"His name is Rayner," Sorin said conversationally, organizing his own hand. "Between him and his network of contacts, we have had eyes on you for a few years now."

"Fucking busybodies," Cyrus muttered, tossing some coin onto the table.

Sorin shrugged, placing his own bet in the middle of the table. "It is my job to protect my subjects' best interests. That includes learning who is robbing them blind."

Cyrus tossed his cards onto the table, pulling the coin towards himself. "Great. You solved the riddle. What are you going to do with me now?"

"Offer you a job."

"Fuck off," Cyrus snorted, picking up the glass and taking a long drink.

Sorin placed his forearms on the table, leaning in to Cyrus. "I meant what I said, Cyrus. You have a unique talent. One I could use in my Court."

"You want me to *work* for you?"

"Work *with* me."

"Semantics."

"I am having some . . . disagreements with the Earth Court regarding Artist fees. I want you to help me with negotiations. Use these skills of yours to help me figure out my best angles."

Cyrus's eyes narrowed. "Then what?"

Sorin sat back, raking the cards in and shuffling them. "If we work well together and get along like I suspect we will, I want you to be my Second."

Cyrus went completely still. "Come again?"

"I know it sounds out of the blue to you, but like I said, Rayner has been watching you for the last few years. He has been reporting back everything he has learned about you. There is a weakness in my Court, and I think you can help fix that."

"Why not make him your Second?"

Sorin glanced at Rayner, and the Ash Rider shrugged.

"Because he is my Third. He is also my personal spy and is often gone for long periods of time. I need my Second to be more accessible."

"You hardly know me," Cyrus said.

"Hence the trial run with the Earth Court, but I think I know enough from what Rayner has gathered. I trust his opinions," Sorin said, dealing the cards once more. "I already have rooms prepared for you if you accept."

"Live here?" Cyrus asked, picking up his cards.

"Rayner has another residence in the city, but he mostly stays here. You are free to do whatever you like, but you will always have rooms available here as well."

The male just stared back at Sorin as if the idea of a place to call his own was foreign to him.

"So let me get this straight: I help you negotiate with the earth prick, and if you get all warm and gooey inside over how well we work together, you want me to be your Second-in-Command. What's the catch?"

Sorin tossed some coin onto the table. "I have my eye on a new general for my forces. She is kind of difficult to get along with. You would have to deal with her."

Cyrus scoffed. "A female? That's the catch?"

Sorin and Rayner exchanged a look. Cyrus had no idea what exactly this *female* could do to him. Rayner was a rare Ash Rider and even he avoided Eliza when she was in a foul mood.

"Fuck it," Cyrus finally said when he won the next round of cards again. "I'm in."

"Why?" Sorin asked curiously.

"Like you said," he answered, knocking back the rest of his drink with a smirk. "I'm excellent at reading people."

Sorin chuckled, glancing at Rayner again. "You in?"

Rayner nodded, grabbing the liquor bottle and bringing it to the table, sliding it over to Cyrus as Sorin dealt him in. He kept his eye on Cyrus while they played. It wasn't his official role anymore, but it was ingrained in him at this point to constantly be guarding his sovereign's back.

Only now that sovereign was more friend-turned-family than prince he served out of any sort of obligation. He'd sworn allegiance to him a year ago, the Mark on his chest proof of that vow. It had been hard to get used to, learning that he could depend on someone else. Trusting after doing so much on his own for so long.

He'd brought Aravis's body back with him that day six years ago. Sorin had performed her Farewell Rites himself. He'd been there waiting for her, just as Rayner had asked him to be in case he did not survive Moranna. Sorin and the Water Prince had stepped in, taking control of everything the moment Sorin had seen him step off the ship carrying Aravis's body wrapped tightly in his cloak. He'd been nothing, going through the motions to get innocent people somewhere safe. He'd never been more grateful to not be alone. To have someone there to take over when he had nothing left to give.

"Since you two assholes apparently know my life story, what's yours?" Cyrus asked, dealing the next hand.

Sorin paused, his glass halfway to his lips, shooting a glance at Rayner. He knew the prince would intervene if Rayner wanted him to, but Rayner just sent the thief a dark grin. "Do you know what a dreamer's lie is?" he asked, picking up his cards.

"Do tell," Cyrus murmured.

"That all nightmares have an end. Some never do. I didn't

know if mine ever would," Rayner replied, tossing coin onto the table to place his bet.

"And now?" Cyrus asked, refilling his drink.

"Depends on the day," Rayner answered truthfully.

Cyrus snickered, toasting him with his glass. "I hear that."

And hours later, when the thief was passed out on one of the overstuffed sofas and Rayner was still seated next to Sorin at the table, sipping on a final glass of liquor, he asked, "What do you think?"

Sorin knocked back the last of his drink, mulling over his thoughts. "He has his own darkness to overcome."

"We all do."

"Do you think he can do it?" Sorin asked, setting his glass down with a faint thud.

"I think he'll make an excellent Second if he can face his nightmares," Rayner answered. "They won't end until he does."

They sat in silence for a long moment before Sorin said, "He will fit in well. Balance us all out, especially once Eliza is ready to be part of this Inner Court."

"You think she will accept?"

Sorin snickered. "A chance to take the position from a male and prove herself? She is as bloodthirsty as they come. You know that."

"And her nightmares?" Rayner pressed.

Sorin's grin fell, his features turning grave. "Together. If we can all learn to trust each other, to depend on each other, we can face those nightmares. If we can do that, we will be a force on this continent."

"It'll take time," Rayner supplied.

"We've got time," Sorin answered. "The war is settling. Our people are safe. We take the time to do this right to ensure they remain so."

"Whatever it takes then," Rayner said.

Sorin nodded. "Whatever it takes."

Leaving Cyrus to sleep off his alcohol in the den, they went up to the floor where their private rooms were located. But when Sorin went to his chambers, Rayner continued up to the top floor. It had been a long night, and the sun would be rising soon.

Fire Court Third.

Another name he now went by.

And as he watched the sun break over the horizon, he couldn't help but wonder what other names the Oracle had glimpsed in his future.

THE REAPER
BONUS EPILOGUE

Sometime Later

"That's who's been stealing from the fruit vendors?" Eliza said skeptically. "He's, what? Maybe twelve years?"

"I was swiping coin at five years, Eliza dear," Cyrus said, trying and failing to hide his amusement.

Rayner suspected he was actually a little impressed with the young male as they watched him swipe another apple while simultaneously slipping coin from a customer's coat pocket.

"What are we going to do?" Eliza asked, crossing her bare arms.

Cyrus gestured to the male. "Go talk to him."

Somehow, the newly appointed Fire General managed to look down her nose at Cyrus while being several inches shorter than him. "Why am I the one going to talk to him?"

"Because you're . . ."

"A female?" she demanded, a brow arching.

"Of course not," Cyrus said quickly, and Rayner snickered. Amber eyes lifted to his in a glare as Cyrus gritted out, "I can talk to him—"

"You *are* a thief," Eliza quipped.

"But I can't right now. I need to get back to the palace. Sorin and I are meeting with the plant guy," Cyrus continued tightly.

"Prince Azrael," Rayner said, his gaze fixed on the male as he crossed the road to another vendor, mingling with the crowd. "One day you're going to slip and call him that to his face."

"Probably," Cyrus said with an uncaring shrug.

Eliza tsked under her breath. "Just go, Cyrus. We'll figure it out."

Cyrus shot Rayner a knowing look before he turned and headed back up the road to the palace.

They didn't experience much crime in Solembra. Not that it was nonexistent, but it wasn't as prevalent as it was in the outlying towns of the Court. In the years since Sorin had started forming his Inner Court, they'd developed a reputation. Not necessarily a bad one, unless you happened to get on their bad side. The other Courts were taking notice. The Fire Court citizens were thankful, and those who had to alter their way of living due to changes . . . weren't so grateful.

"What are we going to do?" Eliza said. "He's too young to face a trial or the cells."

"I'll talk to him," Rayner said.

Eliza's gaze whipped to his. "You?"

"I thought you were opposed to speaking to him?"

"I'm not. I mean, I was. I was opposed to the reason Cyrus suggested it," she retorted. "I'm also not . . . Children are—" She pressed her lips together.

"You don't owe me an explanation, Eliza," Rayner said stoically.

"I know I don't," she snapped.

He sighed internally. He'd known her for years now, and she was still just as abrasive. Every once in a while, a softer side would slip through. It was rare, but happening more and more. When Sorin had said it would take time to break through her armor, he hadn't been kidding. But no one understood wanting to keep to themselves better than he did. Eliza and Cyrus knew little of his history. He wasn't about to try and coerce the Fire General to share hers. It would happen when she was ready.

"You can head back. I'll handle it," he said, watching the boy break away and head down the street now.

Eliza hesitated. "Are you sure? I can help. I didn't mean to imply I *wouldn't*."

"I'll see you back at the palace," he said, moving to the shadowed side of the street.

Before Eliza could reply, he was moving through his ashes. He knew exactly where the youngling was going, and a moment later, he appeared in a dark alley.

Just in time for the male to run directly into him with an *oomph*.

He stumbled back, a curse he was too young to be saying falling from his lips. Then his golden-brown eyes went wide in recognition. He turned to run, but Rayner was faster, moving through smoke and appearing in front of him, once again blocking his path.

The boy's disheveled brown hair was hanging in his face as he slowly backed away, but his features were hard and his eyes narrowed.

"What do you want?" he demanded. "I didn't do anything."

"Starting a conversation like that indicates you're guilty of something," Rayner replied solemnly, his ashes drifting around him and watching the alley entrance. When the young male only clenched his jaw, Rayner asked, "What's your name?"

"I'm not telling you."

"Fair enough," Rayner said. "Do you have a family?"

"Do you?"

"Yes."

He huffed, his hands clenching at his sides.

"We've had reports of thievery around this area of the markets," Rayner continued.

"I don't know anything about that."

His ashes swirled a little faster, and he tilted his head. "Did you know Cyrus was a thief before he became the Prince's Second?"

The boy's eyes widened slightly. "Bullshit."

"I have no reason to lie to you," Rayner replied.

"What does it matter to me?"

"Maybe it doesn't," Rayner answered. "But that same thief saw you today. As did the Fire General. As did I."

"And now you'll haul me away?"

"It's that or speak to your parents," he replied.

The boy's lip twisted in a sneer. "Who do you think sent me out here?"

Interesting.

There were plenty of avenues for those experiencing hardship to come by aid, but there were still some too proud to ask. Others thought illegal activities would be more lucrative and worth the risk. Rayner wondered where his parents fell.

"Do they treat you well otherwise?" he asked.

"We do all right."

"Clearly," Rayner deadpanned. "You have a place to stay?"

When the boy just ground his teeth more and averted his gaze, Rayner added, "I have a place."

"We don't take handouts," the male said sharply.

Ah. So it was the too proud thing.

"Good. I wasn't offering one," Rayner answered. "But I have this place not too far from here. I don't get there often due to my work. Maybe once or twice a year. I need someone to look after it."

The boy eyed him skeptically. "And you want me to do it?"

"If you can handle it. Keep the yard up and the place clean. I'll pay you, and in return, your family can stay there too."

"What's the catch?"

"There isn't one. I need to collect a few things, but I can do that while you tell your parents of the arrangement. I'll be waiting there if they have any questions."

The kid fidgeted, his hands unclenching and fisting again as he clearly debated the offer. If he declined, Rayner would have to follow him home in the smoke and ashes and figure something else out, he supposed. He knew he couldn't help every single person he came across like this, but he made an effort when he could, especially when children were involved.

"I have two younger sisters," the boy said suddenly, then he stumbled back when Rayner's ashes thickened more, rolling across the stone road.

Rayner swallowed thickly, collecting himself and reining in his magic before he said gruffly, "Sorry about that."

The boy nodded slowly. "If it's too many people—"

"It's not," Rayner interrupted. "The house isn't big. Three rooms."

"Better than the two rooms we're sharing now."

"Is that an acceptance of my offer?"

The boy's eyes narrowed once more. "How much you going to pay me?"

"How much do you want?"

He lifted his chin. "Five coins a day."

"Five coins for each of you a day is reasonable."

His mouth fell open. "You're going to pay *all* of us?"

"I assume they'll be helping out if they're staying there too. Seems only fair. Is that sufficient along with room and board?"

Finally, the hard mask cracked, and the boy's eyes fell to the ground. He toed at the dirt, his throat bobbing with a swallow. Then he reached into the pockets of his jacket and pulled out the coin and fruit he'd swiped, holding them out.

"Do you have to tell the prince?" he murmured.

"No," Rayner answered. "He doesn't need to know of any of this."

Sorin wouldn't mind how this was playing out. In fact, he'd probably offer to pay the salary just agreed to and find them another house so Rayner didn't have to give up his. But this was fine. He rarely went there anymore, finding it more convenient to stay at the Fiera Palace, and his own wages were more than sufficient to pay them. He could find another place when the need arose.

"And you can keep those," Rayner added. "I'll take care of the merchants."

The boy nodded, his hands falling back to his sides, still clutching the items.

"There is a caveat," Rayner said, and the boy's head snapped up, anger simmering in eyes that had seen too much hardship. "I require knowing the names of the people I employ."

"Ajax," the boy replied, his relief palpable. "My name is Ajax Conleth."

Conleth.

He tucked the name away to look into later.

Rayner nodded, finally taking a step to the side and moving from his path. "Go fetch your family, Ajax. I'll meet you at the house."

He gave him the address and watched as he ran from the alley, a small grin on his face. After a moment, Rayner followed, paying the merchants as promised. The people Ajax had pickpocketed were long gone, so he couldn't remedy that. Then he made his way to the house he'd owned for decades now.

He didn't have much here. Some old weapons and spare clothing. Methodically, he cleared his personal belongings. The things didn't even fill one knapsack. He'd leave the furniture and dishes. It wasn't much, but he was guessing it'd be more than they had now. With their new wages, they'd gradually be able to afford more.

Checking the time, he knew he didn't have long, saving this final task. He knelt before a trunk in the corner of the bedroom, flipping it open. Pushing aside the blanket, he dug to the bottom and pulled out a pair of shoes.

It was the only thing he'd kept of Aravis's. The shoes she'd held in her hand while her toes had sunk into the sand for the first and only time. He had nothing of Breya's. There'd been nothing for him to keep, and Moranna would have stripped him of it before taking his memories anyway.

He tucked the shoes in the knapsack, carefully wrapping them into the spare clothing before pulling the drawstring taut.

Moving to the front porch, he set the sack aside just as the sounds of giggles reached him. Two young girls were running and jumping around a harried-looking couple. Ajax's sisters. He hadn't known of them when he'd made the offer, but seeing them now made his soul settle. Maybe the Fates were trying to redeem themselves in some small way.

Ajax pulled the male along by the hand. Rayner could only assume it was his father. The male and female looked skeptical, and he was sure they were. It was likely a wild tale their son had returned with. But that was no bother. He'd convince them just as he'd convinced their son.

Because he understood nightmares, and he'd help end as many as he could.

Unrelenting Winds

CHAPTER 1
BRIAR

She's here.

That was all the note said when the Water Prince pulled it from a flurry of snowflakes that had appeared in the air. It was a message from his brother with the same water gifts as his own, but Briar Drayce already knew she had arrived. He could see it in the reflection of the Tana River that flowed through the middle of the Fiera Palace of the Fire Court.

"I have a meeting I need to go to," Briar said, turning to face the others. "Do you need anything before I take my leave?"

Cyrus, the Fire Court Second sighed, but it was the Fire General who answered, flicking her red-gold braid over her shoulder. "You do plenty, Prince. It's our responsibility when he's . . . like this."

Briar studied her for a moment. He'd known her for decades. He'd known all of them for decades at this point, some even centuries. So he caught the flicker of worry in her grey eyes, a brief show of emotion she was always quick to hide.

"Our Courts have never done things alone. This is no different," Briar answered, glancing at the river again. He was late, which was rude in and of itself, but being late to a meeting with a princess was ill-advised, even if he was a prince himself.

"Just . . . don't tell Talwyn," Cyrus said.

"The Fae Queen has her own turmoil she's dealing with. We will leave Prince Azrael to handle her, and we will deal with the Fire Prince," Briar replied. "I will check in later today."

Cyrus pulled on the back of his neck and nodded. "Thanks for always coming here. The sea is . . ."

"I know, Cyrus. It is easier for me to come here anyway. I am the one who can make a portal," Briar reassured him, the sound of rushing water filling the air a moment later as a water portal appeared behind him. Only the Fae Royals had the power to create such a thing.

Nothing else was said as he stepped from the fire palace into his own Court. He paused for a moment in his study, taking a deep breath and letting the sea breeze fill his lungs. The Fire Court may have fire in their veins, but it would never compare to the warmth of the sun when walking barefoot through rolling waves.

The door opened, his Third and his Commander-of-Forces entering, clearly having felt him cross their wards.

"You're never late, and certainly not for a meeting with a Royal," Nakoa said, getting straight to the point. His Commander-of-Forces was tall and broad. He was everything you'd expect of a warlord with his cropped sandy blonde hair, keen turquoise eyes, and brown skin. Marks ran the lengths of his arms, and he never went anywhere without a minimum of five weapons strapped to his being.

"I know," Briar answered, falling into step beside them as they made their way through the halls of the House of Water. "Is she still on the shore?"

Neve, the Water Court Third, nodded, her light golden hair swaying with the movement. "She asked to wait on the beach. Sawyer is with her. Do you want us there with you as well?"

"I assume Ermir is with her?"

"He is not," Nakoa replied.

That made him pause for a moment.

"No," Briar said, mulling over this turn of events. "We all know her . . . personality. I need to be able to focus on what she's saying, especially if she is alone, and the rest of you there spouting your opinions never helps."

"No need to spare our feelings or anything," Neve muttered under her breath.

"You are all busybodies."

"You're confusing us with the Fire Court," Nakoa said dryly.

Briar huffed a small chuckle. He wasn't wrong.

"I don't think there is anything to worry about here, Commander," Briar answered.

"If you think any of us are fine with leaving our prince alone with another Royal, you were smoking mugweed with Cyrus," Nakoa said, his tone making it clear what he thought of the Fire Second. Which was fair. The two had very different personalities. The fact that Nakoa and the Fire General were occasional lovers was the main reason Nakoa tolerated Cyrus and his antics.

"Nothing is going to happen," Briar replied, growing irritated. "It's not a request."

"Of course it's not," Nakoa scoffed.

Something was clearly bothering him today, but Briar would have to deal with that later. He'd kept the princess waiting long enough.

They found her and Sawyer exactly where he'd seen her last on the shores of the sea. Sawyer was strolling beside her, her slippers in his hand as she moved barefoot in the sand. Her light blue gown swished around her ankles. She had to be warm in the heavier fabric the Wind Court favored. She was already turning, whether from hearing their approach or from the winds whispering his arrival to her.

"Princess Ashtine," Briar said with a small bow of his head. "I sincerely apologize for keeping you waiting. I was held up at a prior engagement."

Her head tilted a little to the side as if she heard something, and her silver hair flowed on winds that were more than just the sea breeze. Sky-blue eyes held his as she said, "The Fire Prince has much on his heart these days. Your tardiness is no bother to me."

He gave her a soft smile before turning his attention to his brother. "I have it from here, Sawyer. Thank you for keeping her company."

With pale blonde hair, icy blue eyes, and dark skin, he was almost identical to Briar, even though he was several decades younger. The Staying all immortals went through some time in their third decade of life kept them looking more like twins.

Sawyer's brow arched. "You are taking this meeting alone?"

"Yes. I already discussed this with Nakoa and Neve. The three of you can return to the House of Water if the princess is amenable to remaining by the sea for this meeting," Briar answered, turning to Ashtine in question.

"I am," she lilted in her soft voice, her hands clasped loosely in front of her.

Sawyer held his gaze for a long moment, clearly feeling the same way about this as the rest of his Inner Court. When he didn't move, Briar added, "I've kept the princess waiting long enough."

Sawyer gave a slight nod before exchanging a look with Nakoa and Neve. Briar could already hear the conversation that was going to happen around the dinner table tonight. Again, something he'd deal with later.

He waited until they were well out of earshot before saying to Ashtine, "Can we move a little farther from the water?"

She didn't hide her surprise at his request. "Do you not wish to be near your element?"

"Always," he answered. "But my brother is a busybody and shares my ability to turn water into a looking glass. He is likely watching this exchange at this very moment."

"If you wish to relocate, we can do so. We can move indoors if you wish."

"Not indoors," Briar said, motioning up the beach. "Just away from the water."

She nodded and moved to his side, following as Briar led her over to a small patch of secluded beach. He suddenly realized there really wasn't anywhere to sit unless they plopped down in the sand, and the princess didn't seem like the type who would do something most would deem improper of the title.

"Ermir did not join you?" Briar asked when they came to a stop.

She lifted her chin the barest amount as she replied, "No one from your Court is accompanying you."

"Yes, but . . ." He trailed off, not quite sure how to reply to that without also possibly offending her. "Does Ermir know you are here?"

Ashtine didn't answer for the longest time, but the breeze picked up around them, letting Briar know he'd offended her anyway. "Ermir is handling some things at the Citadel for me. I did not wish to pull him away from those tasks," she finally answered.

Ermir was her Second, but he was also the male who had raised Ashtine. More of a father to her, he'd stepped in when all the Fae Royals had been publicly killed after the Great War had ended. That was when all the territories had been separated. Wards had gone up, and the late King Deimas and Queen Esmeray had convinced the mortals of the realm that the Fae were trying to enslave them all. It was also the late Queen Esmeray who had come to the Courts and slaughtered the sitting Royals before their Courts, not knowing their heirs had been hidden in the crowd. But while Ashtine had not even lived a year of life yet, Briar had been decades old.

He'd stood in that crowd and watched his father, the previous Water Prince, and his mother have a shirastone dagger shoved into their hearts. Sawyer had stood beside him, so much younger, and watched the same horror play out. When they returned to the House of Water that night, Briar had a new crown, new responsibilities, and a new weight on his shoulders. Sorin, the Fire Prince, was the same. The Earth Prince was older than all of them and seemed to handle the transition the easiest, but Ashtine? Ermir hid her away, only letting Talwyn see her, the two females nearly the same age. Ashtine was kept from the public eye until she was ready to take her place as the Wind Princess. Briar still remembered attending her coronation and seeing her for the first time. She was nearly identical to Princess Ophelia, her mother and the previous ruler of the Wind Court, and she'd inherited her mother's Wind Walker gifts to move among the winds and hear their whispered secrets.

But even now, a few decades later, Briar could not recall a single instance where he'd interacted with the princess without one of her Inner Court members with her. If it wasn't Ermir, it was Renly, her Third, or Sion, the general of her forces.

"How can I be of service today, Princess?" Briar asked, ready to get to the point of this meeting, especially if she was here without her Court's knowledge. The last thing he needed was more tension between the Western and Eastern Courts.

"I am here to make a deal with you regarding weapons," she replied.

The portrait of poise and grace, that was the last thing Briar had expected her to say. So much so, that he could only blink a few times, completely at a loss for words. Finally, he said, "Weapons are a speciality of the Fire and Earth Courts, not Water."

"Yes, but imbuing them with magic *is* a speciality of your Court," Ashtine countered. "And that is what I need."

Briar swiped a hand down his face, stealing time for a response. He was even more grateful he'd had the forethought to move away from the water where Sawyer could spy on this conversation. Nakoa would have already shown up here.

"Can I inquire as to why you feel this need?" he asked after several seconds of silence.

"You may," Ashtine answered.

Briar rolled his lips as he contemplated his next words. This was why he didn't want the others here. Conversing with her required carefully phrasing questions and statements. She wasn't purposefully vexing, but others found her oddness irritating.

"Why do you find yourself in need of additional weapons at this time?" Briar finally asked.

"I do not require them for this time."

"For the future then?"

"I do not require them for the past."

He found himself keeping a smile from forming at her response. "That stands to reason," he conceded. "What do you fear the future holds that brings you here with this request?"

He could swear something akin to relief flashed in her eyes.

"The future can hold many things. It is most unpredictable," she replied. "But I fear the Great War was nothing more than one of many."

Briar nodded slowly. "That is natural to fear, but we have all been preparing."

She shook her head, that relief gone and replaced with frustration. "It is not enough. It is not going to be enough."

Briar's brow furrowed. "The Great War has ended. King Deimas and Queen Esmeray have crossed the Veil, likely to the Pits of Torment. Our Courts have known peace for more than a century."

"That does not dismiss bloodshed from coming in the future," she countered.

"I understand, but—"

"You do not," she interrupted, a gust of wind stirring the sand at their feet.

"If you know of a credible threat, you must tell me, Ashtine," Briar said, taking a step closer to her. Her gaze snapped to his, and he winced. "I apologize, Princess. The use of your name was not meant to be disrespectful."

She nodded slowly. Briar was usually fairly skilled at reading people, but not her. He'd never been able to get a read on her, but he'd also never spent much time with her. Certainly not alone like this. And as she stared back at him now, he wasn't sure where this conversation was going to go next, but by the gods was he intrigued.

He was also perplexed because this seemed like a meeting Ermir would definitely want to be present for.

"At the risk of your ire, does Ermir know what you are here requesting?" Briar asked when she didn't speak further.

There was another gust of wind, this one sending sand flying so viciously it stung where it hit the flesh on his bare arms. He was glad his hair was tied up, but Ashtine's blew across her face as a small swirling vortex appeared at the tips of her fingers.

"Do you require the permission of your Court before acting, Prince?" Ashtine demanded, and Briar hadn't known she was capable of such a tone. Her usual mystical lilt was still there, but it was layered with an iciness that had his own Fae nature taking notice and his magic stirring in interest.

"I meant no disrespect, Princess."

"So you have stated, Prince."

Well, fuck. He had no idea how to deal with . . . this. It certainly wasn't how he'd expected this meeting to go today.

"I am taking your continued silence as a denial of my request?" Ashtine finally said.

"That is not—"

"At this point, it is either an approval or a denial," she cut in.

"It is not that simple, Princess. You know this to be true," Briar insisted.

"Nothing ever is," was all she said, and then she was gone, walking among the winds that called to her.

And Briar was left standing on the beach wondering what in the fuck had just transpired.

CHAPTER 2
ASHTINE

The Wind Princess stepped from the winds, only to realize she'd left her slippers in the Water Court when she registered the cool stone of her rooms beneath her feet.

Blood will be shed.

A prince will fall.

The realm hangs in the balance.

A beginning or an ending? Time will tell.

Ashtine released a shuddering exhale. The winds were restless, and it was driving her slightly mad.

She hurried to her dressing room and stripped out of the dress that smelled of the sea, pulling on a fresh gown of deep navy blue with fine white detailing. Shoving her feet into new slippers, she hurried from her rooms, running along the small parapet that connected her quarters to the main building of the Wind Citadel.

He is to the left.

The winds' whispered warning had her taking the next right to avoid Ermir. She loved her Second like a daughter loved her father, but he had grown . . . worried about her these last months. It wasn't surprising, but they didn't understand.

No one understood.

No one else could hear the constant whispered warnings.

She moved down the stairs, taking them two at a time, only

slowing when she reached the main floor. Then she became the poised and collected princess she'd been raised to be.

"Your Grace?" came a feminine voice, and she turned to find her personal handmaiden.

Her dark auburn hair half up, the female's light green eyes held a knowing look, and relief flooded through Ashtine. The female may be her handmaiden, but Ashtine also considered her a friend. She was a few years older than Ashtine and had proven her loyalty more than a few times, keeping quiet about Ashtine's secret wind walkings from the Wind Inner Court. Few knew how often she actually ventured out on her own.

No one knew where she went on most of those outings. Many times, she wasn't even sure where she was going until she got there. Some might find that disconcerting, but she found it freeing. It was the only time her movements were not constantly watched. Guarded. Studied.

Everyone knew she was a Wind Walker. That had been expected considering her mother was one of the few known Wind Walkers in history. Her father hadn't been a Wind Walker, but had been one of the most powerful Wind Fae to exist.

Or so she'd been told.

But it stood to reason, given that pairings among the Royal Fae were often arranged to ensure power was passed down in order for the royal lines to remain strong. Ermir told her often that her parents' marriage may have been arranged, but they had come to truly care for each other in the end. When she was a child, she'd found it romantic and endearing. Now that she was older, she saw it for what it was: a story to make her more amenable to the idea of her own eventual pairing. An heir would be expected of her after all, and everyone would expect that heir to walk among the winds.

As though she had any control over that.

"Noelle," Ashtine said, forcing her breathing to even out.

"Was your outing enjoyable?" Noelle asked.

"It went as I anticipated it would," she answered, clasping her hands in front of her. "I was on my way to the catacombs."

Noelle smiled. "I am not surprised in the slightest by that. Would you like to take your dinner there this evening?"

"Dinner?"

"The meal one eats in the latter part of the evening," came a deep voice from behind her, and Ashtine's eyes momentarily fell closed at knowing she'd been caught.

He knows, the winds whispered.

I am aware. Thank you, she retorted.

As if the winds cared what she thought.

She sighed internally. This is why people thought she was odd. Or part of the reason, perhaps? She honestly didn't know. While others grew up with peers and families, her company growing up was the books in the catacombs. And Talwyn, she supposed, but that relationship was forged out of necessity, even if they considered each other friends now.

"Princess?"

She opened her eyes, finding Renly standing before her, his dark blue eyes studying her carefully.

"Yes?" Ashtine asked.

"Ermir has been looking for you."

"He clearly was not looking in the proper location."

"Or a princess was not where she was supposed to be?" Renly countered, a brow arching.

"Who is to say where one is supposed to be? The gods? The Fates? Time itself?" Ashtine replied.

The ones across the sea.

Enough, she snapped at the winds, her gaze going to where a window was open.

The winds could find her anywhere, but they weren't as loud when the doors and windows were shut. It was part of the reason she spent so much time in the catacombs. No windows down there. Everything was calmer, more peaceful. Even the winds there were more subdued, letting her be with her books and thoughts as she tried to decipher everything they whispered to her.

Noelle cleared her throat lightly, glancing knowingly at Renly before asking Ashtine, "Would you like dinner in the catacombs tonight, Princess?"

"That is unnecessary. I will simply procure food later when I am finished," Ashtine answered, feeling the air stir around her.

The others felt it too, and Renly and Noelle seemed to have some sort of silent conversation. Ashtine had never understood how others could do that. Then again, social cues had never been one of her strengths. It had never really bothered her until recently. It's not as though she hadn't tried, but being so guarded growing up, she wasn't around other children. When her primary sources of company had been mature Fae, fitting in with other children didn't come naturally. Talwyn was the same way, and now, as royalty . . .

Some days, it seemed rather pointless.

She used to prefer the company of the winds over others, but that had changed these past years.

"May I escort you to the catacombs?" Renly asked, pulling Ashtine from her thoughts. She blinked, finding them alone in the foyer. Noelle had disappeared.

"That is not needed," she answered quickly.

"I would enjoy the company," he said, holding out an arm and gesturing for her to move ahead.

She sighed internally again, and Renly fell into step beside her.

His father had served as her mother's Third. From what she'd been told, he'd been killed protecting her mother in the Great War. Renly had spent all his years determined to honor his father's memory by obtaining the same position. It was at Ashtine's own coronation that she had asked him to be her Third, the position having been vacant since his father's passing. While Ermir was like a father to her, Renly was akin to a brother.

Or what she assumed a brother would be like. An older brother, perhaps? She really didn't know.

"It has been a week's time since you have joined your Inner Court for dinner, Princess," Renly ventured as they turned a corner.

Had it truly been that long?

When she didn't answer immediately, he added, "Noelle also informed us you haven't been eating regular meals."

"It may have escaped me a time or two," she replied absent-mindedly.

"One does not simply forget to eat," he said, a hand gently gripping her elbow and tugging her to a stop. When she looked up at him, he added, "Except you. You have a tendency to forget to eat when you are trying to figure out the winds."

"That is an impossible task," she said with a slight scoff.

"And yet you spend hours trying to do just that."

Ashtine pursed her lips, her gaze darting to the side. "I cannot simply ignore their warnings, and that is what is being asked of me."

"Is this about the supposed war again?" Renly asked, and while he tried to hide it, she heard the faint exasperation in his tone.

Most people eventually ended up with that tone when conversing with her.

But the Water Prince hadn't.

If anything, *she* had carried that tone before she'd left.

"Princess?"

"Yes?" she asked, bringing her focus back to Renly.

"We have looked into these supposed warnings numerous times. Nothing has ever come of them. You know this," he said.

"And yet the winds still speak of them."

"The winds know everything and nothing," he said. "You tell me that all the time."

Her fingers curled into the skirt of her gown, and the texture of the material gave her something to focus on. "They are rarely this relentless," she finally answered.

Renly nodded, seeming to mull this over, before he spoke again. "We understand the winds can be prophetic, and we trust you to relay important whispers from them. But you must, in turn, trust us to help you decipher them. Ermir and Sion did so for your mother; let us help you as they did her."

Guilt turned her stomach, and she reached up, tucking her hair behind her arched ear. She offered him an apologetic smile. "Of course I trust you all."

"We take what you bring to us seriously. Truly you know that?"

"Of course."

"We do not simply brush aside your concerns."

"I understand."

His brow furrowed, and he swiped a hand through his hair, pushing out a harsh breath. "Perhaps you should dine with us tonight. We can all discuss your concerns—"

"To what end?" she interrupted.

"I do not understand," he ventured, eyeing her as a gust of air blew through the vacant hallway.

"Each time my concerns are investigated, they come back as unfounded," she replied, turning and continuing on her way to the catacombs.

"We are not simply dismissing them," Renly argued, easily catching up to her with his long strides.

"That is not what I am implying."

"Then come discuss this with us at dinner, Princess," he said again.

She forced herself to halt once more.

Blood will spill.

She may be too late.

The ones across the sea know. Go there.

Go there.

Go there!

I can't go there, she retorted. *No one can go there.*

She can. She must, or the balance will tip and—

"Dinner sounds lovely," Ashtine said suddenly, interrupting whatever Renly was saying.

He blinked a few times before saying, "Okay . . . Ermir will be pleased."

"Shall we go eat?"

"Right now?"

"It is the latter part of the evening, is it not?"

Renly nodded slowly. "Princess, is everything all right?"

But Ashtine only nodded, turning and leading the way back down the same path they'd just taken. Renly spoke to some staff as they passed, asking them to prepare dinner sooner than planned, and she felt a little guilty about the sudden change of plans. But if she wanted some peace from her Court for the next few days, she needed to have this meal with them. It usually kept them placated for at least a week, and then she found it easier to slip away to the catacombs or move among the winds.

Minutes after she'd taken a seat at the dining table, Ermir and Sion, the general of her forces, came through the door, eyes immediately falling to her. She forced a smile, hands folded in her lap.

"I didn't quite believe the note when Renly said you were joining us for dinner," Sion said with a fond smile.

"Why would he lie about something so trivial?" Ashtine asked curiously.

"He only means you have been hard to track down as of late," Ermir answered, taking his seat to her right before reaching over and squeezing her arm gently. "How do you fare, Princess?"

Forcing another small smile, she answered, "Well. And you?"

Ermir chuckled softly, reaching to fill her glass with wine. "I suppose I should have worded that in a different manner. While I am glad you are physically well, despite forgetting to eat several meals, how are you faring otherwise? I know the winds have been troubling you lately, Princess."

Princess.

She knew they called her that out of respect. It was her title, and Ermir had insisted everyone use it because she was so young when she took her throne. He didn't want anyone using her given name as a way to subtly undermine her. She understood that, but hearing Prince Briar use her name earlier in the day had been . . .

She didn't know what it had been, but she suddenly found herself wishing more people used it. Talwyn used it frequently, but that was different. Ermir had stopped using it the day of her coronation.

Now that she was really giving it thought, she couldn't recall the last time someone other than Talwyn had used her given name outside of introducing her.

Waves and winds will call to forces you do not want here, came the whisper, stirring her hair as the winds curled around her ear.

Ashtine reached for her wine, eyeing the open window. It took several seconds before she realized how still and silent the room had become. She found the eyes of her most-trusted on her, full of worry and unease, and not for the first time, she wished her mother were here. Or, at the very least, *someone* else who could hear the constant chattering of the winds.

"How did she manage them?" Ashtine asked into the quiet of the room.

Sion and Renly exchanged a look, but Ermir's features softened in understanding. "Ophelia had centuries of experience with the winds, and even then, there were times she felt overwhelmed by their veiled whispers and ominous chattering."

He could say her mother's name, but not hers.

It made her inexplicably want to throw something.

Power will be resurrected.

Darkness and fire of the stars will draw out the prince who hides in plain sight.

Gritting her teeth, Ashtine pushed to her feet, moving to shut the open window. It wouldn't do any good, but it was an excuse to leave the table for a moment. But as she reached for the small handle, the cry of a hawk had her pausing.

Nasima.

She hadn't seen the silver hawk in several weeks, and a part of her had felt out of sorts that entire time. Something eased in her chest as she spotted the bird gliding on the winds of the Shira Cliffs. The hawk was the spirit animal of Sefarina, the goddess of wind, and she was bonded to Ashtine. She knew her bond with Nasima was unique. She'd seen Talwyn and Prince Azrael with their bonded spirit animals. The wolf and red stag came and went as they pleased, gone more than they were present, but Nasima rarely left Ashtine for more than a day or two at a time. Weeks without her had only increased her agitation.

Instead of grasping the handle, Ashtine extended her hand out into the cool air. Moments later, taloned feet wrapped gently around her forearm, and she brought the bird inside, brushing her fingers down soft feathers.

"Where have you been, my friend?" she murmured. Nasima clicked her beak and tipped her head into Ashtine's touch.

"Did you want the window shut, Princess?" Sion asked, and Ashtine turned to find her general standing a few paces away.

"Yes, please," she answered, returning to her seat and letting Nasima hop to the back of her chair.

"Shall we discuss your concerns from earlier?" Renly asked as staff began setting plates of food before them.

"It seems rather pointless. They are the same concerns we've discussed prior," she answered, studying her plate of food. She wasn't hungry in the slightest.

"The winds still speak of a coming war?" Sion asked with a slight frown on his lips. "Do you feel we are unprepared if such a thing would happen?"

"I am not doubting your skills or your leadership, Sion."

"But you still feel we are not adequately prepared," he repeated, cutting into his meat. "We've increased our numbers, and we've been working on relations with the Witches."

"I am aware of what precautionary steps we have taken," she snapped, her hands flat on the table on either side of her plate.

A warning sound came from Nasima, and Ashtine knew if she looked, her feathers would be ruffled.

Blood will be shed.
A prince will fall.
The realm hangs in the balance.
A beginning or an ending? Time will tell.
The answers lie across the sea.

She didn't want to think about the kingdom across the sea. The kingdom that had been a part of starting the Great War in the first place, then created wards to protect their land while leaving the rest of them to finish the war and suffer greatly for it.

Ashtine stood then, her chair scraping as it slid across the stone floor, and Nasima released an agitated sound. "I apologize," she said, her voice sounding as defeated as she felt in the moment. "You all are correct. I am not feeling well, and I think I will retire early this night."

"Princess—" Ermir started.

But he was cut off when she said, "Good night."

She did not wait to hear their protests or their inquiries as to whether she needed a Healer.

Nasima flew to her shoulder as the dining room doors were pushed open for her, and she made her way back to her private rooms in the Citadel.

But she did not climb into her bed or curl up in a chair before the fireplace. Noelle was already waiting for her, a cloak in hand along with warmer shoes. Nasima trilled a small greeting, gliding to a bed post to wait for her return.

"Be safe, your Grace," Noelle said with a bow of her head as Ashtine pulled the hood of the cloak up over her hair and stepped into the winds.

She would figure this out. It was her duty to her Court to protect them.

She was their princess after all.

Not Ashtine.

Princess Ashtine.

This was her burden to bear.

CHAPTER 3
BRIAR

"Dammit," Briar muttered, realizing he'd left the tip of his quill on the parchment too long, a large blot of dark ink now marring the page.

He placed the writing instrument back into the pot of ink before sitting back in his chair and sighing. His eyes wandered to the open veranda, the gauzy curtains tied back so he could see the waves off in the distance. It'd been six days since Princess Ashtine had been here, and it still bothered him how things had been left. His Court may be part of the Western Courts and hers part of the Eastern Courts, but that didn't mean he didn't like to keep good relations with them. There was enough tension between the Fire and Earth Courts without creating a rift between the Water and Wind Courts.

He'd thought about sending her a message, but he wasn't sure how it would be perceived. She interpreted the world differently than the rest of them did. He didn't want his word choice to be misunderstood. Speaking to her in person would be the most ideal, but he didn't know how to set up that type of meeting without alerting the rest of her Court that she had been here. She clearly wanted that to be kept a secret.

A dinner invitation perhaps? But for what? He'd need to come up with a reason. And why was this so godsdamn difficult? He'd never had a problem communicating with the other Royals before.

Fuck it.

He'd just go to the Wind Court and see if he could speak with her. Say something about needing to . . .

What was he thinking? He couldn't simply *go* to another Court without invitation. Certainly not without some type of courtesy message. The Fire Court? Sure. He and Sorin were close friends and had grown up together. The Wind and Earth Courts? Absolutely not.

With another frustrated sigh, he got to his feet and made his way out to the veranda, leaning against the railing. The sound of the crashing waves usually settled him, but not today. He needed to visit with her. There would be no comforting this unease until he did. It was inexplicable, and, quite frankly, rather annoying that their interaction had taken up so much of his time and energy these last days. On top of all that, if she knew of a credible threat to the Courts, that needed to be discussed.

At least that was what he told himself as he sent a message to Sawyer, Neve, and Nakoa letting them know he was leaving for a bit before conjuring a water portal and stepping into the Wind Court.

He instantly regretted the brash decision when the icy wind of the Shira Cliffs whipped around him. He was in a lightweight tunic and pants, made for the sun and beaches. But he was already here, and there were likely wards alerting Ashtine and her Court. If he simply left, they'd be at his door within the day asking what he'd been doing there. He'd look even more suspicious if he left at this point. Swiping a hand down his face, he moved to face the consequences of his impulsive behavior.

Such impulsiveness was not a normal character trait for him, yet here he was, trying to think of a rational excuse for being in another Court without a moment's notice. He made his way across the stone bridge that stretched across a cavern leading to the Wind Citadel. The domes of the various towers of the fortress reached into the clouds, the Citadel sitting atop the highest cliffs. He didn't even have time to knock before the main door was thrown open, and he stood face-to-face with Sion, the Wind Court General.

The male's light grey eyes studied him, narrowed in suspicion, and rightfully so. His black hair was cut short, and Briar could see the hilt of his sword over his shoulder. Thick arms were crossed over a broad chest, and he said nothing. Just stared at Briar.

"Sion," Briar greeted, falling into his role of prince with practiced ease. "I apologize for the unannounced visit."

"Then what is the purpose of it?"

The demand came from Renly, who appeared at Sion's side. The male wasn't as muscled as Sion and was a little taller, but the small vortex of wind swirling at his fingertips wasn't missed. A reminder of where he was and that, in this place, Briar was not the greatest threat.

Then again, the greatest threat here was the princess housed within the walls of the Citadel.

But Briar smiled warmly, nodding in greeting. "That is a matter I need to speak directly with Princess Ashtine about."

Renly's lip curled into a small sneer. "Then arrange a meeting like anyone else."

"Ah, but I'm not just anyone else, am I?" Briar replied. There was no threat in his voice, but the intention of the words was clear as he held Renly's stare. The pair of them straightened, as if they suddenly remembered exactly who he was.

"You expect us to simply let you speak to the princess unannounced without just cause?" Sion asked.

Briar's smile turned sharp. "You can announce me all you like, but if she is here, I will insist on seeing her unless she is indisposed."

Sion glanced at Renly. "Do you want to consult Ermir?"

Renly continued to stare at Briar. "Ermir is out at the moment." Stepping to the side, he added, "But please come in out of the cold as we discuss this further, Prince."

Briar nodded in thanks, grateful as the door shut out the chill behind him. It may be the summer season, but this far north never saw the heat of his own Court. They didn't say anything about Ashtine not being here, which gave him hope he could make amends with the princess and stop worrying about it. Then he could focus on the countless other things that demanded his attention.

"Can we get you anything?" Renly asked as Briar took in the grand foyer of the Citadel. It had been some time since he'd been here.

"Only an audience with the princess," Briar answered.

"And you will not let us inform her of what this impromptu meeting pertains to?"

Briar shook his head. "It is of a sensitive nature."

Renly seemed to debate his next words, but he finally turned to Sion. "Send word to Ermir. Let him know the Water Prince is here. I am sure he will be most interested in learning that. I will escort him to the princess."

Sion nodded, some silent communication passing between him and the Wind Court Third. Sion left, disappearing down one of the corridors off the foyer, while Renly turned to Briar and said, "This way, Prince."

Each Court had a library, as did the White Halls and Black Halls in the northern and southern parts of the continent, but none of them compared to that of the Wind Court. Its libraries were housed in catacombs beneath the Citadel, spanning the entirety of the structure and beyond. Few knew how big the libraries truly were, only that they were extensive and the Wind Court was extremely protective of the tomes they contained. Visitors were always escorted, never allowed to roam alone, and several areas were closed to outsiders.

Renly led Briar through the winding halls, and they entered the libraries through a large set of double doors that opened into a foyer as grand as the Citadel entrance above. He could count on one hand how many times he'd been here. Once on a tour with his parents when he was a child, and again on a tour when Sawyer was young. The other two times were meticulously planned well in advance, but none of those visits had him this deep in the catacombs as they moved past aisles and aisles of bookshelves. The passages they took seemed to get narrower and narrower, and this deep into the libraries, there were nooks and rooms tucked into the shadows.

It was another ten minutes before Renly knocked on a simple wooden door, waiting for the invitation to enter before pushing it open. Briar wasn't sure if he was more surprised or amused by what awaited them on the other side.

There was a worn plush sofa shoved against one wall, and next to it was a decent-sized table with three chairs around it. The chairs were all different, though. One was a basic wooden chair, while another had a cushioned seat and armrests. The third was completely upholstered and looked more like a chair for a sitting room rather than in this tucked-away study of sorts.

Bookshelves lined two walls, both of them stuffed full with books and ledgers. A low table sat in front of the sofa, and perched on the edge of the cushions was the Wind Princess in a simple dress of soft grey, her silver hair gathered atop her head, and her attention fixed on the three books spread out before her. Several pieces of parchment lay beside her, and she tapped the thin piece of charcoal she was using to write with as she continued to read.

Renly cleared his throat softly before saying, "Princess, you have company."

Ashtine looked up, her eyes widening in surprise when they landed on Briar. That was interesting. She always seemed to know what or who was coming, and he assumed it was from the winds whispering to her. They clearly hadn't warned her this time.

"Prince Briar," she said, gracefully rising to her feet and stepping forward. It was then that he noticed the thick wool socks on her feet. "I was unaware I was to meet with you today."

"It was not planned, and I apologize for interrupting if you are otherwise occupied. I can return another time if you wish," he answered, glancing again at all the books scattered about.

"We tried to schedule another time, but he insisted on speaking to you personally," Renly cut in. Briar could feel the male's glare on him, but his focus was on Ashtine, her sky-blue eyes holding his.

"To tell me we could meet another time if I preferred?" she asked.

Well, when she put it like that . . .

"Yes," Briar answered. "I was hoping to speak with you about a sensitive matter."

Her brows rose so subtly, he almost missed it, but her Third certainly didn't.

"Princess, if you do not wish for this, he can make a proper appointment," Renly cut in quickly.

"It is fine, Renly," she said, clasping her hands in front of her. "You can leave us."

This time it was Renly's brows that rose. "With all due respect, Princess, I cannot, in good conscience, leave you alone with a rival Court."

"Are we at war with them, Renly?" she asked, her tone still light but the air in the room stirring.

"Of course not," he answered.

"Do we have reason to believe the Water Court wishes to start a war by harming me?"

"No, Princess, but you have been—" He cut himself off, glancing at Briar. "I would advise against this."

"Your advice has been noted and taken into consideration," she answered, papers rustling on the table, and pages in books turning. "Renly, if you please," she added, gesturing for him to leave.

Renly's lips were pressed into a thin line, his shoulders tense. Briar couldn't blame him. His Court had acted the same way when Ashtine had visited last week.

"I am not going far," Renly finally conceded.

"I would expect nothing less, Ren," she said with a small, reassuring smile.

"If you need anything . . ."

"I will send word."

With a final hard stare at Briar, Renly turned and left the small room, the wood door creaking as it shut behind him.

Then it was just Briar alone with the Wind Princes, who was

staring at him expectantly. His gaze dropped to the floor, finding her feet in the wool socks again. Her dress was a heavy material too, which only made the lightness of his own clothing that much more noticeable.

"It is cool down here," Briar said, wondering just how awkward this conversation was going to be. He deserved this for being so impulsive in coming here.

"The sensitive matter you wish to discuss is the weather?" Ashtine asked, her brow furrowing.

Briar's lips twitched. "No, Princess. It was just an observation."

"Did you do well in your academics as a child, Prince?"

"Very well," he answered, more than curious about where this line of questioning was going.

"And your studies included geography of the realm?"

"They did."

"Then one would assume you would know the climate differences of our two Courts and not find the chill of the Shira Cliffs surprising," she concluded.

"My trip here was . . . unplanned," he said, unable to hide his smile now.

"So it would seem," she replied. "Would you like to sit?"

"If you would be more comfortable."

"I would," she answered, moving back to the sofa and sitting once more.

Briar opted for a chair near the table, pulling out the cushioned one with armrests and taking a seat. "Again, I apologize for the unplanned visit."

"And the purpose of it?" she asked.

"I did not like how things were left after your visit to the Water Court."

Her head tilted, Briar assuming the winds were speaking to her, but she quickly turned and started gathering the various papers scattered around her. "I appreciate you not speaking of that visit to my Inner Court." She glanced up at him. "Unless you did speak of it?"

He shook his head. "That is not my place, Princess."

She nodded, stacking the papers atop each other. "If I offended you for how I left you that day, I apologize."

"You did not offend me."

Her movements faltered, but she moved on to organizing books. "Forgive me, Prince, but I do not understand what you are asking of me then."

"I am not asking anything of you."

She sighed, clearly exasperated despite her pleasant tone when she said, "Then I do not understand the purpose of this visit."

"You had concerns when you visited me. I do not think you were afforded the opportunity to adequately express them," he answered.

She cleared her throat lightly. "My Court feels those concerns are unfounded. I should not have troubled you with them."

"Do you feel they are unfounded, Ashtine?" Her gaze snapped to his, and he winced. "I apologize for the use of your name. Again."

"No one uses my given name. Only Talwyn on occasion."

"I apologize."

"I find I do not mind when you say it," she replied.

He wasn't sure what to say to that.

"Would you like me to abstain from using it?"

"No. I do not think I would like that," she said in her usual lilt as she returned to straightening her books and papers.

Briar looked around the room, noting the untouched tray of food and full glass of water on a small cart that had been shoved into the corner. "Can we return to the earlier discussion? Do you feel the concerns you came to visit with me about are unfounded?"

"I wish I could say yes, but it would not be a truthful answer," she replied, still not looking at him.

"Then tell me of them," Briar said, settling back into the chair and resting his temple on his fist. His hope was she would relax more if he did the same. "Tell me why you wish to increase your weapon stores."

Her movements had stilled once more, and she finally lifted her gaze to his. "If you are asking this to simply placate me, I do not wish to discuss this with you."

"I would never disrespect you in such a way, Ashtine."

Her stare swept over him, and she subtly nodded as if in agreement to something unheard. "The winds are restless. More so than I have ever experienced."

"The sea doesn't speak to me, so I need you to expand on that," he said, using these quiet, private moments to study her. The way she nodded to herself as she processed his words. The way she continued to fidget with the books and papers while they conversed. How she would steal glances at him, a worry in her eyes that he didn't understand.

"The winds carry secrets of the past and present," she said, her lilt softening. "They speak of things long past and paths of the future. They speak nonsense and truth, riddles and facts."

"That is a heavy burden to bear," Briar said gently.

"My mother did it with grace. Or so I have been told. I often wish she were here to give advice because . . ."

He waited, but when she didn't continue for a full minute, he pressed, "Because what, Ashtine?"

Her eyes lifted to his again at the use of her name, and for the life of him, he couldn't understand the reaction. Unless she was speaking literally and that *no one* other than Talwyn used her given name.

"I would ask if they spoke the same way before the Great War began," she whispered. "The winds speak of bloodshed. They speak of a prince falling. They speak of beginnings and endings and the balance tipping. And I am expected to understand it, and I cannot. Despite my days spent in this room among texts, I do not understand."

"It is often said the winds know everything and nothing," Briar said. "How can you be expected to understand everything they whisper to you?"

"Is that not my role as their princess?"

"Your role is to make the best decisions for the betterment of your people. Not to decipher ramblings that may mean nothing," he countered.

She shook her head in disagreement, but she said nothing.

"Does your Inner Court expect you to know? Does Ermir? Renly? Sion?" Briar demanded. He tried to keep his tone neutral, but if they were placing such expectations on her shoulders . . . It made him irrationally angry.

"No," she said. "Quite the opposite actually."

"You stated they feel these latest concerns are unfounded."

"I did."

"And you disagree."

"I do not know, and I find that aggravating," she answered.

"And you are down here seeking answers?" Briar asked.

"I spend much time here, but yes. I am seeking answers."

"Then I offer my assistance."

She went preternaturally still in the way only the Fae could. "Why?"

"Because if you believe we have reason to be concerned, then I owe it to you, my own Court, and this realm to look into them," Briar answered, standing and moving to sit beside Ashtine on the sofa. He reached for a book on the table as he said, "Show me where to start."

CHAPTER 4
ASHTINE

Blood will be shed.
A prince will fall.
The realm hangs in the balance.
A beginning or an ending? Time will tell.
The answers lie across the sea.

Ashtine stared up at the ceiling of her dark rooms, nestled under blankets and furs. The sun would rise soon, and she hadn't slept. Her fingers dug into the soft coverings, and she shifted, curling onto her side.

Power will be resurrected.
Darkness and fire of the stars will draw out the prince who hides in plain sight.
She may be too late.

Her windows were closed. The doors to her balcony were locked tight, but the winds still found her. They still kept her awake. They were still incessant.

Prince Briar had visited twice more in the last two weeks. Her Court was uneasy every time he was here, and she did not entirely blame them. Each of them had tracked her down individually and tried to ease into a conversation about what they were doing, but her answers never placated them. They had insisted on dinner as a court tonight, again expressing concern she wasn't eating, and Briar's increased visits had been brought up once more. Ermir had started the conversation, backed up by Renly and Sion, but she'd had trouble focusing on what they were saying. It had been a warmer day and all the windows had been opened.

The winds had been loud, and it now carried over into the night.

The realm will fall to one.
Blood will stain the lands.
Those across the sea know.
Go there!

She flung the blankets off, sliding from the bed and going to her dressing room. Shucking off her nightclothes, she slipped on a lightweight cream dress, leaving her hair unbound. She didn't bother with shoes. They wouldn't be necessary where she was going.

Five days.

It had been five days since Briar's last visit. The winds were . . . different on the days he was in the Citadel libraries with her. Perhaps it was simply because she was in the catacombs, but this wasn't the same. She could feel the winds stir, but they were quieter. The incessant whispers were occasional murmurs that she found easy to ignore if she wished.

And it was because of that she found herself stepping into the winds and then onto the shores of a beach.

Winds and waves. The balance tips.

Stop, she retorted, but there was no bite in her mental reply. She was too exhausted to feel the annoyance.

Blood will be shed.
A prince will fall.
Answers lie across the sea, locked away and hidden.

Gritting her teeth, Ashtine moved down the beach until the waves rolled over the tops of her feet and her toes sank into the wet sand. She'd hoped it would ground her for some inexplicable reason. It did nothing of the sort.

Blood will spill.
Enough! she snapped.

Find the one to cross the sea.

"Be still!" she cried into the night, her voice breaking as another round of waves rolled to shore.

He comes.

She turned just as a water portal appeared, and the Water Prince stepped onto the beach. Wearing only loose linen pants, the moonlight reflected off his dark skin, and his white hair appeared nearly as silver as her own beneath the stars. He went still when he spotted her, as if he hadn't expected her to be there. But that couldn't be right. Why else would he suddenly come to the beach at this exact place and moment in time? She'd assumed he'd felt her cross into his Court. All the Court Royals could feel when great power entered their territory. Most of their Inner Courts could feel it too.

"Princess Ashtine," he greeted, stopping several feet away from her.

"Prince Drayce," she returned in kind.

His icy gaze swept over her. "Are you well?"

Her smile was forced as she turned to face the waters once more. "Do you ever attempt to outrun the waves?"

"No. They call to me, and my soul answers," he replied, moving to stand beside her before facing the sea as well. "But the waves are not as capricious as the winds."

Ashtine glanced at him side-long, finding him with his hands clasped behind his back and eyes closed. Only the sounds of the waters stirred the night. Even the winds had gone still.

"I used to feel such things about the winds until days of late," she said softly.

Briar turned, and she felt his gaze on her. "How else can I be of aid, Ashtine?"

Ashtine.

Her name from his lips brought her the grounded feeling she'd been seeking by coming here. It had not been the beach or the waves, and something uneasy crept up her spine at the idea of that.

It was dangerous to seek such respite in another, and it was foolish to find it in a prince from a rival court.

"I should not have come here uninvited," she said suddenly, taking a step back from him.

"Did I not do the same to you mere weeks ago?" he countered.

"Yes, but you had a purpose."

"You do not strike me as someone who takes aimless actions."

She wasn't someone who did that.

And she had come here with a purpose. She just hadn't expected him to be the one to fulfill what she was seeking.

"The winds are not as volatile when I am around you," she said suddenly. "I do not understand why. Even now, they do not speak when they have tormented me all night. All day. Too many days and nights."

His brow furrowed. "Ashtine, when was the last time you truly slept?"

"It was so long ago, I cannot recall," she whispered. Before he could say something further, she asked, "Why are you on the shore at this hour?"

"I also find sleep evading me as of late," he sighed. "I was hoping Abrax would be waiting for me as he often is, but I was gifted your presence instead."

"Abrax finds you often?" she asked, speaking of the water horse that was the spirit animal of Anahita, goddess of the seas and water. Abrax was bonded to Briar in the same way Nasima was bonded to her.

"He does," Briar answered. "Others simply do not see it as he cannot perch on my shoulder."

A breath of laughter escaped her. "You jest."

He glanced over at her and smiled. "I do."

Her head tilted. "You do so often?"

His small smile faded. "Not as often as I once did."

"What changed?"

"The world is ever-changing," he answered. "Do not let me keep you," he added as he lowered to the sand.

Ashtine nodded, trying to decipher what she should do. She wanted to stay. There was a peace here that was evading her at home, but not if he wanted her to leave.

"You wish to be alone?" she finally asked.

"I simply do not wish for you to feel obligated to stay," he answered, resting his forearms atop his bent knees.

She nodded again. "Are you opposed to me staying?"

He looked up at her, his brow pinched. "Of course not, your Highness."

Another nod, but still she didn't move to sit. Or leave for that matter.

"Do you wish to stay?" Briar asked after an extended stretch of awkward silence.

"I do."

A soft smile appeared. "Then sit, Ashtine."

"But if you wish for me to—"

"Do you always overthink?"

A frown pulled on her mouth. "I am well aware that others find me perplexing, Prince Drayce. I find social situations just as bewildering."

"Is that what this is? A social situation?"

"I don't know because—" Then she glimpsed the smile he was fighting. "You are teasing me," she said in irritation.

"I would say you read social situations just fine, Ashtine," he said with a small huff of laughter. Patting the space beside him, he added, "Please sit. It would be a pleasure to spend this time with you."

Ashtine gave a sharp nod of her chin before she lowered down beside him, digging her toes deep into the sand.

"If you are allowing me the informality of addressing you by your given name, I am going to insist you do the same for me," he said after several quiet moments.

"What?" Ashtine asked, confused as she watched him lift a hand and begin to toy with the surf as it rolled in. Tendrils of sea water threaded between his fingers, staying with him when the waves rolled back out.

"You called me Prince Drayce earlier. Briar will do."

"Do others call you Briar?"

"My friends do." He turned to look at her as the water spiraled into a mini-cyclone in his palm. "I also want you to know I do not find you perplexing in the slightest."

"You are teasing me again," she said, averting her eyes and dragging a finger through the sand.

"Not at all, Ashtine," he replied. "I find you to be many things, but perplexing is not one of them."

Lifting a hand, she let a small whirlwind of air twist in her palm, matching his water cyclone. "I do not know how to respond to that."

"There is no need to respond to it," he answered. "Do the winds bring new murmurings that have kept you from sleep?"

"No. Only more of the same," she sighed.

"I can see how that would keep sleep at bay."

"Ermir told me my mother wrestled with the winds as well, but he can offer no guidance as to how she managed them."

"Have you found anything that quiets them?"

Ashtine lowered her whirlwind to the ground, letting grains of sand join the swirling air. "They are not as loud in the libraries, but I think that is because there are no windows or doors. It keeps them somewhat contained. Or perhaps I am simply reaching for some semblance of reprieve."

"Did you find a reprieve when you came here tonight?" Briar asked, back to letting his magic wind between his fingers, small droplets landing on the sand as it moved.

"Not particularly. Not until—"

She cut herself off, because even she could recognize how inappropriate that sounded. How it was something that shouldn't be entertained.

That *couldn't* be entertained.

"Until what?" Briar asked.

"There is no hiding from the winds," she answered instead. "What are you running from this night, Prince?"

"Briar," he corrected with a small smile.

He let his magic dissipate before leaning back on his hands.

Stretching his legs out before him, he stared out at the sea. He was completely relaxed and at peace alongside the element he commanded. She used to have that with the winds. Walking among them was a freedom she'd cherished, and their whispered secrets had made her feel special as a child. A gift when so much had been taken from her. As she'd aged, they'd become as much a part of her as her silver hair and lilting voice. But they'd also become as symbolic as her title. The Wind Princess and Wind Walker. That was what she was to most.

"Ruling is a privilege we are given," Briar said into the summer night. "But some days, it is heavy and feels more like a burden. Would you agree?"

"I would," she replied without question. "But if I am adding to that burden—"

"You are not," he interrupted, pinning her with soulful eyes. "I have lived far more decades than you and know this cycle well. Times change. Trials come. Peace reigns, until it doesn't. I can feel the shift, and so can you."

"You believe me," she said in realization, staring back at him.

He nodded. "Many feel it, but many also choose not to acknowledge it. I cannot entirely blame them. I can see the value in clinging to the peaceful times before they are gone, but we do not get such a privilege."

"Because we have the privilege of ruling," she said softly.

"Exactly," he replied. "You are wise beyond your years, Ashtine. Do not doubt yourself."

"A task easier spoken than carried out."

"Agreed."

She relaxed more, wondering just how long they could sit on a shore before either of their Courts realized their sovereign was missing.

"I find it doubtful that is what is keeping you from sleep this night," she said after several minutes of comfortable silence.

"Because you are wise beyond your years," Briar replied.

"You tease again," she said, but she felt a small smile pull at her lips. Briar only smiled as well, continuing to stare out at the gently rolling waves. Her head tilted, silver hair slipping over her shoulder. "Do you do this often?"

"Do what?"

"Sit on the beach in the night with another and tease them?"

Briar slowly turned to face her again and studied her for a long minute. She wasn't sure why, but usually when someone did that it was because she said something they found odd.

Finally, he answered, "I often find myself on the beach. It does not matter the time of day. Rarely with another. If there is, it is often Sawyer or Sorin."

Ashtine nodded, processing all of that before she said, "How does the Fire Prince fare?"

"How is Queen Semiria?" Briar countered.

That was a fair response. The Fae Queen and the Fire Prince had been close. Mentor and mentee for all of Talwyn's childhood. Ashtine had often found herself jealous of their relationship. Ermir was like a father, but the Fire Prince and Talwyn had been different. Niece and uncle, perhaps? Again, Ashtine wouldn't know, but the sudden disappearance of Queen Eliné had left their relationship broken. She wasn't sure it would ever be repaired at this point.

"Talwyn has the Earth Prince. Azrael is a knowledgeable and loyal Second," Ashtine answered. As an afterthought, she added, "And she has Tarek."

Briar nodded. "Having people who care is only valuable if one is willing to let them do so."

"The Fire Prince does not let you offer comfort?"

"Centuries of life together, and he still pushes others away," Briar sighed.

"Surely he just needs to find his way. He and Queen Eliné were close. He was her soulmate," Ashtine pondered aloud.

"Yes, which makes her sudden disappearance all the harder on him, but he won't fucking talk about it," Briar gritted out.

She waited for the apology that always followed after someone cursed in her presence. Not that she cared, but everyone treated her differently. Even Talwyn and Azrael conversed differently when she was around, but the apology never came from Briar. From what she knew of the male, he didn't appear to act any differently around her. In fact, he was the only one who seemed to treat her the same as everyone else. No one ever *teased* her. Perhaps Renly had when she was younger, but after her coronation, that had ceased.

"But you do not need to hear of my burdens this night," Briar went on. "If a war is on the horizon, the other Courts need to be made aware."

"I have tried," Ashtine sighed.

"Have you?"

She lifted her gaze to his, a bit taken aback. "Did I not come to you and seek your aid? Did you not initially dismiss my concerns?"

"I do not recall dismissing your concerns."

Ashtine sat up straighter, her eyes narrowing. "You denied my request."

"I never spoke such words. I wanted to discuss things further—which is a rational request when someone is asking to increase their stores of magically enhanced weapons—and you became upset and left before we could do so," Briar said simply.

"I— That is not—" Ashtine snapped her mouth shut as she started to sputter, something a princess was never to do.

"If others are not taking your concerns seriously, it is because you are allowing such a thing," Briar said.

Ashtine could only gape at him. "You believe I *allow* others to dismiss me?" she demanded, failing to keep the incredulity from creeping into her voice.

"What is your explanation?"

"I do not have one," she retorted. Briar's brow arched, and the mannerism only served to make her more upset. A gust of wind swept along the beach, grains of sand and droplets of water splattering against her skin and marring her gown. "I have never considered you a rude person, Prince Drayce."

"I have never considered you meek, *Ashtine*," he replied, still calm and collected as he got to his feet.

Ashtine scrambled up as gracefully as she could beside him. "I am not that," she retorted, air swirling beneath her and lifting her feet a fraction off the ground.

Briar glanced down before bringing his gaze back to hers. "You certainly shouldn't be," he replied. "Not with the power that runs in your veins and not with the title you wield. But I stand by what I said, your Highness. If your concerns are not being taken seriously, it is because you are allowing it. Feel free to stay on these shores as long as you wish."

A water portal appeared, Briar retreating through it a moment later, leaving her standing on the shore beneath a sky slowly taking on the colors of dawn. A flash of faint silver light appeared a second before Nasima's cry mixed with the sound of the waves.

The realm hangs in the balance.

A beginning or an ending? Time will tell.

Biting down on a cry of frustration, Ashtine stepped into the winds that tortured her and went home.

CHAPTER 5
BRIAR

Fuck!

That was all he had time to think as he rolled to the side, but not before he conjured a wave of water to meet the wall of flames coming at him. And not before he sent an ice dagger flying.

The Fire General lifted her sword with a second to spare, the dagger shattering into tiny crystals when it collided with her blade.

Briar rolled onto his knees before pushing to his feet. Eliza's skills never failed to impress him, but it wasn't a surprise. She and Nakoa trained together and trained their forces together, and he'd lain awake all night with an idea rolling around in his mind. The problem was, he didn't know how to approach his Inner Court or the Fire Court with the idea because relations with the Eastern Courts were strained enough as it was.

"Step behind your foot instead of in front," Nakoa said, and Briar turned to find him approaching Thia, one of Eliza's soldiers. "That will allow you to pivot easier."

Thia nodded, taking in every word and testing out the maneuver while the rest of them looked on.

"Where's Cyrus?" Sawyer asked, coming up beside them.

Eliza clicked her tongue in annoyance. "Cyrus is never up this early."

Sawyer huffed a laugh. "He sleeps in while his mate reports for training?"

"Every fucking day," Eliza grumbled, sheathing her sword down her back and flicking her red-gold braid over her shoulder. "Anyway, is there a particular reason you joined us this morning?"

Sawyer looked at Briar expectantly, because he too had been confused when Briar had suggested a trip to the Fire Court as the sun rose. He hadn't been planning on bringing Sawyer with, but his brother was getting nosy. Briar knew the moment he suggested joining forces with the Eastern Courts for training, Sawyer would inundate him with questions. Maybe he should have approached Ashtine with this idea first, but he wasn't sure when he'd be seeing the Wind Princess again after the way he'd left her earlier that morning.

"Is Sorin doing any better?"

Eliza crossed her arms, looking past him and watching the rest of her soldiers going through their morning training routines. Her shoulders tensed. "That is not what you came here to ask me because you already know the answer."

Fair point.

Briar pushed out a harsh breath, tugging on the band that kept his hair tied back. Nakoa had joined them now, his turquoise eyes narrowing as he studied his prince. "I came to get your thoughts. Both of you actually. We train our Courts together, teaching our armies to work together and use their magic as one. Perhaps, now that we are all under one queen, we should be doing so with the other Courts as well."

Eliza slowly slid her gaze back to him, and Nakoa blinked, a scowl pulling on his mouth. "Talwyn is only ruling in Eliné's stead right now," Sawyer cut in. "Technically, that's not even her role. It would be Eliné's Second—"

"Who is too lost to his own inner turmoil to properly do so," Nakoa interrupted, rubbing at his jaw.

"Which would then fall to her Third, which is you," Eliza continued, jerking her chin at Briar. "So I suppose the decision is yours."

"That's not how this works, and you know it," Briar retorted. "I came to ask your opinions on the matter."

"Why now? Eliné has only been gone a little over a year. Even when she was here, the West and East didn't mingle much," Sawyer said.

"That was due more to the feud between the Fire and Earth Courts than anything," Briar argued.

"Question still stands. Why now?"

Definitely should have done this when Sawyer wasn't around.

"It was merely an idea. It would give our forces new training activities rather than the same old, same old, and it could build relations," Briar said. "Seems like a grand idea all around."

Eliza flicked her grey eyes up to Nakoa, who had folded his arms across his chest once more. "It's not a terrible idea, but with so much animosity between the Earth and Fire Courts, I don't know that it would work."

"So we start with the Wind Court," Briar said with a shrug.

Eliza scoffed. "Luan would see it as a slight against him if we went to the Wind Princess and not him. And the Earth Prince isn't the only issue here. There is also Talwyn."

They all fell silent. No one needed to ask what she meant. The growing rift between the Fire Prince and the Fae Queen of the Eastern Courts wasn't a secret by any means.

"Something to think on then," Briar finally said.

"Sure," Eliza replied, her eyes narrowing as Cyrus came sauntering down the path from the Fiera Palace. "Do not distract my soldier," she yelled at him.

Cyrus merely threw her the middle finger before wrapping his arm around Thia's waist and bringing his mouth to hers.

"One of these days I am going to set him on fire," Eliza grumbled.

"Wouldn't do much seeing as he's also a Fire Fae," Sawyer replied.

"Eyebrows take a while to grow back," she returned with a shrug.

Briar huffed a laugh turning to Nakoa. "Are you staying for a while?"

Nakoa nodded. "I'll send word when I need a portal home."

"Actually, I was planning to spend some time in the libraries here. If that's all right with you?" he asked, his gaze shifting to Eliza.

But before she could answer, Cyrus was there, Thia tucked into his side. "Of course, Drayce. Whatever you need."

"Thank you," Briar answered, turning and beginning the walk up the path Cyrus had just come from.

Sawyer fell into step beside him, and he didn't miss that his brother had gone quiet. He knew the interrogation was coming, and within minutes of stepping into the libraries, he started.

"What is really going on, Briar?" Sawyer asked, his voice low as they began wandering among the various rows of books. When Briar didn't answer, he pushed, "Does this have anything to do with why you've been going to the Wind Court lately?"

Briar threw a glare at his brother. "Maybe let's not discuss this in another Court's palace."

"Apparently, this is the place to discuss a multitude of things, including new training regimens you haven't even proposed to your own Inner Court yet," Sawyer went on, his tone hard. "What the fuck, Briar?"

Briar sighed as they climbed the stairs to the next floor. "I know, Sawyer. This last year has been hard on all of us."

"Shutting the rest of us out is not the answer. You can see what it's doing to the Fire Court."

"I know."

"Do you even know what we're looking for here?" Sawyer asked as they made their way through the stacks of books on the third floor.

They had a library in the Water Court, of course, but the Fire Court library was second to only the Wind Court catacombs. And, again, Briar wasn't sure when he'd be going back there again. The truth was, he'd been a dick to Ashtine. He'd likely spoken to her in a way no one ever had, and while he stood by what he said, he'd said that to create distance between them. He'd been far too close to crossing a forbidden line. Or maybe not crossing it completely, but definitely pushing invisible boundaries.

"Yes. No. Sort of," Briar answered absent-mindedly.

"That is not helpful in the slightest," Sawyer replied in annoyance. "If you had an idea, we could at least ask Eliza where to look. There are *seven* levels in this library, Briar."

"I know how many floors there are," Briar retorted. He always simply looked through the books Ashtine had already collected when he was looking for answers with her. "Texts about the Great War and Avonleya," he finally added.

"Avonleya?" Sawyer said, coming to a standstill. "What could we possibly need to know about Avonleya?"

"I don't know," Briar answered. "That's why I'm looking for books about the kingdom."

Avonleya.

The kingdom locked away to keep the rest of the realm safe. Or that was what King Deimas and Queen Esmeray had tried to rewrite into history. The truth was they had brought war to Avonleya when their monarchy had denied them something they wanted. The Fae Courts had fought alongside Avonleya, and that was why the then Court Royals had eventually been executed. While everyone had been at the public slaughter, the Court capitals had been ransacked and precious texts destroyed. It had been expected. It was why the hidden heirs had been dispersed among the crowd. No one would have suspected they'd be there to watch their parents be sacrificed in the name of setting an example.

He rounded the corner, taking the stairs to the next floor. Honestly, he had no idea where to look for anything in here. He'd simply been hoping that a change of scenery might help him sort everything out.

There was no warning when a figure stepped from the lingering smoke of the lit brazier along the wall, but Briar was used to the Ash Rider suddenly appearing. Whereas Ashtine could walk among the winds anywhere, Rayner needed smoke or ashes to move among. It hindered his movements, but only slightly.

"I asked Eliza. She said the main floor houses books about Avonleya, but there aren't many," Rayner said in his low voice, black hair falling across his brow and into his grey eyes that swirled like smoke.

"You spoke to Sawyer, then," Briar said, only now realizing his brother hadn't followed him up the stairs.

"He said he'd rather not wander around aimlessly the entire day. He also said to tell you he'd meet you downstairs when you were ready," the male said, crossing his arms and leaning a shoulder against the wall. "Something we need to be aware of?"

"No. I mean, I'm not sure yet. Is Sorin here?"

Rayner's features seemed to darken, the smoke in his eyes swirling faster. "He went to his mountain chalet."

"Fuck," Briar muttered. Eliza and Cyrus had conveniently left that part out. "Not letting anyone in?

"Has he ever?"

Briar didn't need to answer. The mountain chalet was where the Fire Prince went to sort himself out. The problem was, he'd never let another soul into that grand mountain estate. Wards kept everyone out, but the gods knew they'd tried. When Eliné had first left, Sorin had spent almost a month there and only came back to the Fiera Palace when Eliza had threatened to burn his mother's garden to piles of ash. Drastic measures, sure, but it'd done the trick. Now he only stayed gone for a day or two. Most of the time.

Normally, Briar would have talked through all his thoughts about Ashtine's concerns with him, but Sorin had his own turmoil to deal with. He didn't need Briar's piled on top of everything else right now.

"Thanks for the help, Rayner," Briar said, turning to head back down the stairs.

"Drayce," Rayner called out.

Briar looked back over his shoulder to find him pushing off the wall.

"Was he like this after the Royals were killed? His parents?" Rayner asked.

"No," Briar answered. "He grieved, of course. We all did. Together. But he's never been like this."

The unspoken hung in the air between them. They didn't know how to help him, and they didn't know if he'd ever be the same.

Rayner was gone in the next blink, and Briar made his way back down to the main floor. It took a few minutes, but he found Sawyer at a table situated beneath a window. There were a few books on the table, and he dropped into the chair across from his brother. Someone had brought them a pitcher of water and glasses, and he poured himself a cup.

"The staff is locating more," Sawyer said. "But they warned me that a lot of the information contradicts itself."

"That's not surprising," Briar muttered. He and Ashtine were having the same difficulty with the texts in the Wind Court, and that only seemed to aggravate her for some reason. He was still learning how to read her, so he hadn't pushed.

No.

That wasn't it.

He was learning to read her too well, and that was a problem. He shouldn't know that she was getting aggravated when she smoothed her hand over the page, as if hoping the text would change. He shouldn't know that she preferred wool socks over slippers or boots. And he shouldn't know that if he used his water gazing magic on the water in his glass, he'd find her in her cozy nook in the catacombs because, although they brought her food and drink there, she never touched it, giving him the perfect view to observe her.

"I found something that should be of interest to you," Sawyer said, sliding an open book across the table.

Briar picked it up, skimming the page, then let the book fall to the table. He met his brother's gaze, icy blue eyes that mirrored his own.

"You've been spying," Briar accused.

"You've been sneaking around," Sawyer replied, not a hint of remorse in his tone.

"This," Briar said, tapping the pages of the book, "is not something that needs to be worried about."

"If you say so," his brother said, reaching for another book. "I just thought it was something you should keep in mind."

The text Sawyer had shown him spoke about Fae powers not crossing, specifically those of powerful bloodlines. It was common knowledge that the Courts did not mix bloodlines. It wasn't unheard of for the common, less powerful Fae, but strong bloodlines? It was taboo on many levels, and the only way around it was if you were twin flames. A fated bond could trump the unspoken laws of old, and even then, the Courts would have issues if Royals formed a union. There would be worries about heirs and an imbalance of power and—

And none of this mattered because that wasn't why he was spending increasing amounts of time in the Wind Court.

That wasn't why he was wondering if she'd remembered to eat today.

That wasn't why if Sawyer weren't sitting across from him, he would have already spelled the water in his drinking glass to watch her comb through texts.

This was to keep their Courts safe and prepare for war, not create more division among them all.

He sighed, glancing once more at the warning his brother had offered before flipping the book shut and reaching for another.

Perhaps distance would be the wiser option.

CHAPTER 6
ASHTINE

She took a deep breath as she stepped from the winds and stood before the White Halls. The sprawling castle was Talwyn's home. Or rather, it was the home of the Queen of the Eastern Courts. It was situated at the northernmost point of the Tykese River on the border between the Fire Court and Wind Court.

Eliné, Talwyn's aunt, had resided in the Black Halls. It was the sister castle at the mouth of the Tykese on the southern part of the continent between the Water Court and Earth Court. Talwyn had been Queen of the Eastern Courts for several decades, her aunt slowly easing her into the duties, but Eliné had still been highly involved in the affairs of the Eastern Courts. She'd still been heavily guiding her niece, and this last year without Queen Eliné had taken its toll on more than the young queen.

Still, Ashtine had grown up with Talwyn, and when she had become queen, she had asked Ashtine to be her Third-in-Command. With Eliné around, Ashtine had found her duties hadn't changed much, and now with the upheaval of recent events, she wasn't sure what was expected of her. Technically, Talwyn didn't rule over all the Courts. The Fire Prince would be the acting sovereign until evidence of Eliné's death was undeniable, she provided a means to step down, or all the sitting Royals came together and made a unanimous decision to let Talwyn take both thrones.

The Western Courts would never allow such a thing.

The lost one approaches, came the whispered murmur of the winds seconds before the heavy front doors of the White Halls opened.

Talwyn stepped through, her mahogany hair braided back. Jade green eyes fixed on Ashtine, her features taut. She wore a white tunic with fitted brown pants. It was her usual attire. She didn't have her fighting leathers on, but there were various daggers in place. Her customary twin blades were also absent, and Ashtine tilted her head at that observation. She always had at least one on her.

"Why are you standing out here?" Talwyn asked, her tone brusque. She always spoke like that, though, even before her aunt's abrupt disappearance. But there had once been an underlying softness, and that was still usually reserved for Ashtine. Not this morning, apparently.

That was fine.

Ashtine was on a peculiar edge herself. Briar hadn't been to the Wind Court in weeks. In fact, she hadn't spoken to him since the morning he'd all but dismissed her on the beach. He'd sent a few messages to see if she'd learned anything more, but after the second one, Ashtine had stopped bothering with replies. If he'd suddenly become too busy to help her like he'd offered, that was fine. She didn't need to appease his guilty conscience, or whatever it was he was trying to do. It confused her, and things that confused her made her irritable.

Like the nonstop chattering of the winds about war and bloodshed and the land across the sea.

And Briar's words constantly replaying in her mind: *If others are not taking your concerns seriously, it is because you are allowing such a thing.*

Her winds swirled, tossing her flowing hair across her face, and the queen took notice. Talwyn could command the winds as well. She could also control earth elements, along with Shifter magic she had yet to delve too deeply into. But despite having wind magic, the winds did not accost her as they did Ashtine, and the queen could not walk among them.

Talwyn's tone had softened a touch when she stepped to the side, making room for the Wind Princess to pass. "Come inside, Ashtine. Have breakfast with me."

Ashtine wasn't the least bit hungry, but she nodded once. "Thank you," she replied, moving gracefully through the entry and into the halls. The warmth of the castle wrapped around her, but she didn't feel it. Not as the winds immediately started a tirade.

The rivers will run red.
The lands will be divided.
Which side will you choose?
Which side will she choose?
Across the sea.
The balance tips.

"Ashtine." Her name was sharp on Talwyn's tongue, but her given name pulled her from the winds' grasp. Talwyn was the only one who used it.

And the Water Prince as of late. Or at least he had been.

"I have never seen you look so . . ." Talwyn trailed off, her gaze sliding over Ashtine as the princess pulled her cloak from her shoulders and passed it off to the waiting staff. "Are you unwell?"

"Why do you ask such a thing?"

"I have not seen you in some time. You are pale and thin, and you seem . . . haunted."

Ashtine fell into step beside the queen as they made their way to the dining room. "I do not have phantoms disturbing me."

"No, not—" Talwyn cut herself off. "I simply mean you appear troubled."

"We are all troubled in these times," Ashtine replied, nodding to the male who pushed the dining room doors open.

But her steps faltered when she entered and found another male already seated at the table.

A snake in the grass.

For once, Ashtine wasn't sure if those were the whispers of the winds or her own thoughts.

The male was as surprised as Ashtine as he quickly pushed to his feet, the sound of his chair scraping against the stone floor sounding in the room. He rounded the table, bowing at the waist before straightening and saying, "Princess Evermorn. What a delightful surprise this morning." Then he turned to Talwyn. "Did you forget to inform me of a morning meeting, Moonflower?"

"I am not required to inform you of anything," Talwyn retorted. "But no. I was on my way down to breakfast when I felt her cross my wards. It was an unplanned visit, but one I am happy to be surprised by."

A small smile tilted on Ashtine's mouth, and for the first time in weeks, she felt some of the tension ease from her being. There was a sense of familiarity with Talwyn. Something that came from growing up together.

"Sit. Let's eat," Talwyn said, gesturing to the spread of food as she moved to her place at the head of the table.

"After you, your Highness," Tarek said, stepping aside to let her pass.

Tarek Ordos.

The Third-in-Command in the Earth Court under Prince Azrael and Talwyn's twin flame. Although, the pair were still in their Trials.

The twin flame bond was a mysterious twist of fate if Ashtine was being honest. Those who believed they'd found their twin flame were Marked to see if the connection settled into place and to initiate the Trials. There were five parts to it, and each piece had to be fulfilled in a test of sorts. Each couple was different and so each Trial was specific to them. The Marking itself was a powerful enchantment that called from soul to soul. It created a literal offering of a piece of themselves to one another. If they had truly found each other, the Mark branded itself permanently to their skin, and the bond became unbreakable. However, if a bond was initiated and the couple were not twin flames, the Mark slowly faded over time, and the pieces of soul offered faded with it. Many believed they had found their twin flame but were too afraid to test it against the Marking, so they were content to simply join in a union of marriage as mates and husband and wife.

Ashtine had not witnessed many true twin flame bonds in her two centuries of life, and even before she was born, accounts of them were few. Cyrus and Thia were twin flames. Having completed their Trials, their twin flame bond was fully anointed. Tarek and Talwyn were the other, assuming they completed their Trials someday. They'd accepted the bond over a decade ago and still had not progressed through another Trial. Cyrus and Thia had completed their bond in under two years.

A prince hides in plain sight.
Allies will turn.
Across the sea—

Her fingers curled into her palms, nails digging into her skin as Ashtine took her seat to Talwyn's left, and her head canted to the side when Tarek took the seat on Talwyn's right. This was an informal breakfast, but tradition mandated that that seat was for the Queen's Second. Prince Azrael. Not Tarek. This only changed when a union had taken place, and even then, he would sit in the chair Ashtine currently occupied.

"Did you wed since I saw you last?" Ashtine asked.

Tarek paused his reach for a platter of sausages while Talwyn choked on the sip of juice she'd just taken.

"No. Why would you ask that?" Talwyn asked once she'd finished coughing.

"To receive an answer."

"Right," Talwyn muttered, setting her glass down. "Why do you think I have married?"

"The seat Tarek occupies is not his."

Talwyn glanced at Tarek briefly before looking at Ashtine once more, clearly noting her odd mood. Tarek, however, had gone stone-faced, his jaw tense and pale green eyes fixed on Ashtine with an unimpressed stare.

"Azrael is not here," Talwyn said. "Would you like him to sit at the other end of the table?"

"It does not matter to me where he sits," Ashtine replied. "But I think it matters to *him*."

The unimpressed stare morphed into a glare as Tarek gritted out, "What dishes can I pass to you, your Highness?"

"I am not hungry," Ashtine said, toying with the silverware beside her plate.

"You look like you need to eat," Talwyn said pointedly, spearing a piece of melon with her fork.

"Is Prince Azrael visiting today?"

"I see him often, as I see you, but we correspond daily."

Ashtine's brow furrowed. "That did not answer my question."

"No, Prince Azrael is not visiting today," Talwyn amended, trying to pass her a plate filled with pastries.

Ashtine shook her head, waving the dish away. Her hand fell to the tabletop where she tapped her finger, her nail clicking.

"What brings you to the White Halls today, your Highness?" Tarek asked.

"A prince who hides in plain sight," Ashtine said, looking past him to the window beyond. "Why is that open?"

"Are you cold?" Talwyn asked.

"No."

"Then why does it bother you?"

"It does not."

Talwyn set her silverware down, pushing her plate aside. The weight of her full attention landed on Ashtine, but before she could speak, Tarek said, "What do you mean, 'a prince who hides in plain sight?'"

"It could mean many things," Ashtine murmured.

"But you have an idea?" Tarek pushed.

"She doesn't know," Talwyn said.

"Surely she has an inkling," Tarek argued.

"That is not how the winds work."

"She is a Wind Walker," he replied. "Her entire purpose is to communicate with the winds."

"The winds speak like an Oracle," Talwyn said tightly. "Only Ashtine cannot have a conversation with them. She can only hear their chattering."

"And she has been doing this for decades," Tarek said, clearly growing agitated. "One would think she'd have learned to understand them in some way."

"One would think you'd speak more respectfully to your *queen*," Ashtine cut in, her lilt sharp as the air around the room stirred. A moment later, a hawk's cry sounded before Nasima appeared at the window, perching on the ledge.

"I am not speaking to her as my queen right now," Tarek replied flippantly. "I am speaking to my twin flame."

The silver bracelet coiled around Talwyn's wrist shimmered, and Tarek's eyes dropped to it before meeting her gaze again. Ashtine watched, somewhat fascinated, as his features softened. "I did not mean to upset you, Moonflower."

She ventured east, whispered the winds.

Ashtine slid her gaze to Talwyn. "Did you visit the Wind Court recently?"

Talwyn slid her plate back in front of her, watching Ashtine carefully. "Do you think I would visit your Court but not visit you?"

Ashtine tapped her nail again absent-mindedly. "Visiting me is not a requirement of visiting the Wind Court."

"Ashtine, I—"

"But I would have felt you enter the Court," she continued, as though she hadn't heard Talwyn speak at all.

But if she hadn't come to the Wind Court that only left the Witch Kingdoms, and why would she go there? It was common knowledge Talwyn and the High Witch did not get along.

There was a long moment of silence before Talwyn lifted a hand, a swirl of leaves appearing and disappearing, taking a message to someone.

"We need Azrael for breakfast?" Tarek asked shortly, apparently knowing who Talwyn had sent the message to.

"No. I need my Second because Ashtine is troubled by something," Talwyn answered.

"We don't even know if that is true," Tarek argued. "Furthermore, how will Azrael help with that?"

Lies and truth, who can tell?
Enemies or friends?
She will come.

Who will come? Ashtine wondered, desperate to understand something. Anything. Desperate for a reprieve from—

The rivers will run red.
The lands will be divided.
Which side will you choose?
The war only sleeps.

Answers lie across the sea, Ashtine recited in her mind.

Go there!

She sighed. *I cannot go there. I do not wish to go there.*

Reaching out, she stroked her fingers along Nasima's feathers. She wasn't sure when she'd stood and made her way to the window, but she hadn't heard the last several minutes of conversation between Talwyn and Tarek.

The guarded prince arrives.

She didn't need the winds to tell her Prince Azrael was here. She knew the male's heavy footsteps and heard them seconds before the dining hall doors opened once more. More out of habit than anything, Ashtine turned and nodded in greeting to the Earth Prince. His earthy brown eyes were scanning the room before him, but she'd already turned back to the window.

He trusts no one.

He is smart, Ashtine retorted.

Which side will he choose?

"The winds' whispers are vague and often nonsense," Azrael was saying. "They could mean nothing, but they could mean everything."

"She has to have some idea," Tarek was arguing.

"What stakes do you have in this revelation?" the Earth Prince countered.

The rivers will run red.

The lands will be divided.

"There is a war coming," Ashtine said, fingers gliding over Nasima's head once more.

The chatter ceased for a moment, the silence deafening.

Tarek was the first to speak. "The war ended centuries ago."

"The end of one war does not prevent the rise of another," Azrael replied from where he stood near the table, his arms crossed.

"There have been no indications of war. Does this have to do with Avonleya?" Talwyn mused.

"Avonleya can do nothing locked behind their wards," Tarek scoffed.

"They incited the Great War. I am sure they can incite another."

"We are well prepared for a war. All the Courts are after everything that transpired before," Azrael said.

Answers lie across the sea.

Her hands fell to the window ledge, fingers curling. The whispers of the winds mixed with the arguing of her peers.

If others are not taking your concerns seriously, it is because you are allowing such a thing.

Briar's words rattled in her mind among everything else.

And it was all just so fucking loud.

"Enough!" she cried, whirling from the window. A gust of wind rattled the dishes on the table, and Nasima let out an anxious cry. Everyone stilled, turning to her.

"Ashtine?" Talwyn ventured.

Both Azrael and Tarek had stepped in front of her, standing in defensive positions. It was only then that Ashtine realized her feet weren't on the ground. She was floating a few inches above the floor, the winds keeping her aloft.

Control was as fleeting as the winds right now, and she grappled to find any semblance of it. A princess was to never lose control over her power, her Court, her demeanor.

And she found she did not care in this moment. That was both stupid and dangerous.

"War comes. Prepare or don't, but with war, death comes to claim what is his. The rivers will run red. The lands will be divided, and the survival of the realm hangs in the balance," Ashtine said, holding Talwyn's gaze. "Do with that knowledge what you will."

"Ashtine—"

But she was gone among the winds before she could hear them speak further.

Before she lost any more control.

She'd already lost her sanity.

And she wondered if she'd ever know peace again.

CHAPTER 7
BRIAR

Abrax shook his head, water from his mane spraying with the motion. His white coat glimmered in the hot summer sun, and Briar was thankful for the water that flowed as his mane and tail. The mist was a welcome reprieve from the heat.

He'd come out here when he'd seen Abrax running along the rolling waves. The sea was choppier than usual today, the sweltering sea breeze a little more haphazard, and Abrax seemed to be enjoying the chaos as he ran. Abrax wasn't alone, however. A silver hawk was soaring in the air above him, swooping down and brushing the tips of her wings along his mane and coat.

And where Nasima was, the Wind Princess usually wasn't far behind.

He hadn't seen her in weeks, and shortly after that, she'd stopped responding to his sporadic correspondence. Not that Briar could blame her. After his conversation with Sawyer, he'd made the wise decision to distance himself from the princess. If Sawyer was noticing, her Court was noticing too, and the last thing they needed was to incite rumors or suspicion. He could still aid her from here. Or that had been his thought until she'd stopped replying to him.

That wasn't the only part of his plan that had failed, though. Despite his best efforts, his mind wandered to her multiple times a day. When she'd stopped replying to his correspondence, he'd forced himself not to send a water message to Ermir or Renly to check on her wellbeing. More than that, he'd forced himself not to go to the Wind Court himself. Showing up unannounced once had been suspicious enough. To do so again would make things worse.

What things?

Things he tried not to think about.

Things that had made him keep himself busy, running himself ragged and trying to keep from thinking thoughts he had no business letting enter his mind.

Yet when he saw Nasima, he had known. He'd immediately gone to one of the shallow dishes of water, drawn a quick enchanting Mark, and found her exactly where he knew she'd be: walking along the shore in the same place where they'd sat and spoken in the early morning hours nearly a month ago.

He'd felt her cross into the Court, of course, but it was only a matter of time before others noticed her presence as well, especially if the wind continued to increase.

Nasima swooped down again, the tips of her wing brushing Briar's cheek as she did so. Then she circled before coming to settle on his shoulder moments before Ashtine came into view. She was no longer walking among the waves, but lying flat on her back in the sand. The closer he got, the more of her he took in. Her gown fluttering in her winds; her silver hair blowing across her face. Her hands rested at her sides, swirling vortexes at her fingertips. Her eyes were closed, but he knew she was aware of his presence.

"Princess," he greeted, stopping several feet away.

She didn't move. Didn't even bother acknowledging him. He took a few steps closer, then faltered. This close, he could see how pale she was. Her complexion was fair to begin with, but this was . . . not that. She looked frail, as though she wasn't getting enough sleep or eating properly. It was rare for a Fae to fall ill. They were not plagued with sickness like the mortals of the realm, and while they didn't need as much food and rest as a mortal, their power reserves depended on both to remain at their strongest. The more powerful one was, the more maintaining those things was crucial, and yet the Wind Princess was lying on the shores looking as if death himself was courting her.

It wasn't until Nasima took to the air once more, a soft cry coming from her, that Ashtine blinked her eyes open. She appeared almost startled.

"You came," she lilted. "I did not think you would."

Guilt gnawed at him, but he didn't let it linger. "Are you well, Princess?" he asked, taking a few more steps until he stood right beside her. Peering down, he held her stare as she mulled over his question.

"Is anyone ever truly well?" she finally countered. "Or do we all simply mask our ailments?"

"I . . ."

"I do not require an answer," she continued, her eyes falling closed once more.

Movement in his periphery had him turning to find Abrax making his way forward. He bent his head, huffing into her hair, and Ashtine smiled. Or tried to. It certainly didn't reach her eyes when she blinked them open, stroking a hand down Abrax's muzzle. He huffed softly into her hand again.

"Would you like to come up to the House of Water?" Briar asked, crouching beside her.

"That is not necessary."

Except that it probably was. This area of the beaches was close enough to the House of Water it was patrolled regularly. She would be discovered soon. If not by his guard, then by his Inner Court.

"Please come with me," he said gently, extending a hand to her.

"It is not necessary," she repeated.

He smiled softly. "Please come join me for the midday meal. Or at the very least, come out of the sun. Your fair skin will burn quickly here."

"Fae heal just as quickly."

"Ashtine."

Something in her eyes cleared a little at her name, and he reached for her hand. When she didn't resist, he curled his fingers around hers before pulling her to her feet. A moment later, he guided her through a water portal directly into his private rooms. They were less likely to be interrupted here, and he was certain Ashtine didn't want others to see her in this state.

He sent a request for a light meal to be prepared before he said, "I am going to change quickly if that is all right with you?"

"It will not bother me if you change."

"Would you like different clothing?"

Her brow furrowed. "Do you have female clothing in your rooms?"

He stifled his huff of laughter. "No, Ashtine, but I could have some procured for you."

She waved him off, moving to pull the open window closed before examining the ledge that ran along the perimeter of the room. The ledge was halfway up the wall, and the top of the ledge was shallow, allowing water to pool and flow. It was for aesthetics as much as it was security. The more water around the Water Prince, the more powerful he would be.

Briar let her be, going to his bedchamber to change into a set of fresh pants and tunic that weren't damp from the spray of the sea. When he returned, he found her on the other side of the room, far from the windows and balcony doors. She was studying a large map of their continent that was mounted on the wall, a hand raised and her finger tracing along the western edge of the map.

"Food will be delivered shortly," Briar said.

"I am not hungry."

Briar shrugged, moving to her side and clasping his hands behind his back. "That is no bother. I can eat, and you can tell me what brings you to the sea this day."

Her finger paused, head tilting to the side. "I do not always know where I will find myself when I walk among the winds."

"Are you saying the winds brought you here?"

"No. It was simply a statement."

"What is the most obscure place you have found yourself?"

She stepped closer to the map, her finger sliding along until it hovered over the mortal kingdom of Toreall and the Dresden Forest.

Briar's brows rose. "We cannot access our magic in the mortal lands. The enchanted wards prevent it."

"The winds forewarned me that I would need Talwyn's ring," Ashtine replied.

"Her Semiria ring? You stole it?"

"Is it stealing if an item is returned before someone realizes it is missing?"

He couldn't stifle his laughter this time, and Ashtine finally turned to look at him. She eyed him for a moment, looking at him as though she'd never heard such a sound.

"You find amusement easily," she murmured, turning back to the map.

"Do you not laugh on occasion, Princess Evermorn?" he asked in a teasing tone.

"I do not remember the last time I found something joyful enough to produce such a sound," she answered. Before he could comment on that, she asked, "What if history is wrong?"

"That is . . ."

He was going to say an odd question, but that wasn't necessarily true. He just needed to work out what she was trying to say. Their times in the Citadel catacombs had allowed him to slowly start learning to converse with her, but it still took a conscious effort to understand what she was truly saying. So instead, he studied her for a moment. Watched her bring her focus back to the Edria Sea and trace along the left side of the frame while rolling her words around in his mind.

Finally, he asked, "What history do you question?"

"All of it," she replied. "Some texts I have read suggest there is power that once walked our lands, but no longer does. But does that mean it left our world altogether? Or does it simply mean it has been trapped somewhere else?"

He watched her trace the edge of the frame again, understanding finally dawning. "You speak of Avonleya."

"You lived decades during the war."

"Yes, but I was born long after the Avonleyan Wards went up. I was born well after the wards around the mortal lands were erected. I remember my parents trying desperately to keep the peace with Deimas and Esmeray," Briar answered.

"And yet their blood was still spilled."

He swallowed thickly as the memories flashed in his mind. Standing stoically beside his brother and Sorin. Hidden among the crowd and glamoured. Forcing himself not to react, not to make a sound. Slipping a hand over Sawyer's mouth to keep him quiet when he couldn't stifle his cry.

"Yes, it was," he finally managed to say, just as a knock sounded. "Leave the food outside, please," he called.

"I apologize," Ashtine said. "I did not mean to stir such memories."

He lifted his hand, as if he was going to touch her, then quickly dropped it when he realized what he was doing. "Still reading social situations just fine," he replied with a sad smile before he moved to retrieve the food.

When he returned, tray in hand, he asked, "Do you like fish?"

"I am not opposed to a creature that lives in the sea," she returned, her tone slowly returning to her signature mystical lilt.

Briar smiled, placing the tray on the small dining table near the balcony doors. There was seating for four, though when he dined in his rooms, he was usually by himself.

"I should have asked if you enjoy eating seafood. Fish. Shellfish," he explained, lifting a lid off a platter of salmon and lobster.

She took a single step closer, then stopped. Her hands were at her sides, fingers curling into the fabric of her gown.

"If you do not, I had chicken prepared as well," he added in a hurry, revealing the other platter. "There is also fruit, bread, and cheese."

"But I told you I was not hungry?"

It was a question, and he picked up one of the two stacked

plates. "You did, but if that has changed, there is plenty here," he replied, beginning to fill his plate.

He was cutting a piece of bread from the loaf when he felt her approach. It took everything in him not to react as she peered over his shoulder. "I have dined with you in the Water Court before."

"You have," he agreed.

"But I was never served that," she continued, and he knew she was referring to the oysters.

"I hoard them," he said matter-of-factly.

There was an extended silence before she said, "I find that amusing."

"Would you like to try one?"

"Does that not defeat the purpose of hoarding them?"

He huffed a laugh. "I suppose it does, but I am willing to do so."

It was another few seconds before she gave a decisive nod. "Then yes, I would like to try one. And some fish. I do enjoy the food when I visit."

"Noted," he replied with a smile, placing his full plate before a chair. "You can have this plate. I will make another."

Ashtine stumbled back a few steps, her gaze darting to the balcony doors. "You can eat, Prince. I will wait on the sofa. Or perhaps I should simply take my leave."

Briar set the empty plate he had just retrieved back down, turning to face her. "Did I offend you in some way?"

"No," she answered, shaking her head and taking another step back.

"If I did, I apologize."

"I did not mean to come here," she said, more to herself than to him.

"You can always come here," he replied, moving closer to her.

Her focus snapped back to him. "That is a foolish statement. Impulsive visits cannot happen. This should not have happened. I will go."

On instinct, he lurched forward, because he didn't want her to go anywhere. She was clearly upset, and he reached out, clasping her elbow. Wind Walkers couldn't travel with a passenger, so she wouldn't be able to leave if they had physical contact.

"Ashtine, wait—"

But a violent gust of air slammed into him, and he was thrown backwards. Tendrils of water from the ledges leapt out, wrapping around his arms and waist and keeping him on his feet. More importantly, his magic kept him from colliding with the table full of food. The force of Ashtine's magic, however, had still blown the smaller plates to the floor. Bread and cheese splattered against the balcony doors and grapes rolled across the marble floor while the dinnerware shattered.

He lifted his gaze to find Ashtine standing with a curved sickle blade in her hand. The weapon's blade was white and silver. Skystone, he realized. Her reaction had certainly caught him off guard, but it shouldn't have. Ermir would have made sure the last Evermorn heir could protect herself. Her childhood spent hidden away would have included all manner of training and that would have continued. Sion wouldn't have let her stop.

"I would not harm you, Ashtine," he said cautiously. "I only wished to speak with you more before you left. I did not wish for you to leave."

"I can feel your wards, Prince Drayce—"

"Briar," he interrupted.

Her lips pursed. "I can feel your wards. I cannot walk among the winds from your rooms."

She wasn't wrong, but he hadn't been thinking clearly when he thought she was going to leave upset. Again.

"I admit I acted impulsively," he replied. "I did not wish for you to leave."

"You stated that, but I do not think I believe it."

"Why would you doubt my words?"

"Because you ceased your visits."

She said it so simply. No bite or bitterness to her tone. Just a statement of what was.

And it made him so uneasy because he did not want that to be her impression of him. She didn't realize that—

"I understand I can be vexing," she lilted, dropping her arm, but her grip remained on her weapon.

"Vexing. You think I stopped coming to see you because I find you vexing?" Briar repeated.

She gave a curt nod of her chin. "I do not fault you for it."

He moved then, quickly in the way the Fae could, but so did she. In the next blink, he stood in front of her, and she had her blade raised once more, the edge at his throat. He let her keep it there, but he also placed the tip of his finger beneath her chin, tipping her head back and keeping her eyes on his. "I find you clever. I find you captivating. Alluring in a way I have never experienced. I find you so incredibly enthralling that my thoughts wander to you multiple times a day. But I find you anything but vexing, Ashtine Evermorn."

"Why?" she asked, and gods. It wasn't breathy or teasing. She was truly asking why. Because she was Ashtine. The princess who saw the worlds differently than the rest of them.

"Because you are a breath of fresh air, my dear," he answered.

Her brow furrowed. "That is . . . nonsensical."

"Very much so," he agreed. "It is nonsensical that even with a blade at my throat I am contemplating if the inevitable injury would be worth it to press my lips to yours."

Ashtine stepped back, her weapon still poised as she stared at him for a long second. Two. Three. He gave her time, letting her process. Then she slowly lowered her blade as she said, "It is nonsensical that I am not opposed to that. It breaks laws of old."

"It is nonsensical that I do not care," he replied.

"You should care, Prince Drayce. Breaking the laws of old angers the gods and Fates."

"Briar."

"What?"

He closed the space she'd put between them, but she didn't raise her weapon again. "Stop calling me 'Prince Drayce,'" he said, the words laced with a primal growl. "And I do not care. In this moment, the only thing I care about is your permission to take what I want."

"It is not that simple—"

"It is either an approval or a denial," he cut in, echoing her words from weeks ago. He was being pushy, but he didn't care about that either because he'd been thinking about this since the morning hours they'd spent talking together on a beach.

"We will regret this," she whispered.

"I do not think I could ever regret you, Ashtine. Yes or no?"

"Yes."

She'd scarcely whispered the word when his lips were on hers, breathing in her approval. His hand cupped her jaw, tipping her head to the perfect angle to deepen the kiss while his other arm wound around her waist, pulling her into him. In the back of his mind, he registered the sound of her blade clinking against the floor when she dropped it. Then soft fingers skimmed along his cheek, and her other hand curled around his forearm.

Ashtine pushed onto her toes, seeking more from him, and his magic pressed against his skin in approval, seeking her wind, her air, all of *her*. Gods, if they weren't careful, this was going to be far more than a kiss. If their magic became involved, this would become so much more.

She must have had the same thoughts because she broke the kiss first, but she didn't move away. Their bodies were still pressed together, and when she tilted her head, silver hair flowed on her phantom winds.

Winds that had been absent until this moment.

"I am sorry I stayed away," he murmured into the space between their lips. "Never again. If you need me, I will be there. With you. For you."

His thumb brushed along her cheekbone, and an expression he couldn't read filled her features. She finally took that step back from him. "I should return, but I require a water portal to leave your quarters."

"I invited you for a meal, and we have not dined together," he argued.

"I did tell you I was not hungry."

"Then meet me on the shore before the sun wakes."

"Perhaps."

"I will be waiting."

"And if I do not show?"

He stepped into her once more, brushing a soft kiss to her lips and savoring the taste of her. "Then I shall wait the next day and the next and not regret a moment of it."

"Be well, Briar," was all she said, her fingers dragging along his bare forearm as she moved past him.

He didn't reach for her again. Didn't try to keep her any longer. He conjured a water portal, and the Wind Princess didn't look back when she stepped from his rooms.

CHAPTER 8
ASHTINE

She hadn't planned to go there.

When she'd stepped from the White Halls, she'd wandered for a while, letting the winds take her where they would. And when they'd dumped her on the shores of the Water Court, she hadn't had it in her to truly care. Anyone could have found her. His Inner Court would have likely felt her cross into their territory, but Briar would have felt it first. She didn't know what she'd do when they came for her either. But no one would find that out of the ordinary.

She was the sheltered, peculiar Wind Princess who spoke in oddities and was difficult to understand. Hard to converse with, yet simple to dismiss. Easy to pass her concerns off as the idle chatter of the breezes and lack of faith in her advisors.

For weeks, Briar's words had plagued her as much as the winds, and she'd realized he'd been right. But how does one demand consideration for something no one can understand?

So for a few moments, she'd dropped to the sand and tried to simply exist. She'd said her piece. She'd passed the winds' warnings along. What the others chose to do with those cryptic words wasn't her concern.

And yet she knew it wouldn't be enough either.

Not as her winds swirled around her, throwing her hair across her face and whispering more and more as the waves methodically rolled to shore. She'd been so distracted by their newest musings, she'd missed Briar's arrival. But with each passing minute of his presence, the winds had quieted, and when Abrax had let her run her fingers along his muzzle, she'd found the smallest breath of peace she'd been seeking for months. Years. Decades.

Ashtine had expected to go back to the House of Water and dine with him, but she had not anticipated being escorted to his private quarters. It had made sense, of course, but after his weeks of silence, it had still been a surprise.

But not as surprising as his admission to wanting to kiss her.

Not as shocking to her desiring the same thing.

Not as unforeseen as both of them giving in to that longing.

And now she was confused about more than the winds.

She moved to her bathing room, peeling off her dress. Now that she was feeling more herself, she realized how sweltering it had been in the Water Court. She bathed, wishing she could take her time in the water, but consequences for her brash actions earlier in the day would certainly find her soon. Sure enough, she'd been in the bath all of five minutes when she felt the power cross her wards. More than one.

A light knocking sounded, and Noelle entered the bathing room. "I apologize for the interruption, your Grace, but Ermir asked me to tell you Queen Talwyn is here along with Prince Azrael."

She was already moving to retrieve towels and preparing to help Ashtine get ready.

"Is Tarek also present?" Ashtine asked.

"No, your Grace."

Ashtine nodded. "Renly and Sion?"

"Are also here."

She nodded again, already tired at the thought of dealing with all of this. She was also a touch annoyed that the winds could plague her with ominous warnings but not warn her about who was coming to her Court.

Perhaps useful information would serve us all better, she snapped internally.

Answers lie across the sea. Find the one to go there.

By the gods, she sighed, standing from the bath so abruptly, water sloshed over the sides.

Noelle was there, handing her a towel before helping her squeeze the water from her hair. Long before she was mentally ready, she was making her way down to one of the meeting rooms near the main foyer. The room fell silent when she entered, everyone but Talwyn getting to their feet and bowing or nodding. It was ridiculous, really. These formalities were pointless after centuries together.

"Princess," Ermir greeted, everyone returning to their seats after she'd taken her place at the other end of the table, opposite Talwyn. "Queen Talwyn and Prince Azrael were just telling us of your visit earlier today."

"I was unaware my movements were being monitored and reported," Ashtine replied.

"That is not what we're doing," Talwyn said.

"My misunderstanding. To what do I owe the visit?"

Everyone in the room shifted in their seats, but it was the Earth Prince who said, "You cannot be serious."

"I am usually quite serious."

"You came to the White Halls, told us a war was coming, and then you left. Surely you recognize we would have questions after all that," he said in disbelief.

"One would assume you would have questions," she agreed.

"And what do you have to say about it all?" Azrael demanded.

Ashtine tilted her head, folding her hands in her lap. "I have nothing to say."

"You have . . . How can you—"

"Stop, Az," Talwyn interrupted. "I'll handle it." Turning her attention back to Ashtine, she said, "We have questions, but do you have any answers, Ashtine?"

"I do not know your questions," Ashtine answered. "But if you are asking of the rivers running red, the lands dividing, and the survival of the realm hanging in the balance, I have been searching for those answers for months. I have the same questions you do."

"If you have been searching for answers for months, then why do you just now bring them to our attention?" Azrael cut in.

Ashtine's gaze slid to him. "As you said, the winds' whispers are vague and often nonsense. They could mean nothing, but they could mean everything."

"We are talking about a potential war," the Earth Prince snarled.

"I am aware."

"You cannot keep a war threat a secret for months, Princess."

"Not informing you does not mean it was kept a secret, Prince Luan," she replied, the air in the room stirring.

"If I may," Ermir cut in before Azrael could speak again. "As you know from working with the late Princess Ophelia for decades before her death, the winds are not an Oracle. It has long fallen to the Wind Court to investigate and try to interpret the songs of the winds. That is why our library is so vast."

"The fact remains that a potential war should be brought to our attention," Azrael argued.

"Prince, do you know how often the winds speak of war? Of death? Of bloodshed and any number of catastrophes?" Ermir replied, his tone getting sterner.

Ashtine had only heard him speak this way a handful of times. It was his power stirring the air in the room now. Not hers.

"They speak of peace and prosperity just as often," Ermir went on. "They carry news from other continents, other realms. They carry history. Not just ours, but of the stars. When we say the winds know everything and nothing, we mean just that. We do not dismiss things lightly, but to assume we have kept a threat of war a secret is insulting to our princess and our Court as a whole."

Talwyn's gaze was moving between Ermir and Azrael, clearly trying to decide if she should intervene. She was the youngest Fae at this table. Ashtine was older by mere months, but half of the Fae in attendance had fought in the Great War. And *all* of them, save for the females, had been alive during it.

"I meant no disrespect, Ermir," Azrael said. "I remember well how Ophelia was often plagued by the winds."

That had Ashtine leaning forward in interest.

"But I also remember a war fought and lives lost," the Earth Prince went on. "I would be failing my own Court if I simply sat back and did not pursue a potential threat."

"That is understandable," Sion chimed in. "We would do the same, and we have. The princess came to us with these whisperings months ago, and we have been looking into them ever since. We know it plagues her. We can see it consuming her. We are not blind, but we have found nothing to substantiate it. Bringing it to your attention without proof brings just as many obstacles."

"What if there was proof?" Talwyn cut in.

"What do you speak of?" Ashtine asked, and even she could hear the desperation in her tone.

The concerned looks from around the room told her everyone else could hear it too.

"There are . . . rumors. Of a weapon hidden in the mortal lands," Talwyn said.

"Rumors?" Sion asked with a frown. "We cannot act on rumors."

"The source is credible."

She ventured east, the winds whispered.

"You spoke to the Oracle," Ashtine said in realization. "That is why you went to the Witch Kingdoms."

"When did you go there?" Prince Azrael demanded, turning to the Fae Queen. "And who escorted you?"

"I went myself, Az," Talwyn sighed.

"To the fucking Witch Kingdoms?"

"Yes," Talwyn snapped. "Maliq was with me," she added, referencing her wolf spirit animal.

"By the gods, Talwyn—"

"Who or who did not accompany her is not important," Ashtine interrupted, the chatter around the table falling silent. "What did you learn, Talwyn?"

"I was told that a weapon hides in the mortal lands. I was told how to retrieve it, but that the time is not right," she explained.

"And when will the time be right?" Azrael asked.

"I was only told I will know. That's it. That's all she would say. But the weapon will determine the outcome of centuries of conflict."

"A war that was not won but only sleeps," Ashtine murmured.

Feelings of relief at knowing she wasn't losing her mind warred with dread at learning the winds weren't just chattering nonsense.

"So where does that leave us?" Azrael asked.

"On the precipice of salvation and destruction," Ashtine answered.

"That is . . . not helpful."

"You believe now is not the time to seek this weapon?" Renly asked, sitting forward to peer at Talwyn down the table.

"The Oracle was clear the time is not now. She insisted I would know when the time was right to retrieve it," the queen answered.

"And how will you find such a thing? Let alone retrieve it? Do you even know what it is?" Sion asked.

"I am still working on the strategies, but when the time comes, I will be prepared," she answered, sitting taller and lifting her chin. "In the meantime, we use the time we have to prepare." She met Ashtine's gaze again. "And if you learn anything more, Ashtine . . ."

"The information you have provided may be useful," Ashtine said, the burden and expectation of what she was weighing on her once more.

"We will help her," Ermir added. "As the princess said, your information helps us narrow down our search."

Talwyn nodded, glancing at Ashtine quickly before saying, "While this is pressing, we have time. None of us need to stress over it."

"Understood, your Majesty," Ermir answered.

Ashtine had stopped listening though.

A prince hides in plain sight.

Beginnings and endings.

A world the gods forgot.

There must be balance.

A genesis brings death.

"Is there anything else I am needed for?" Ashtine asked suddenly, the winds so loud now she could scarcely hear herself speak.

"No," Talwyn said slowly. "Will you come for dinner tomorrow evening?"

"Will I dine with you?" Ashtine asked.

Princes fall. Kings rise. The realms will divide.

"Why would I invite you to dinner with someone else?" Talwyn asked.

"That would indeed be odd. Dinner sounds lovely. Thank you."

Then, before anyone else could speak, she was moving among the winds.

The rivers will run red.

The winds swirled around her.

Allies will stand on opposite sides.

They carried her where they willed.

Across the sea the cursed one rules.

She let them have her for so long, she lost track of time. Minutes became hours, and still she stayed among them because while the winds were her freedom, they were also her prison.

Across the stars, he waits for vengeance.

Ermir had spoken so much truth in that room, but one thing she was sure they were all wrong about was the winds speaking nonsense. Their chattering may be nonsense in this moment, but a decade from now, would they say the same? Or were warnings for another world carried to her across the voids and stars between the realms? Either way, she did not believe them to be nonsense. The winds were rarely wrong.

It wasn't until she glimpsed dark skin and pale blonde hair sitting on a shore that she realized how late it was. She'd been wandering among the winds for hours if it was nearly dawn, but she didn't step from them now. It was for the best. The winds wouldn't let her linger. They would pull her somewhere else soon enough, so for the briefest of moments she let herself remember what it had been like.

His lips on hers.

How he'd tasted of the sea and sun.

How he'd been demanding yet soft with how he spoke to her, touched her, when everyone else in her life was careful and wary.

How she'd wanted more. So much more.

How she had sent her magic to him, hoping he'd lose as much control as she was.

She'd been with males before. Not many due to her obvious peculiarities, and they were never more than physical needs being met or curiosity being satisfied. But this had been different, and she was unsure how to feel about any of it.

But she knew she could not meet him tonight like he'd requested.

She knew it broke laws of old.

That waves and winds would tip the balance.

Still, she found herself returning among the winds the next morning before the sun woke, and he was there, just as he'd said he would be. He was there the next and the next and the next, simply waiting.

He'd promised he would always be there. With her. For her.

But he didn't know what she knew.

He didn't know what the winds had whispered to her while she'd lain on that shore the day he'd kissed her.

A prince of water will fall.

CHAPTER 9
BRIAR

"I am surprised you haven't brought up training with the other Courts again," Sawyer said as Briar sat with his brother on the banks of Anahita's Springs. The water was said to be blessed by the goddess, and it was where the Water Fae imbued weapons with magic. Not only water magic. Any weapon could be imbued here. The element of the Fae dipping the weapon into the waters determined what magic would imbue the weapon.

The Springs were also connected to Briar and Sawyer, the only two known Water Gazers in the realm.

"No one seemed keen on the idea," Briar mused, watching the images in the water before them. Of course he'd come here with the intention of seeing if Ashtine was in her catacomb nook, but Sawyer had already been here. He wasn't about to send his brother away. This was the one place they both felt connected to their parents. Their mother had been a powerful water Fae, but it was their father who had been the Water Gazer. It was hard enough for Fae to conceive one child, let alone two. Both of those children receiving the Water Gazer gift contributed to the idea that the Drayce bloodline was blessed and favored by Anahita.

He'd also come here because there was a storm blowing in from the north, and the Springs were more sheltered from the elements.

"Right. It has nothing to do with the fact that you stopped visiting the Wind Court," Sawyer said, drawing his own enchantment to change the view he was watching in the water.

"What do you want me to say, Sawyer?" Briar asked.

His brother shrugged. "Thought maybe you'd want to talk about it. Sorin is . . . unavailable, and you've been preoccupied. Not to mention that for weeks you've been going to the same place on the beach every morning before dawn."

"Your spying habit is becoming annoying," Briar muttered.

"You're just jealous because it's easier for me," Sawyer replied, pulling the small mirror from his pocket. It had belonged to their father, and Sawyer had been enamored with it as a youngling. It had only seemed fitting that Sawyer have it when their parents were killed, but the mirror was imbued with the power of the Springs. Their father always told them the goddess herself had given it to the first Drayce Water Prince. That was the legend anyway.

"Either way, I thought I'd let everyone sit with the idea for a while before bringing it up again. I still believe it would be a good idea," Briar said.

"Quit trying to change the subject," Sawyer said, dipping a hand into the Springs and letting water pool in his palm. "Tell me about the Wind Princess."

"There is nothing to tell."

And that was the truth, as far as he knew. Sure, he could tell his brother about a kiss that happened over a month ago, but what was the point when it had meant nothing? At least to her. That was clear by the fact that she never showed on the beach, but he still waited, night after night, despite knowing it was likely pointless.

Ashtine wasn't wrong. A relationship would break laws of old and likely incite the wrath of the gods. She wouldn't risk that. He shouldn't either, but that didn't stop him from replaying the kiss over and over. Each day, the memory of how it felt to touch her faded a little more, and he found himself desperate to preserve it. He hated that if they were anyone else, no one would care. He'd spent time with plenty of females. But because of their godsdamn titles, the mere act of spending time together caused speculation. Sure, the speculations were true, but that was beside the point.

"Fuck!" Briar shouted as something icy hit him right in the face. He lurched to his feet, finding his brother laughing. Looking down, he found the snowball already melting in the summer heat. "Ass," he muttered, wiping at his face.

"It is rude to ignore someone when in their company," Sawyer replied, scooping more water and freezing it to snow.

"I swear to Anahita, Sawyer, if you throw that at me—"

But they were cut off by the piercing cry of a hawk.

A cry he knew.

"Is that—"

"Yes, it is," Briar interrupted, trying to see through the trees that kept the Springs secluded.

What would Nasima be doing here unless Ashtine was with her? But he would have felt her cross the wards.

The hawk finally broke through, gliding above the small body of water in tight circles. Her wings brushed the surface, sending rings rippling to the edges as she screeched another cry.

"I have never seen her apart from Princess Evermorn," Sawyer said, almost in awe.

"It is rare," Briar agreed, but something wasn't right. He could feel it in the way Nasima circled again, her cries almost desperate. Without thinking, he raised an arm. The silver hawk immediately flew to him, taloned feet wrapping around his forearm.

"Briar . . ." Sawyer trailed off, staring at him. "Tell me again how you haven't been spending time with the Wind Princess."

"I haven't seen her in weeks."

"That doesn't erase the past."

"Nothing has happened," Briar retorted.

"That doesn't erase the wish that something had," Sawyer countered. He said it softly, almost gently.

But this had nothing to do with wants or desires. Something was wrong, and he'd promised Ashtine he would always be there. With her. For her.

It wasn't even a question when he conjured a water portal, stepping through to the same place he had a few months ago. There was no hesitation this time. No trepidation or overthinking what he was doing as he strode across the bridge and up the Citadel steps. And just like the time before, the door was opened by Sion.

"Prince Drayce. Sawyer," the Wind General said, his features grim.

It was only then that Briar registered how godsdamn windy it was here. Sure, it was the Wind Court, but these were brutal gusts. He suddenly wondered how he hadn't been tossed right off the bridge and into the chasm it spanned. The clouds swirled just as violently, and Nasima loosed another cry as she battled against the gales, taking to the sky.

Sion stepped aside, letting them in. Briar hadn't even thought about Sawyer following him, but he should have expected it.

"This is not a good time," Sion said, shutting out the raging wind.

"Where is she?" Briar demanded.

"You really need to make appointments for these meetings, Prince," Sion tried again.

"Noted. Where the fuck is she?"

Sion straightened at the tone, instinctively going into a defensive position. His hand twitched toward a blade strapped to his waist, and his features hardened. "She is not available right now. I can send word when she is feeling better."

"No. Take me to her. It is not a request, Sion. Take me to Ashtine now," Briar snapped, the temperature in the foyer dropping dramatically.

"Briar, calm down," Sawyer murmured, bringing a hand to Briar's shoulder. A little louder, he added, "Nasima came to fetch him, Sion."

"What the fuck is going on?" Renly demanded, coming up behind Sion. His glare was enough to make any other Fae shrink back as air swirled at his fingertips. "The princess is unavailable. Surely Sion told you this."

"He did. I did not care. Take me to her," Briar answered. "Or I will find her myself."

"They claim Nasima summoned them here," Sion cut in, eyeing the Drayce brothers.

"Bullshit," Renly spat. "I know you are a Fae Prince, but that does not mean you get to come to another Court and make demands. The princess is unavailable. If you take one step more into this Citadel, I will assume you are here to harm her and act accordingly."

"You cannot be serious," Briar snarled.

Sawyer's grip on his shoulder tightened. "Do not start a conflict here, Briar."

"There will be no conflict as long as I can lay eyes on her," he bit back. "If not her, then take me to Ermir."

"He cannot leave her side—" Renly started, but a faint flash of light cut him off.

When it faded, Abrax stood between the Water Fae and Wind Fae. He reared up, Renly and Sion both cursing as they lurched out of the way, but Briar was already moving. His own water magic propelled him up, and he was scarcely astride the spirit animal when the horse bolted forward. Staff cried out and jumped aside as they moved through the Citadel. If he wasn't so focused on seeing Ashtine, he'd find the scene comical. A horse galloping through the halls of a palace.

Two Fae scrambled to open the doors that led to the grounds behind the Citadel, and Abrax burst through. Briar didn't question how he knew where to go. He was too busy using his power to stay astride now that he was back out in the swirling winds.

Abrax skidded to a halt at the base of steep stairs that climbed up a cliff side and into the dark clouds. Briar knew that at the top of those steps was a courtyard that was believed to be as blessed as Anahita's Springs. Skystone was found there. Stone that was said to be wind-kissed by Sefarina. Briar had never been inside the courtyards. In fact, the base of these steps was the closest he'd ever been.

Nasima's cry carried to him again, and it spurred him into motion. He took the steps two at a time, praying to the gods he wouldn't lose his footing. The climb took longer than he would have liked, and the gusting winds didn't help matters. He was out of breath when he reached the top, but he found Ermir there, standing outside the archway that was the entrance to the courtyard.

The air around them turned so cold, Briar could see his breath. He wasn't sure if it was the wind raging or his own fury.

"Why are you not with her?" Briar demanded, staring at the Wind Court Second.

Ermir calmly turned to face him, worry and sorrow mingling on his features. Speaking loud enough to be heard over the howling winds, he said, "Prince Drayce. I am so sorry you made the climb up here, but she cannot see you today."

"She will see me, but that does not answer my question," Briar growled. "Why the fuck are you out here when she is in there? Something is clearly wrong."

"The winds can be all-consuming," Ermir said, turning back to face the archway.

Briar finally let himself look as well, and his breath stalled. There was a whirlwind inside the courtyard, leaves and dust swirling among it, but he couldn't see Ashtine.

"Where is she?" Briar asked, taking a step forward.

"In the center of it," Ermir answered.

"Again I ask you: why *the fuck* are you out here when your princess is in trouble?"

"I cannot help her," he answered, and Briar could hear the angst in his words. He wanted to, but he wasn't even trying.

Ermir lifted a hand, his magic wrapping around them and creating a barrier against the storm. They could still hear it, but at least they didn't need to yell to be heard. "Ophelia would experience the same at times," he said.

"And you stood back and did nothing? Nothing helped?" Briar asked, his gaze fixed to the courtyard.

"We tried," Ermir said. "For decades. But it is a burden of a

Wind Walker. Only they can find what quiets them. Ophelia struggled, just as I have seen Ashtine struggling these last years."

"You have seen her struggling and done nothing?" he sneered.

"Do not presume to know the inner workings of our Court or the winds, Prince," Ermir said. "You think I enjoy seeing her like this? She is like a daughter to me. If there was anything I could do, I would."

"And Ophelia never found a way to balance her gifts?" Briar asked.

"Not until Ansel," Ermir said, referencing Ashtine's father. "Even then, it took time. Their union was arranged, like all royal joinings are, but he found a way. He was the only one. I pray to Sefarina that Ashtine will find that peace one day. But today is not that day, and I have no choice but to watch over her while she suffers."

"Let me into the courtyard," Briar said, because standing back wasn't an option.

He'd promised her he would always be there for her. Even if they could never be anything more, he could do this. Not stand back and watch, but he could step into her suffering and let her know she wasn't alone in it. No one else might understand the winds, but that didn't mean she needed to endure her fate alone.

Ermir shook his head. "It is too dangerous, Prince."

Briar turned, a dagger of ice forming in his hand. "That is my risk to take. It will be a risk you take if you deny me again, Ermir. Let me into the courtyard."

The older Fae's eyes went wide, bouncing between his face and the dagger. "Prince, you overstep—"

The dagger flew, grazing Ermir's shoulder enough to cause blood to well. Another dagger had already formed. "The next one will not leave a simple scratch, Ermir," Briar warned.

He'd expected rage, but the Second only studied him for a long moment before nodding. He lowered his magic, the winds so forceful once more that Briar stumbled forward and the ice dagger was ripped from his hand. He pushed against the wind, following

Ermir to the archway. The Second sent a small burst of his magic through the archway. It glowed faintly, and he motioned for Briar to enter.

Each step forward felt like pushing against ten warriors in training. More than once, he stumbled back, losing ground. Even using a shield of his own magic didn't aid him. He was exhausted when he finally broke through the whirlwind, using his water gifts to wash the dust from his eyes. He had hoped there would be a calm at the center, but while the winds didn't assault him like they had outside her storm, what he found had him rushing forward.

Ashtine was there, on her knees and face in her hands. Her hair appeared to have once been intricately braided, but now it was a wild mess of knots. She was barefoot, and a cloak was nowhere to be seen. Her gown was sleeveless, and the skirt was as tossed about as her hair.

"Ashtine."

Her name got caught in his throat, but she still somehow heard it. She slowly lifted her head, dull sky-blue eyes meeting his. She was as white as a phantom. Even her lips were bloodless, but the dark circles beneath her eyes told him she hadn't slept in days, possibly weeks.

Briar lowered to his knees, wanting to reach for her, but not sure if he should. Truth be known, now that he was here, he had no godsdamn idea what to do or how to help her.

"Ashtine," he said again. "Tell me what I can do."

"You came here." It wasn't a question, and gods, she sounded so incredibly tired.

"I told you I would always be here for you, my dear," he answered.

"You came," she repeated, as if she didn't believe he was kneeling in front of her.

"I did."

"Why?"

"You called for me. Or I suppose Nasima did the calling," he replied.

"They are quieter when you are near," Ashtine said, her voice somewhere between an awed whisper and a sob. "I do not understand why."

"Then I will stay. We can understand tomorrow," Briar said. Looking around, he found her storm had lessened some. The winds still swirled, though not as violently. He could see glimpses of the gleaming white skystone. "Do you wish to stay here? In the courtyard?"

"I wish for a bed and to sleep. That is all I wish for. It is all I have desired for days," she said, still not moving.

"Then let's do that."

"The winds do not let me," she whispered. "They never cease."

"But they are less in the moment, yes?" Briar asked, unable to help himself as he reached out and pushed her hair from her face. Her eyes fluttered closed for the briefest of moments. "Speak, Ashtine." He didn't say it harshly, but it was a command to answer.

"Yes," she murmured. "Because you are near."

"Then I will stay near. Are you ready?"

He didn't wait for an answer this time. He stood, then he bent and scooped the princess into his arms. She didn't fight him. There was no protest. She only sighed, a sound born out of weariness, and rested her head against his shoulder.

But the whirlwind around them faded, the gales slowing until they were nothing more than a gentle breeze stirring around them. He imagined this was the way the courtyard normally looked. Peaceful and stunning with the skystone glinting in the midday sun.

As he approached the archway, he saw Ermir standing on the other side, a cloak in his hands. Standing next to him was Sawyer. When he stepped out of the courtyard, Ermir placed the cloak over Ashtine without a word.

"I will be staying with her," Briar said to the Wind Court Second. "It is not a request."

"Indeed, your Highness," Ermir replied. "Had you attempted to leave, I would have asked you to stay."

Briar glanced at his brother, who only gave a small nod of his head, before they turned and followed Ermir. He carried Ashtine all the way down those steep stairs. The courtyard was warded. There was no way to make portals at the top. But Ermir did not take him back to the Citadel the way Briar had come on Abrax.

Instead, Ermir veered left, leading them through a small grove of evergreen trees. They emerged sometime later, where the Second pulled open a door that would have been easily missed without guidance.

"The princess's safe route," Ermir explained as they entered a dark passageway. "I do not wish for her to be seen in such a state."

Briar made a sound of acknowledgement. Ashtine hadn't said a word, and he hoped that meant she was asleep. They climbed several flights of stairs before he was led into a set of rooms he could only assume were Ashtine's private quarters.

"Her bedchamber is through that door," Ermir said, nodding to a doorway. "Send word if you need anything. Her handmaiden, Noelle, may be in and out. She can be trusted."

"Thank you, Ermir," Briar said.

"No, Prince. I believe it is I who should be thanking you," the Second replied.

Briar only nodded before carrying Ashtine through to her bedchamber. He wasn't sure what Sawyer was planning to do, but he also didn't care as he gently laid Ashtine down. He removed the cloak and replaced it with a heavy wool blanket, but the moment he stepped back, her eyes opened, finding his.

"You will stay?" she asked.

"If you wish," he replied, but that was a lie. He wasn't going anywhere, even if she wished him gone.

"You will still be here when I wake?"

"I will always be here for you, Ashtine. Sleep."

But it wasn't until he'd removed his boots and climbed atop the bed next to her that she finally found rest. Her fingers curled into his tunic, keeping her tethered to him. The sound of wings rustling drew his attention to the window where Nasima was perched on the ledge. She clicked her beak, feathers rustling again.

"Thank you," Briar said softly.

The hawk made another clicking sound before she launched back into the sky.

CHAPTER 10
ASHTINE

If this was a dream, she did not wish to wake.

Not only because it was the first truly restful sleep she could remember in years, but because she was surrounded by the scent of the sea. The winds were there. She could feel them gently flowing around her, but they waited. All her life, the winds had spoken when they wished. Now they waited until they were summoned. A give and take. A balance. A peace she had desired for months. Years. Decades, if truth be told.

Ashtine took a deep breath, curling more into the male beside her and soaking in these last moments of calm. She wasn't fool enough to think this could continue, but she was wise enough to take the reprieve while she could.

Opening her eyes, she found Briar propped on several pillows, one arm behind his head. His other arm was curled around her, fingers making a light sweeping motion along her waist and hip. If he knew she was awake, he didn't reveal it, and she took the time to truly study him. His pale, blonde hair was such a stark contrast to his dark skin. It reached his shoulders and made his icy blue eyes stand out even more. He appeared completely relaxed as calloused fingers continued their same path. Had he simply . . . lain here this entire time?

Glancing at a window, she found the light of a dying day. The sun was nearly set. Someone, she assumed it had been Noelle, had been in the room and lit candles and sconces and tended to the fire. There was fresh water on the bedside table, along with a plate of dried meat and cheese, although the food appeared untouched.

He had to know she was awake. Fae could sense the smallest shift in breathing, and in the silence of the room, he could detect a change in heart rate, but neither of them spoke. Was that normal when waking next to someone? She wouldn't know. This was a new experience. While she had been intimate with males before, it had been only that. She had never woken next to one. Never spent an entire night with someone. She'd never actually *slept* next to another in her centuries of life. How odd to still experience new things even after over two hundred years of living.

Minutes passed. Briar's fingers never ceased their movement, and she was nearly lulled back to sleep until a burst of flames appeared next to Briar's head. He sighed, pulling the message from the fire and scanning it. Then he tossed it aside, propping his arm beneath his head once more.

"You must go," Ashtine said, loosening her grip where her fingers were still curled into his tunic.

"It can wait," Briar answered, shifting onto his side. He propped his head on his fist, staring down at her. "How do you fare?"

"My wellbeing need not be your concern."

"And yet it is," he countered. "Ashtine, what happened?"

"That question is too broad, and I find it confusing to answer."

He nodded in understanding, contemplating his words before he spoke again. "What drove you to the courtyard today?"

"The winds are unrelenting," she answered, rolling away from him and onto her back. "Is this common practice?"

When he didn't answer right away, she glanced at him, finding his brow pinched in confusion. It was an expression she was far too used to.

"You do not need to supply an answer," she added, turning away and trying to find the resolve to get out of the bed. She knew this stolen peace would shatter the moment her feet touched the floor. But fingers were gripping her chin, gently turning her back to face him.

"Do not dismiss me, Ashtine," Briar said, the words somehow both gentle and commanding all at once. "I simply need a moment to discern what you are saying and how to respond."

"I understand I am—"

"I swear to the gods, if you say you are vexing, I will become upset," he interrupted, and the temperature in the room dipped. "I am learning how to speak with you, but you must give me the chance to do so. I do not become impatient with you. I request the same courtesy."

Ashtine's eyes narrowed. "You are impatient at this very moment."

"Impatience and displeasure are different."

"You do not need to spend time learning how to communicate with me."

"You misunderstand me," Briar said, leaning imperceptibly closer. "I *want* to learn how to speak with you."

"Why?"

He huffed a small laugh. "I can see I was not clear when I kissed you weeks ago. I want to learn everything there is to know about you, my dear. If you are amenable to that, please clarify what you were referring to when you asked if this was common practice."

Ashtine was silent, mulling over his words before saying, "I find you both intriguing and perplexing, Briar Drayce."

"And I only find you captivating, Ashtine Evermorn," he replied, his thumb brushing along her bottom lip. "Now tell me."

She nodded once, gathering her thoughts. "I simply wonder if it is common practice to wake next to someone and have a conversation."

"That depends."

She rolled towards him once again because no one had taken the time to learn how to speak with her, let alone try to explain social expectations to her. It was just understood she would be the

Wind Princess with her head in the clouds and whispered nuances in her ears.

"What are the qualifiers for such an interaction?"

"It is quite common to ask of another's wellbeing, but in this case, I am a friend who is worried after finding you in such a state earlier today," he answered.

She nodded slowly, processing that. "So if we were not friends, the interaction would have been different?"

"If we were not friends, it would have been inappropriate for me to sit in a bed next to you while you slept," he replied. "Then again, it was likely inappropriate either way."

"Because of our titles," she said in understanding.

"Fuck our titles, Ashtine," he replied. "When it is just us, I care little of our titles. It was inappropriate because while you slept I let my mind wander to what it would be like if I could steal kisses and touches without worry."

"It breaks laws of old," she whispered.

"But to answer your question," he went on, ignoring her comment. "If *that* were us, I would have still asked how you were faring when you woke. Then I would have kissed you until we were both breathless."

"That would never happen. I have magic of wind and air," she answered.

He huffed a laugh. "Then my lips would have likely strayed away from yours. Ideally, I would already be wearing little clothing, and you would be in the same state."

"Your thoughts wandered too far," she admonished.

He caught some strands of her hair, winding them around a finger. "You wish to stick with conversation then?"

"I . . ." She watched him for a moment, seeing his lips twitch. Her eyes narrowed. "You are teasing me again."

"I would never, my dear."

"You are a liar, Briar Drayce."

"Perhaps," he conceded, releasing her hair, before rolling to his back and stretching.

"But I . . ." she started, pausing when he turned to look at her again.

"You can speak plainly with me, Ashtine. Always."

"I know. I simply . . . I enjoy this," she said. "I did not think I would."

He smiled softly. "As do I."

"I think I would enjoy the intimacy as well."

His blue eyes seemed to darken. "We could put the theory to the test?"

"That would be unwise," she replied, but her eyes darted to his mouth anyway.

He moved fast, and she let out a small gasp as he rolled, hovering over her. "I tell you I have spent the last hours thinking of what it would be like to taste you again, and you tell me *that?*"

His voice was a sensual purr that she felt in her soul, making her toes curl in a way she'd never experienced. Was *this* what such intimacies were supposed to be like? She truly didn't know, but gods, did she want to find out.

"Tell me not to kiss you, Ashtine," he murmured, his face so close to hers they were sharing breath.

"Why would I say that if it is what I wish for?" she replied, her features scrunching in confusion.

"By the gods," he muttered right before his mouth landed on hers.

His lips moved, insistent and demanding, but she didn't care. Everyone was always so gentle with her. Sharp canines nipped at her lower lip, and another gasp slipped from her. Briar used the moment to slip his tongue into her mouth, tangling with her own. And she wanted more, just like the last time they'd kissed. Her hands looped around his neck, fingers twining into his hair. He was still propped up on one arm, but his other hand was roaming. Rough fingertips traced her jaw, her throat, her collarbone. She was the one shoving at the blankets, giving him room to explore further, but his hand slid back up and cupped her jaw. She was about to protest until he broke the kiss and his mouth followed the same path his hand had. Down her throat, her collarbone, and her magic was restless, seeking out more as much as she was.

"I was wrong," she said, and Briar paused, lifting his head to look at her in question. "I did not think I could be breathless, but I am."

He laughed, a real one, before he kissed her again, this time rolling to his back and taking her with him. Another laugh sounded, but this was her own. She sat up, staring down at Briar beneath her. Her knees were on either side of his hips, her gown bunched up. His hands were on her thighs, and he was watching her in wonder. Not the curious air of bewilderment, but as if he were truly enamored by what he saw.

"I do not laugh often," Ashtine said, more to herself than to him.

"It is a beautiful sound," he answered, a hand skimming up her side and down her arm, where he interlaced their fingers. "You are still rather pale."

"I am fair-skinned."

"This is more than that, Ashtine. Tell me what drove you to the cliffs today," he said softly, bringing her hand to his mouth and brushing a kiss to her knuckles.

"I already told you this. The winds are unrelenting," she answered.

"Still about a coming war?"

"Yes, among other things. They speak so often, so quickly. So many things all at once . . ." She trailed off, the peace she'd been basking in already dissipating with his line of questioning.

Ashtine pulled her hand from his grip before sliding off him and slipping from the bed. Briar let her go, but he followed, getting to his feet just as quickly.

"Tell me one," he said, reaching for her hand once more and tugging her to stop.

"Tell you one what?"

"Tell me one thing the winds say that drove you to the cliffs."

She barked another laugh, but this one was humorless and

harsh. "So you can carry such burdens too? I cannot do that to you, Prince Drayce."

He snarled as he yanked her into him, tilting her head back with his finger while his other arm wound around her waist. "Stop trying to distance yourself from me, Ashtine. We can share burdens. We are not designed to face this life in solitude. We have centuries. What would be the point?"

"Then why was I given a gift no one else possesses?" she cried, and Briar's eyes went wide, his grip on her falling slack. "I was given a gift that so many covet, but they should not, Briar. The winds are both loving and cruel. Their gifts are a blessing and a curse, and you rarely know which until their musings come to fruition. What good is knowing of the happenings in other realms? What is the purpose of driving me mad until I wish I were anyone but who I am? I cannot use these warnings to protect my people. I cannot use their omens to warn the realm. I cannot understand any of it."

Her power gusted, blowing through the room with such force the plate of food beside the bed was overturned and pillows were tossed to the floor. Frames slipped from the walls, glass cracking, and pages rustled as books fell from shelves.

"Ashtine."

His voice was soft and so full of an understanding he could not possibly possess, but he pulled her into his chest, arms wrapping tightly around her.

They come.

It was barely a whisper from the winds before there was a knock on the door. "Princess? Prince? Is everything well?"

Ermir.

"We are fine," Briar called back, keeping her close. "Give us a minute, and we will be out."

"Do you always speak deception, Prince?" she asked, her voice muffled as she kept her face buried in his tunic. She was anything but fine. She was certain she had never been *fine*.

"It was not a lie," he said, a hand smoothing down her hair. "You are not fine right now, but I refuse to believe this was the life fate wanted for you. We will find harmony with the winds, Ashtine."

"It is not possible."

"And yet you told me they are less when I am near," he countered.

"You cannot be with me all the time, Briar."

"Perhaps not, but I can be there when you need the reprieve until we figure it out." He took her shoulders, gently easing her back. "But you must make the choice to let me help, Ashtine."

"I fear the more time I spend with you, the more I will desire things we cannot have," she whispered.

He smiled, but it was a sad tilt of his lips. "We will figure that out too."

"And if we do not care for the outcome?"

"Our friendship will remain," he answered, swiping a thumb across her cheek. It was only then she realized she was crying. "Do you need another moment before we join Ermir in your sitting room?"

Ashtine nodded, stepping from his touch and retreating to her bathing room. She took her time dragging a brush through her tangled hair, a product of the windstorm she'd summoned.

A storm Briar had walked to the center of to find her.

A storm no one else had dared to even try to help her manage.

But he'd dared.

Foolish or brave, she could not decide.

She changed into a fresh dress, pulling on wool socks rather than slippers, before she stepped back into her bedchambers. Briar was standing near the window, hands clasped behind his back, but he immediately turned when she emerged.

"Are you ready?" he asked.

No.

"Yes," she answered with a tight smile, but the look Briar returned told her he saw right through it. Then she wondered when she had learned to read social cues. Except she hadn't. She was only learning to read *him*.

Briar moved to her side, his hand falling to her lower back as he pulled open the bedchamber door and guided her through. She should care that Ermir was seeing him touch her in such a way, but after everything that had happened that day, she doubted it would matter in the end.

She wasn't met with one male in the sitting room, however; she was met with two. Ermir and Sawyer both stood when they emerged, both of them bowing their heads.

Ermir stepped forward, reaching a hand for her, but she found herself drawing back and stepping into Briar. Her Second's brow arched, while Sawyer sent a knowing look to his brother.

"What is the plan here?" Sawyer asked.

"I received a message from the Fire Prince. I was planning to go visit with him tonight," Briar answered, his hand sliding lightly up and down her spine.

"That is not what I meant, and you know it," Sawyer countered. His gaze flicked to Ashtine then back to his brother.

"I do not understand what you are asking," Ashtine said.

"Are you going to speak of the clear relationship between the two of you?" Sawyer asked plainly.

"Sawyer," Briar warned.

"There cannot be a relationship," Ermir cut in. "Old laws of the gods forbid such a thing, but that was not what this is. Is it, Princess?"

"Of course not," she answered, Briar's hand pausing before it slid back to her lower back once more and lingered.

"Bullshit," Sawyer scoffed, folding his arms across his chest. "There will be pushback, but it would be better to come forth with this from the start."

"Calling the Wind Princess a liar is ill-advised," Ermir cut in, his tone condemning. "But if Briar can help her learn to manage the winds, we welcome his aid."

"Even if that was all this is, which I still very much doubt, the Water Prince and the Wind Princess working so closely together ought to be disclosed."

"People will not understand," Ashtine said, shaking her head. "It breaks laws of old, and they will make other demands to prove it is not more."

"What other demands?" Sawyer asked, still eyeing them both.

"The Courts will push for both of them to take partners," Ermir explained. "But that should start being discussed either way. It is long past time—"

Ashtine tensed, but Briar said, "That does not need to be discussed at this moment after the day we have experienced."

"I think this does need to be discussed before we leave this room," Sawyer argued.

Briar didn't appear bothered in the slightest as he smoothly stepped in front of Ashtine. How he'd known that's what she needed, she didn't know, but his presence between her and the others eased something in her chest. It was a statement. He was choosing her—and whatever this was—over their Courts.

He couldn't do that. They couldn't have this.

"We will discuss this at home, Sawyer," Briar said.

"Godsdamn right we will," his brother retorted, the room starting to feel chilly as the siblings argued.

Ignoring his brother's retort, Briar turned to face her. "You will be all right if I leave?"

Of course not. The moment he left, the winds would pounce.

"Yes," she answered, stepping back from him and forcing a smile. "Thank you for today. Be well, Prince."

His eyes narrowed, and she knew he was upset over the formal address, but he couldn't choose her.

She wasn't an option for him to choose.

"The next day and the next and not regret a moment of it, Ashtine," was all he said before he turned away from her. "Ermir, do not hesitate to send a message."

"Of course, Prince," her Second answered, but his gaze was pinned on her.

Sawyer followed Briar from the room, the door clicking shut behind them.

"I will ask once, Princess: is it more?" Ermir said, watching her closely.

The balance tips.

She forced her smile brighter, suppressing the wince as the winds descended. "No, Ermir. The wrath of angry gods is not something I seek," she answered. "Is dinner nearly prepared?"

He studied her a moment longer before nodding. "It is if you are feeling well enough?"

"I would enjoy a meal with you," she answered, placing her hand in the crook of his arm when he extended it to her. She let him lead her from the room as the winds followed.

Lies and truth, who can tell?

Maybe she was the liar in all of this after all.

The rivers will run red.

A genesis brings death.

A prince of water will fall.

She breathed deep and wished she was still lost to her dreams.

CHAPTER 11
BRIAR

He stared out at the sea, the waves rolling to shore in a rhythm that had soothed him all his life. His hands were in his pockets, and his sleeveless tunic was still warm, even with the stars standing watch while the sun slumbered. Water brushed his bare feet as it ebbed and flowed, and he toyed with the element as he waited.

He'd spent the entirety of the afternoon and evening with Ashtine, and he hadn't lied to her. He *had* thought about what it would be like to steal moments with her, but he'd also thought of all the reasons why they couldn't have that. Their Courts would never stand for it. The other Royals would never agree to such a power pairing. Not to mention the gods who forbid such a thing since the First gods and goddesses emerged from the Chaos.

And still he did not care when he definitely should.

A faint breeze had him smiling, and he didn't bother looking behind him when he said, "I knew you would come tonight."

"This will break laws of old," Ashtine said, coming to stand beside him.

"It does not have to."

She looked up at him, and he finally turned to face her. In the moonlight, her sky-blue eyes appeared almost silver. Her hair flowed on winds of her own making, and her silvery gown was light-weight and sleeveless. She'd dressed for his Court tonight.

"How can it not break laws of old?" she asked. "Our power is immense. It is why we carry our titles, and while the old laws are not officially our laws, they—"

"I think we simply take the trials as they come," Briar interrupted. "I know you have reservations, Ashtine, and I will not try and sway you if it is not something you want."

"But you know it *is* something I desire," she insisted. "You should be telling me all the reasons we should stop this. Both of our Seconds tell us this is ill-advised."

She was both right and wrong. While he didn't know what Ermir had said to her, Sawyer hadn't once told Briar not to pursue this. He had only cautioned him, telling him to think of the implications. And tonight, when they'd returned from the Fire Court, he'd only told him again that if this moves forward, they should be upfront with everyone rather than keep it a secret. Despite that, secrecy was their only option if they wanted time to learn about each other without the involvement of the rest of the Courts. Maybe it would be short-lived in the end and the commotion would be pointless.

That was what he told himself as he said, "We do not know what the future holds, Ashtine. We will go mad trying to figure it out."

"You speak of the winds?" she asked, stepping closer.

"I speak of life and fate and the days ahead," he answered. "I speak knowing we have centuries ahead of us, and we deserve happiness and something for ourselves, despite our titles and responsibilities."

"We *are* our titles and responsibilities. You cannot deny that simply by speaking it," she argued.

"Then we keep this for ourselves."

"You will be content with stolen moments and secret meetings?" she asked.

"I will steal whatever time I can from fate if it means being with you," Briar replied, taking her hand in his and bringing her fingertips to his lips. "I will never regret a moment of it."

She was silent for so long, Briar thought she was going to deny him. He'd let her go, of course. If she did not want to risk it, he understood. He would move on at some point, but he'd always spend his days wondering what it would have been like. *That* he would regret. Never knowing, but feeling in his soul he had missed out on something that even the gods would envy.

"I do not know how to navigate something like this," she finally said.

"Neither do I," he answered, tugging her closer.

Ashtine shook her head. "No. I mean, I . . . This is a social situation I am unfamiliar with."

He tried to hide his smile, but couldn't as he reached to tuck her hair behind her ear. "My dearest Ashtine, this is anything but a social situation."

"Oh," she murmured. "In that case, I do not understand what this is at all."

"Neither do I," he repeated. "We will discover it together, I suppose."

It was a moment before she nodded. "That sounds like something I would enjoy."

Brushing his thumb along her cheek, he asked, "Have you slept tonight?"

She shook her head. "I spent the hours debating if I would come to you."

He knew that. Having been in her private bedchamber, he could now use his water-gazing gifts to enchant the water there. He'd done so tonight, not entirely trusting her to summon him if she needed him.

Without a word, he conjured a water portal, guiding her through into his private rooms, just as he had before. Ashtine looked around the space, a frown forming.

"There is only a sofa and chairs in here," she said.

"It is a sitting room," he replied.

"I have only been intimate in a bed. Is a sofa the same?" she asked, her head tipping to the side as she studied the furniture.

"I was attempting not to be presumptuous," he replied. "However, apparently you had presumptions of your own."

"I did assume this situation would involve a bed," she retorted.

He rolled his lips, fighting the smile, but when she glanced at him, he couldn't hide it.

"Briar Drayce, it is rude to continually tease me when I do not understand when you are doing so," she chided.

Reaching for her and intertwining their fingers once more, he said, "This situation indeed involves a bed for the sole reason that neither of us has slept tonight. The intimacy part will be left up to you to decide."

He pulled her to the bedchamber, candles already lit to illuminate the room. There wasn't a fire because the heat of the summer still permeated the air, but—

"Do you want the windows and veranda doors closed?" he asked, while she again took in his space.

"No," she murmured. "The winds are calmer when I am with you."

"Are they silent?"

"Not silent. They simply . . . wait for me. Until I am ready to hear them," she answered.

"Then we need to figure out how to carry that over whether I am with you or not," he said.

She sighed, and he could hear the exhaustion in that single breath. "I have tried for decades. They do what they wish."

"Our magic is not meant to control us, Ashtine," he said gently.

"The winds are different."

He didn't think that was true, but he also recognized this wasn't the time to argue with her. Instead, he asked, "Do you wish to rest in that dress, or would you like to borrow a shirt?"

She turned to him, her expression one of curiosity. "One of yours?"

"I do keep only my clothing in this space."

"You jest."

"You are a quick study," he said with a wink.

Ashtine clicked her tongue in annoyance. "Again with the teasing." Then she added, "Different sleeping attire would be appreciated."

He nodded, retrieving a light-weight tunic that would be more than oversized on her frame. While she changed, he did the same in the bathing room, and when he returned, she was already nestled on the bed.

"You will stay? Like before?" she asked the moment he stepped back into the room.

He smiled softly, making his way to the bed and blowing out the candles as he went. "I am stealing every moment I can with you, Ashtine."

She smiled at that, and it was one of the most beautiful things he'd seen. He immediately made a silent vow to pull more of those smiles from her. And laughter. He wanted to hear more of that from her too. She deserved to smile and laugh. She deserved so much more than duty to her people and indiscernible musings from the winds.

He'd been settled in the bed beside her for several minutes when he said into the fading dark, "Ashtine?"

"Yes, Briar?"

He smiled at his name on her lips. "Can I kiss you, or would you prefer to sleep?"

"I enjoy kissing you," she answered.

That was all he needed to roll onto his side, moving closer until his lips met hers. A contented sigh came from her when he deepened the kiss, parting her lips and seeking her tongue with his own. For a long time, they lay there, tuning out the world, until Ashtine murmured, "Am I still to decide the intimacy?"

"That choice is always yours," he answered, pressing another kiss to the corner of her mouth.

"If I tell you I wish for more this night?"

He smiled against her skin as he pressed a kiss to her jaw. "I will ask if you are certain."

To his pleasant surprise, she pushed his shoulders, nudging him onto his back and climbing atop him, settling against his already hard length. "I rarely speak unless I am certain," she said. "But I will ask if you are certain as well. I will understand if you change your thoughts on the matter."

"I am not changing my mind, Ashtine," he answered, his hands sliding up her bare thighs and slipping under the shirt she wore. His thumbs made idle circles along her hips as he added, "But should I ever question things or feel differently, I will tell you. And I request you promise the same transparency."

Her smile was soft and tender as she leaned down, brushing her lips along his. "I can agree to such terms."

"Good," was all he said before he gripped the hem of the shirt and pulled it over her head. Then he was rolling them over so she was lying beneath him. Her silver hair fanned across the pillows, and her body bared to him had him swallowing down the possessive growl that rumbled in his chest.

He didn't feel worthy of seeing her like this, let alone having the privilege of touching her, but he wasn't about to question it now. Not when he'd wondered about this moment for months. Not as her winds wrapped around him in a gentle breeze, making his entire body shudder with want.

He dragged his fingertips along her throat, across her collarbone, and down until he was cupping a breast in his hand. Then he was sucking her nipple into his mouth, unable to help himself when she arched into his touch. Her hands were roaming too, gliding along his back and arms. Fingers tangled in his hair, and he let his magic rise to the surface, turning his touch cold and making her gasp at not only the contrast, but his magic seeking out her winds.

For a long while, he was content just to feel her beneath him, stealing all those touches and kisses he'd told her about. It wasn't until she was moving beneath him, hips seeking more, that he finally pulled himself away long enough to remove his pants. Seconds later, he was settling between her thighs.

"Ashtine—" he started. He was going to ask her if she was sure, give her one last opportunity to tell him to stop, but then she was reaching for him, dragging his mouth back to hers. People had been second-guessing her her entire life. He wasn't about to do the same when she had made her desires clear.

Her hips rose again, grinding against him, and he groaned when he felt her already ready for him. If there was still any question about whether she was sure, it was gone now. Sitting back, he slid his hands beneath her, lifting her ass and angling her hips before sliding in, and by the gods. She had said she hadn't taken many lovers, but he hadn't been prepared for exactly what that meant. She was so godsdamn tight and warm around him that he was biting down on a curse.

Ashtine reached up, her thumb smoothing along the crease between his brows. "Are you well?"

He nodded, choking on his huff of laughter because it was such an Ashtine question in this moment, and he was more than all right. "I just need a moment. Are *you* all right?"

She smiled, her fingers sliding down his torso and making his stomach cave at her touch. "I am happy with my choice to both stay here and share a bed with you."

Fuck, he couldn't focus on what she was saying or how she was saying it with her fingers tracing the indents of his abdomen, let alone his cock being buried inside her. He hoped this wasn't one of her veiled sayings with layers of meaning because all he could do was say, "I'm glad you stayed too, Ashtine," before he curled over her, covering her body with his and kissing her slowly.

Another groan clawed up his throat when he moved excruciatingly slowly, but if he moved too fast, this would be over just as quickly. He could feel the perspiration on his nape and chest, and it had nothing to do with the summer heat. This was all the princess beneath him as she wrapped her arms around his shoulders, pulling him closer still and rolling her hips in a way that ground her center against him.

Briar buried his face in the crook of her neck, kissing and sucking as she stroked her nails down his back. He thrust into her lazily, giving her the time needed to get to the same place he was. When her movements started growing desperate, he reached between them, circling and rubbing at her center until her breaths were short gasps and her nails were digging into his flesh. That was when he finally let himself take what he'd been desperate for.

It didn't take long when his thrusts were deep, fast strokes, and she buried her face in his chest as he held her close, finding his own release. He'd expected this to be good. Their odd connection was too intimate for it not to be, but he hadn't expected . . .

He simply hadn't expected this.

That was all he could think after they'd both cleaned up and were back in bed. Ashtine curled into him, her head on his shoulder. He wrapped an arm around her, tucking her in impossibly closer and pressing a kiss to the top of her head.

"Briar?" she asked in a sleepy murmur.

"Yes, my dear?"

"The winds . . ."

She sighed into him, her breath coasting across his bare chest, and he traced his fingers along her arm.

"Tell me, Ashtine," he urged.

"They speak of a prince of water falling."

His movements paused, and she stiffened against him. "I upset you. I apologize."

"No," he said, resuming the soothing strokes of his fingers. "I am not upset. I am told the winds speak of past, present, and future. Perhaps they speak of my father. Or a prince in another realm."

"And if they do not?"

"We will go mad trying to figure it out," he answered, pressing a kiss to her brow when she looked up at him. "Did we not agree to take trials as they come?"

"We did," she answered. "But that does not quiet the worry."

"Worrying about something that may not even come to pass steals joy from the present."

"Perhaps," she murmured.

She was asleep before she breathed another word, and he certainly wouldn't wake her when sleep came easily after months of insomnia. And as the first light of day filtered into the room, he sent a message to his Court telling them not to expect him for meals today.

CHAPTER 12
ASHTINE

She'd been in the Water Court for four days.
Four days since she'd been home.
Four days since she'd walked among the winds.
Four days of a peace she had never thought she'd know again.

Her days were spent in Briar's rooms or on the shores of the sea. Her nights were spent in Briar's bed, both pleasure and rest being found.

She shifted on the sofa she was lounging on as she remembered waking to Briar's head between her thighs that morning, a soft smile forming. Then that smile widened as she realized she had smiled more in the last four days than she could remember doing in the last four years.

Briar was also making sure she wasn't only fulfilled intimately, but physically as well. She slept soundly next to him, and he made sure she was eating. There always seemed to be food available no matter if they were in his rooms or on the beach, and she'd finally been given the opportunity to try these oysters he hoarded. She'd decided he could keep those for himself, but she did enjoy the food of the sea, particularly the fresh fish they had for dinners. Their cuisine in the north tended to be more fowl and animals of the earth.

Ashtine readjusted the book she was reading where it rested against her bent knees. Briar had secured texts from the Fire

Court library, and she had been leisurely reading through them the past few days. Briar, of course, had things to tend to, but he never left her alone for long. However, they'd agreed to gradually make his absences longer in the hope that she and the winds could come to an . . . understanding. She had been hesitant, but he'd reassured her she only needed to send a wind message and he would return immediately should they become too unrelenting.

The first day of this had been . . . taxing. The winds sought her out, and she'd had to summon Briar more than once. Then it had become a battle of wills, hers versus the winds that had controlled her for centuries. Even now she could feel them drifting around her, wanting to come closer. She lifted a hand, air swirling in her palm and pulling more wind towards her.

Breaking laws of old angers more than just gods of past, they whispered.

There are dozens of realms. They will care little for this one, she replied, turning the page of the book.

Tempting fate tips the balance.

Allies will stand on separate sides.

A prince of water will fall.

She tensed, wondering if they would continue, but the winds curled around her, flowing through her hair, before letting her be.

A slow give and take.

Testing limits.

That was what they were learning.

Briar's Inner Court were the only ones who knew she was staying here. She and Briar had discussed it over a midday meal that first day. They'd woken when the sun was high, and he'd retrieved a silk robe the color of the sea for her to wear while he'd simply donned pants. A spread of food was waiting for them, and they discussed how to move forward. They agreed to keep it a secret for now, not wanting more turmoil among the Courts. More than that, if war was truly coming, this was not the time to push against long-standing traditions. But if she were staying here for an extended period, his Inner Court needed to know, especially if they were venturing down to the water.

Sawyer was her escort whenever Briar could not be with her, and they'd formed the start of a friendship of sorts. At least, she thought that was what it was. He was like his brother in so many ways, and despite his words at the Wind Court, Sawyer never brought up disclosing the relationship again. He was carefree and jested as much as Briar, but he was astute and observant. She suspected he knew more than he let on about many things.

That was why when the knock sounded, she assumed it was Sawyer or Neve. She did not expect Briar to come through the door, and she certainly did not expect Ermir to be with him.

You could not warn me of this? she demanded of the winds.

But they were silent.

Traitors, she muttered, to which she felt them kiss her cheek before moving on again.

"You are well?" Briar asked, coming to a stop beside her as she closed the book and set it aside.

"Yes, thank you," she answered, immediately standing and falling into her role of princess. Admittedly, a role she had been enjoying the reprieve from. "Is there news I need to be aware of?"

"Relax, my dear," Briar answered, his hand running the length of her spine and instantly making her tension ease. "Ermir wishes to speak with you, but only if you are amenable to that."

"Of course," she answered, glancing at her Second. But Briar was gently taking her chin between his thumb and forefinger, turning her back to him. She felt a shield slip into place around them, keeping their words for their ears alone.

"If you need more time or do not wish to do this right now, simply say the word," he said.

"I cannot avoid him nor my duties for days on end, Briar," she answered. "This is one of those things we must learn to navigate."

"You are not meek, Ashtine Evermorn. You are their sovereign, and while you indeed have a duty to your people, your Inner Court answers to you. Do you understand?"

She smiled softly up at him. "I do."

He held her gaze a moment longer before releasing her chin and letting his shield disperse. Stepping back from her, he added, "You know what to do should you need me."

Ashtine nodded, looking at her Second once more. He was waiting patiently near a window, his hands clasped behind his back. He did not look upset or worried, only calm and welcoming, as she had always known him to be.

The door clicked shut behind Briar, and she smoothed her hands down her dress. It was nothing like what she wore at home. Neve had brought her clothing, and this teal dress was lightweight and revealing. Sleeveless, it dipped low in the front, reaching halfway to her navel, with the same in the back. The fabric was partially sheer in some areas, and slits up the sides allowed for air movement in the oppressive summer heat.

Ashtine cleared her throat lightly before saying, "I apologize for my extended absence."

Truth be told, she hadn't expected him to come looking for her. It wasn't uncommon for her to disappear among the winds for days on end. Although perhaps four days was pushing it.

"It is I who should be apologizing to you, Prin— Ashtine," Ermir said, regret filling his features. "May we sit?"

"Of course," she answered, perplexed by his admission as she reclaimed her spot on the sofa.

Ermir took an armchair across from her, the low-lying table laden with plates of food situated between them. He glanced at the plates, then back to her. "You have been eating. I am relieved to see that."

She was unsure how to answer that, so she simply folded her hands in her lap. "May I inquire what you feel the need to apologize to me for?"

Never one to skirt around what needed to be said, Ermir shifted in his chair. "I should have handled all of this differently. I observed your mother battle the same persistent winds, and I felt just as helpless then."

Ashtine looked away at the mention of her mother. The one person who would have had the capacity to truly understand what these last months, years, and decades had been like.

"Ophelia managed the winds as gracefully as you do, even before she learned how to live in harmony with them," Ermir went on.

"There has been nothing graceful about how I have managed the winds in my years of life," Ashtine replied. "I have allowed them to control me and drive me mad."

"You did the best with what you were given," Ermir countered gently. "That is all anyone could ask of you."

She met his silver stare at his words. "Much is asked of me because of both my title and my gifts."

"I know, Ashtine. You were born with the weight of ruling from the moment you entered this world, and I . . ." He released a harsh breath, shifting once more. "I tried to shield you from so much. I wanted you to experience life before you were thrust onto a throne, but time was not on our side."

Ashtine nodded. She knew this. Knew that all Ermir had done when raising her was trying to not only prepare her for her role but also keep her from expectations as long as he could. There was no preparing her for battling the winds, though, let alone finding a way to love them. For a time, she had. Ermir and others made sure to constantly tell her how special her gifts were.

"You said my mother eventually found a way to live in harmony with the winds," Ashtine mused, forcing herself not to break her stare with Ermir.

"She did," her Second answered, relaxing back into his chair some and crossing one leg over the other. "As you know, unions are traditionally arranged for the Court Royals. Your mother was no different. Ansel was a powerful Wind Fae. It was a union planned from birth despite them not joining in marriage until Ophelia was well into her second century of life."

"I know of this history," Ashtine cut in. "What I do not know is how she harnessed the winds."

Ermir smiled at her sharp tone. "There is much of her in you. The grace and poise, but the tenacity and authority as well. Know she would be proud of you, Ashtine. So incredibly proud."

She swallowed against the emotion threatening to spill from her eyes, but she remained silent, waiting for him to answer her question.

His smile faded, that same regret filling his features as before when he said, "I have always known how to calm the winds that plague you."

Ashtine was on her feet before she realized she had moved. Wind tore through the sitting room, sending books and food to the floor. Her feet weren't even on the ground. "And you have held your tongue for decades?" she demanded. "Despite seeing me slowly succumb to madness?

"Let me explain," Ermir rasped, and it was only then that Ashtine noted her raised hand and realized she was cutting off his air supply. He was strong, but she was more so.

She immediately dropped her hand. "My apologies," she said tightly, her toes making contact with the marble floor.

"Do not apologize to me. You have every right to be angry with my actions."

"You made . . ." She rolled her lips, trying to figure out how best to word what she was feeling. "You made me feel meek and inadequate for my role, Ermir. You made me feel as though I was failing my Court when my concerns were continually dismissed."

"They were never dismissed, Ashtine. We wished to take some of that burden from you, not laden you with more. However, despite our best intentions, we see our actions were misguided. Please sit and let me explain."

"I do not wish to sit," she snapped.

Ermir nodded, folding his hands as he spoke again. "Your mother found harmony with the winds after she and Ansel were united."

"You are saying I must find a partner? Wed? That is a ludicrous statement, Ermir," Ashtine said.

"You misunderstand," he answered, shaking his head. "I have told you many times that while their union was planned, your parents eventually came to care deeply for one another. She found a haven in Ansel, and he did for her what none of her Inner Court had ever been able to achieve. She often said the winds were quieter when he was near. Over time, I witnessed your mother find a balance with the winds. I do not know her secrets beyond that. I wish I had wisdom to impart, but I do know that when their chattering became relentless, she and Ansel would disappear for days at a time." He smiled softly. "Albeit, not to the sea."

Ashtine had slowly lowered back to the sofa while he spoke, and now her fingers curled around the edge of the cushions.

"You believe Briar is this person for me? You believe . . . We cannot be together, Ermir," she said, voicing the concern that was old as time itself.

"I am centuries older than you, Ashtine, but my senses are just as sharp. I know well what has been happening here."

"Well, yes, but one could assume it was simply physical needs being met," she replied, not meeting his gaze.

"I believe fate brings some people into our lives for a reason," Ermir answered. "I believe Prince Briar is one of those people, and I believe you owe it to yourself to learn what that reason is. If a relationship with him for a time is what you need to learn that reason, then that is your choice to make."

"Why did you not tell me of my mother sooner?" Ashtine asked after several quiet moments.

Ermir sighed again. "I did not wish for you to search for another simply as a means to an end," he answered. "Did I hope that one day your union would bring you the same reprieve? Of course, but I did not want to push you towards such a thing when you were already overwhelmed with omens and duties. Perhaps you will find that same reprieve with another in the future, but if you can find it with Prince Briar for now, I cannot fault you for that."

She mulled the words over. The thought of finding another did not sound appealing, but surely that was simply because this was so new. Something forbidden made it all the more exciting, and perhaps Ermir was right. She and Briar had discussed not worrying about future trials until they came to pass. And while they certainly needed to think about the future, that didn't need to keep them from enjoying the present. They both knew this could not last forever. They both understood this was only for a time, and Briar had promised he would always be there for her, with her, whether they were lovers or simply friends. But she would never regret this and what they had found together.

That was what she told herself later that night as they lay next to each other, both having found their pleasure again. He was on his side, head propped on his fist, while his other hand traced along her bare skin. Down her arms, up her sides, along her breasts. They'd enjoyed a quiet dinner tonight on his veranda, but she needed to return to the Wind Court tomorrow. It was time.

"Tell me what worries you carry, my dear," he murmured, leaning down and brushing his lips along her cheek.

"They are too vast to speak in one night," she answered. "And I do not wish to spend my final night here speaking of them."

"Final night does not seem accurate."

Ashtine frowned. "I already told you I must return home when the sun rises."

"If you think we shall not have another night together, you are mistaken. It may not be the next night, but I already swore to steal any time with you I can. Do not make me a liar, Princess Evermorn," Briar replied, nipping at her shoulder before dragging kisses along her throat.

She huffed a laugh, lifting her chin to give him more access. "I cannot simply come to the Water Court at will, Briar."

"Of course you can. I have altered my wards. You can wind walk or portal here whenever you desire."

"And you can portal north just as easily," she countered.

He lifted his head to meet her gaze. "You wish for me to stay with you? In the Wind Court?"

"I know you are delicate in the cold, but I can secure wool socks for you," she replied, running her fingers along his muscled chest.

Briar barked a laugh. "Are you teasing me?"

"I am attempting it," she answered. "Did I do so correctly?"

Another laugh fell from his lips as he brought them to her own. "You did, my dear. You absolutely did."

CHAPTER 13
BRIAR

Several Months Later

"You cannot charge the Earth Court more for your services," the Fae Queen said from the head of the table.

"Why not? He charges our Court more for his services for obtaining Marks," Cyrus replied.

Briar rubbed at his brow. He had to give Cyrus credit. Going head-to-head with Talwyn Semiria was a bold choice in its own right, but he was handling her well. He supposed this was why he was the Fire Court Second. The fact that he was the one here arguing with her rather than the Fire Prince himself had been a sore subject from the start of this meeting.

"You have your own Fae to give Marks," Talwyn said with a sneer.

"Good thing Eliza isn't here for that statement," Sawyer muttered under his breath, and Briar was inclined to agree. He was certain that Nakoa was talking the Fire General down at this very moment, but he threw a warning look at the glass of water in front of him. Nakoa and Neve were on the other side, watching the proceedings, and Eliza was with them.

"Perhaps if the Fire Prince would bother to show up to a meeting, he could negotiate properly," Prince Azrael said, staring down his nose at all of them from his place at Talwyn's right.

Glancing up, Briar caught Ashtine's stare where she sat across from him, straight and poised. Nasima was at her shoulder, and the princess tilted her head, clearly hearing the winds.

She'd learned much these past months, and they made it a point in their stolen time together to give her time to practice the balance with the winds rather than simply letting them have their way with her. He'd learned much too. Communicating with her was getting easier, but it still took conscious effort. Learning what made her body hum, however, was a different story.

"Do fees need to be decided today?" Ashtine asked, looking away from him and at her queen. "The weapons have not been created yet. Perhaps that should be the primary focus."

"And who is funding these weapons if fees are not decided beforehand?" Cyrus demanded. "Furthermore, the Earth Court creates their own weapons. Why do they need those of the Fire Court?"

"This argument is trying and old," Ashtine lilted. "Fiera steel is only found in your Court, just as skystone is only found in mine. This war already brings division. Adding to it will only serve defeat and death."

Cyrus made a face telling Briar he had no idea what she meant by that, but Briar knew.

"I believe the Wind Princess is saying that we should be working together rather than finding more reasons to bicker among ourselves," Briar supplied. "This coming war will divide the realm enough, and we will not survive it if we cannot figure out some way to find peace among ourselves."

"Then perhaps the Fire Prince should be attending these meetings instead of sending his Second and Third," Talwyn gritted out. Her gaze slid to Cyrus, winds stirring around her and energy sparking off the silver bracelet coiled around her wrist. "Tell him that should he ignore my summons again, I will collect him myself."

"With all due respect, your Majesty, you are queen of the Eastern Courts, not yet of the Western Courts," Rayner replied, his voice deep and solemn.

"I will talk to Sorin," Briar cut in. "In the meantime, I think we move forward with all Courts producing weapons. Fees can be discussed when we reconvene. Sawyer and I will have a better idea of how many weapons can be imbued at the Springs in a given time period by then. We can also begin the inter-Court trainings."

Talwyn looked at Ashtine. "You are still amenable to your forces training with the Water Court?"

"I have no feud with the Water Court that needs to be considered," Ashtine replied.

"Right," Talwyn muttered. "Do you need assistance working out those details?"

"That is not necessary."

"Great. Anything else, or are we done here?" Talwyn demanded.

When no one spoke, she stood, Azrael and Ashtine standing with her. The three of them left the meeting room, and Briar pushed out a long breath. That could have been worse.

"Can I get a portal, Drayce? I need to go punch Sorin in the godsdamn dick for making me deal with this today," Cyrus said.

"Tell him I will visit tomorrow," Briar answered, conjuring a water portal.

Cyrus waved him off as he and Rayner stepped to their Court.

Turning to his brother, Briar started to speak, but Sawyer cut him off. "I will keep watch and give you as much time as I can."

They left the room together, taking the familiar paths through the White Halls. But when they reached the main foyer, Briar slipped down a corridor used by the staff. She was already waiting for him, a small swirl of wind at her fingertips.

"How do you fare, Briar?" Ashtine asked, head tilting back as Briar never slowed, walking right into her space.

He didn't answer. He only took her face in his hands and kissed her soundly. His tongue dipped between her lips, desperate and wanting. He'd been waiting for this moment all day. She hadn't been in his bed for over three weeks.

"Not nearly as well as I will be after tonight," he answered when he finally broke the kiss. "Our plans remain?"

"They are unchanged," she agreed, hands slipping from his shoulder and falling to his chest.

"Thank the gods," he replied, before capturing her mouth with his once more. His hands slid around her hips, gripping her thighs and hoisting her up. Pressing her against the wall, her legs wrapped around his waist. Each stroke of his tongue and caress of his hands made promises of what was to come tonight, and the small sounds coming from her told him she was as desperate as he was.

The warning dusting of flurries from Sawyer came far too soon, and he lowered Ashtine back to the ground, brushing the snowflakes from her hair. "Tonight?"

"Tonight," she agreed, brushing one more kiss to his lips.

She took a step back, but he caught her hand, sky-blue eyes finding his in the dim lighting.

"The winds? You are well?" he asked, studying her.

She smiled, a small, soft thing that only made him want to tug her back to him all over again. "They speak of a genesis."

"What does that mean?"

"I suppose time will tell," she answered. "Worrying about it now steals the joy from the moment."

His lips tilted up. "That is does, my dear."

"Be well, my heart," she said, and then she was gone among the winds.

And he was left counting down the hours until she flitted back into his rooms and wondering how long he would be content with stolen kisses and touches. But it was enough for now.

UNRELENTING WINDS BONUS EPILOGUE

Sometime in the Future

He was pacing in his rooms. Not even the gentle sound of the sea through his open balcony doors could soothe him right now.

Ashtine was supposed to be here nearly three hours ago. Granted, this wasn't entirely unusual. They both got caught up in one thing or another, making them late for their far too infrequent meetings these days. He would have sent a note by now. Ashtine, on the other hand, probably hadn't even realized just how late she was. The worry was likely for nothing, but here he was, worrying nonetheless.

He was debating sending his own note after another thirty minutes slipped by when the cry of a hawk reached him. His stomach sank in relief, but it was short-lived when Nasima appeared alone.

When no silver-haired beauty followed her.

The silver hawk swooped into the room through the balcony doors, gliding to the back of a chair where she perched. Large, round eyes stared at him, her beak clicking in admonition. As if he should already be somewhere else.

He took a step closer, reaching out a hand to slide his fingers over soft feathers. "Where is she?"

Her head tipped to the side, examining him, and even after all this time, he still had to force himself not to fidget under the spirit animal's scrutiny.

"Is she with the winds?" He paused for a beat, then added, "Or at the Citadel?"

Nasima let out a screech at that, her wings flaring out before nestling against her body once more.

It was all he needed.

"Thank you," he said with a small bow of his head.

He moved to grab a cloak, the northern part of the continent experiencing the harsh winter months right now, as he debated where to portal to. Her rooms were where he usually went, but he doubted she was there. It was late, so there shouldn't be many roaming the Citadel, but their relationship was still a secret. If anyone other than Sion, Renly, or Ermir spotted him, he would need to explain the presence of another Court's prince sneaking around in the midnight hours.

He was still debating when Nasima let out another loud screech, the cry grating to his ears. Clearly, the time for weighing his options was over.

Summoning a water portal, he stepped into Ashtine's quarters, finding them empty as expected. He moved quietly through the bedchamber, pausing to listen for a beat, before continuing to the sitting room.

Renly quickly pushed to his feet from where he'd been seated in an armchair, relief visible as he took in the prince. "Nasima found you then," he greeted.

The worry Briar had been feeling increased tenfold at the words. It had been ages since they'd had to intervene and send Nasima to him. "What is wrong? Where is she?"

"Nothing is wrong yet," Renly said. "But it is a pattern we recognize."

"Where is she?" he repeated again, unable to keep the low growl from his voice.

"In the catacombs. Her usual room. Take the back stairs. You won't be seen," Renly answered. "Sion will meet you there to admit you into the libraries."

Briar was already moving, having traversed the hidden stairwells with Ashtine numerous times at this point.

"Prince Drayce," Renly called after him, and Briar paused, looking over his shoulder. "Noelle reported she has not eaten today."

Godsdammit.

"Send food down. I'll see to it," Briar replied, already moving once more.

His steps were quick as he descended the stairs all the way to the catacombs, and he found Sion in the hall, just as Renly had said. Not even the usual sentinels stood their guard at this door tonight.

"Prince," Sion said with a nod of his head. "Everyone is in bed. You shouldn't encounter anyone else," he continued, letting his magic identify him as he pushed open the heavy doors to allow him entry.

"Thank you, Sion," Briar replied. "Renly is having food prepared and sent."

"Noted."

Then he was rushing through the shelves and stacks of books until he came to the nondescript door. He knocked twice before pushing it open, Ashtine having murmured a distracted response.

And there she was, sitting on the edge of that worn plush sofa, books and scrolls scattered around her. Feet in wool socks. A cold cup of tea off to the side and an uneaten meal in the corner. She didn't even look up as she turned the page of a book, and then seemed to compare it to something on the scroll.

"It's cold here, my dear," he said, leaning back against the closed door and smiling as she jumped at the sound of his voice. "It's why we agreed to meet in my Court tonight."

"Briar," she breathed, rushing to stand, then stilling to look helplessly around at all the texts scattered about. "I am late?"

"Only by a few hours," he replied with a wink.

"That cannot be true."

Briar arched a brow.

"I mean, it *can* be true, but it seems unlikely," she amended, her eyes darting from him to the clock on a shelf. "Oh."

His smile fell then, and he moved deeper into the space, coming to a stop before her. He took her shoulders, gently running his palms down the length of her arms and back up again. "I am told you have not eaten today. Why did you not summon me if the winds have been—"

"It hasn't been the winds," she interrupted with a soft sigh, pulling from his touch and lowering back to the sofa.

He followed, settling beside her with their thighs pressing together as he reached to tuck her hair behind her ear. "Then what is keeping you from me, my dear?"

Her eyes fluttered closed at his touch, and he gave her a moment to breathe deeply. "Talwyn grows more insistent about this weapon with each passing day."

"She is pressuring you on this?" he demanded, working to keep his voice even. "The Oracle told *her* of the weapon. Not you, Ashtine. It is ultimately her responsibility."

"Yes, but I am her Third, and more importantly, I am her friend. I wish to be of aid to her. She is suffering more than she lets on."

"I am not dismissing your noble intentions," he said gently. "But just like with the winds, Talwyn's claims on your time cannot overtake your own wellbeing. You need to eat. And rest. And not miss important meetings."

She huffed a laugh at that, turning to him. "I apologize I lost track of the hours."

"No need," he replied. "We will make the most of what time we have left tonight. Renly is sending food."

As if in summoning, there was a knock before the door opened and Sion appeared, a tray in hand. Relief flashed across his face when his gaze fell on his princess, and he turned to swap the tray with the old one.

"You are well, Ashtine?" he asked when he faced them once more.

"We are. Thank you, Sion," she replied with a nod.

The male's gaze slid to Briar, and he gave him a slight nod. Sion left, and Briar stood to retrieve the plates of food. Small portions of roasted lamb and potatoes, bread and honey-glazed carrots. He wasn't remotely hungry, but he picked at his food anyway as Ashtine ate, telling him of her research in between bites. When her food was nearly gone, he slid more of his onto her dish. He was sure she knew, but she said nothing.

When both plates were nearly emptied and set back on the tray, Ashtine settled into his side, her feet tucked under her. A comfortable silence fell between them while Briar dragged his fingertips up and down her arm.

He hummed softly. "If Sorin weren't in such a dark place right now, I would tell him of our relationship so I could take you to the hot springs within the Fiera Mountains."

She tilted her face up to him. "There are hot springs there?"

He nodded. "They are divine. One of the few things I like more about the Fire Court. One would think the Water Court would have hot springs."

"There are no mountains in the Water Court," she reasoned. "And they are the Fire Court. It does make sense that they would have them."

He grunted his disagreement.

"I wonder if they are similar to the ones within the cliffs," she mused.

Briar stilled. "What?"

Her brow creased. "I do not know how to make that statement clearer."

He swallowed his huff of laughter. "I did not know there were hot springs within the Shira Cliffs."

She nodded. "They are quite lovely."

"And why haven't we visited them?"

Her lips turned downward. "It simply never occurred to me."

He gently extracted her, getting to his feet and reaching for her hand. "Then let's go."

"Now?" she questioned, but letting him pull her up anyway.

"I don't see why not."

"It's the middle of the night, Briar."

"And neither of us is sleeping, Ashtine."

"Obviously," she grumbled, and he loved these moments. The moments when she could grumble. When it was just her and him. Not a prince and princess. Not rulers. Just the two of them with something they were keeping hidden from the world lest the realm tarnish it.

Briar squeezed her fingers in his palm. "Shall we?"

A smile graced her lips, and they quietly crept from the small room, making their way out to the hall where Ashtine could conjure a wind portal. A moment later they stood in a cavern, moss and flowers scattered along the floor and walls, and strands of ivy draped along the ceiling. And just as she'd said, a large pool stretched out before them, steam rising from the surface. The air was thick with humidity, and he immediately set his cloak aside.

Turning to Ashtine, he said, "Remind me why you have never brought me here before?"

She smiled, bending down to remove her wool socks and placing them with his cloak. "I often forget it exists. I rarely have time to visit."

"We will have to remedy that," he said, stripping off his tunic and toeing off his boots.

Ashtine was already at the water's edge, walking through the edge of the warm water. "Ermir would bring me here from time to time when I was a child. But as I got older and my responsibilities increased, those visits became less and less. Until eventually, they simply . . . ceased. I didn't even notice." She turned to face him once more, opening her mouth to speak more, but her eyes went wide. "You are naked," she blurted.

He smirked because she wasn't wrong. He'd stripped down completely. If they were going to get into that pool together, he wanted her to be naked as well.

Closing the distance between them, he reached for the skirt of her dress, pausing. But she only lifted her arms, letting him slide the garment over her head. A moment later, she was as bare as he was, and he held her hand as they waded into the water until it covered her chest and lapped at the base of his. Skimming his palm along the surface, the water gently eddied and swirled around them.

Her hair still piled on her head, she moved out further until she was swimming rather than touching the bottom, and she turned back to look at him. "How does this compare to the hot springs in the Fiera Mountains?"

"A thousand times better," he answered without hesitation, following her path.

"They are that different?"

"The ones here include a naked princess."

She laughed, the lilting sound a beautiful melody to his soul. He reached out, finding her hips and tugging her into him. Her legs wrapped around his waist, soft parts of her pressed against hard planes of him. Her arms wound around his neck, and then she was kissing him, letting him taste what he'd been craving for weeks.

This was worth the secrets and the sneaking around. This was worth the late nights and meetings under the stars. But there was a part of his soul that was getting restless. Not to leave her. No, if anything, it was becoming clearer and clearer with each day that would never be an option.

She pulled back, pressing her brow to his, and her breaths quick as they both sucked in air. Her fingers toyed with his hair, and those piercing sky-blue eyes held his.

"Someday things will change," she lilted.

"I know," he answered.

"I fear what those changes may hold."

"We don't worry about it now."

"Sometimes that is not possible, despite best efforts."

"I know," he said again, brushing his lips along her cheek. "I am trying to find a way."

She leaned back to see him better. "You are?"

"I refuse to believe what we have is a mere coincidence," he answered, pulling her with him as he swam closer to the edge. "And I refuse to lose something we both deserve to have."

"Briar, we can't—" She paused, clearly trying to phrase whatever she wanted to say correctly. "We both knew what this was going into it."

"That's just the thing, my dear," he replied, pressing his back to the stone wall of the spring. "I don't think either of us knew what this would become going into it."

"But we did. We agreed," she insisted.

"I distinctly remember us agreeing to not knowing what this was. That we would discover it together," he said, his mouth finding her neck, gently kissing and sucking.

"That is true," she breathed.

"And I've discovered that I will fight for us to keep this happiness we've found," he murmured against her skin. "If you will do the same."

Her head tipped back, and he cradled it in his palm as his lips moved higher.

"Yes," she sighed, melting into him, and her pleasure pulling her under. "If we can find a way, I would wish to keep this forever, my heart."

There was no more talking then as kisses turned into more. As hands roamed and primal needs took over.

But she'd given him permission to find another way, and he wouldn't stop until they could keep this forever.

AN EXCLUSIVE Q & A WITH MELISSA K. ROEHRICH

CAUTION: CONTAINS PLOT SPOILERS FOR LADY OF DARKNESS SERIES

Q: What was your main inspiration for the *Lady of Darkness* series?

A: *Lady of Darkness* was born in a time when I was battling darkness of my own. We had lost two girls in second-trimester losses in successive pregnancies, and I was broken. But we can't stay broken when we have families and jobs and responsibilities. We keep going through the motions, trying to survive. I needed someone to tell me that it was okay if all I did some days was survive.

I've always been an avid reader, but that escape wasn't enough anymore. So I started writing. It became my escape, and my place to process my own grief and trauma. Scarlett and crew saved me in more ways than one, and it's because of them I learned that darkness isn't such a bad thing once you learn to befriend it.

Q: What was the first scene you wrote?

A: I truly don't remember what the first scene was that I wrote. I do know it was banter between Scarlett and Sorin. *Darkness* and *Shadows* were written at the same time, and then split into two books. Nuri, Cyrus, and Eliza weren't even in the first drafts.

Can you imagine? Obviously the story grew quite a bit from those first words.

Q: You write from the perspectives of so many different people. Do you find any particular characteristics trickier to write? The softer types like Ashtine, as opposed to the more assertive types—of whom there are plenty in the series?

A: Yes and no. Talwyn was hands down the hardest to write in the *Darkness* series. I absolutely loved her character arc. It is one of my favorite arcs I've written to this day, but when I write those POVs, I'm deep in their feels and in their minds. I knew her motives, knew the mistakes, knew the guilt and the anger. Making sure that's conveyed while still staying true to their character can be challenging.

Oddly enough, Briar was also somewhat challenging to write because that male has zero red flags. Haha!

Q: Is there a difference in writing male and female characters?

A: I actually prefer to write male characters and find them easier to write. I don't really know why. I've never been able to pinpoint a reason. I think it's just a personal preference at this point.

Q: The world building in the *Lady of Darkness* series is incredible, with so much backstory that readers learn with each new book. How much of these intricacies did you know when you started writing *Lady of Darkness*?

A: I had the main continent completely mapped out and knew where all the territories were, the strengths/weaknesses of each, etc. But I really enjoyed slowly building the world and expanding it with the reader as we went on the journey. I knew the backstories of our main characters, but the side characters told me their stories when they were ready. (And some of them demanded POVs. Looking at you, Cyrus . . .)

Q: Are any of the characters based on you or anyone you know?

A: I wish I knew some Fae to base them on! But no, none of them are based on anyone I know. However, all of my characters have little pieces of me sprinkled in, some more than others. My main goal is to make them diverse and ensure they each have their own personality.

Q: If the *Lady of Darkness* series was made into a film, who would you cast as the central characters?

A: I laughed when I read this question because my team and readers ask me this all the time, and I truly have no idea. I don't watch much TV or movies, and I don't follow celebrities closely, so I really can't fancast the characters because I don't really know who anyone is. Haha!

Q: The series has some weighty, dark moments, especially Mikale and Alaric's treatment of Scarlett. How did it feel to get this out of your head onto paper?

A: When I'm writing, I'm deep in the mind and headspace of the characters, and it definitely affects me. It's something I've had to make a conscious effort to monitor, especially in the beginning of a series when the characters are experiencing all the major trauma, grief, etc. I feel their depression, angst, anger—whatever it may be—on a soul-deep level. While working through that on paper with them is cathartic, I always have to be mindful of my own mental health while doing so and making sure those feelings of helplessness, hopelessness, intense anger, etc. don't bleed over into other areas of my life.

Q: Which authors do you like to read?

A: I don't read nearly as much as I did before I started writing, but that doesn't mean I don't have around nine bookshelves packed full of books! The list of authors is endless, from trad to indie. I'm also a complete mood reader, so that very much dictates what I pick up at any given moment. I can't read fantasy when I'm deep in a writing project, but in between books, I usually devour a few. I'm in between projects right now and have books by Shannon Mayer, Miranda Lyn, LJ Andrews, Mikayla Hornedo/Nelle Nikole, and Emma Hamm downloaded onto my Kindle.

When I'm deep in writing, my go-to is dark and gritty romance. I eat up that trauma and drama! Some of my recents have included CE Ricci, Penelope Douglas, Sierra Simone, and Harley Laroux. And sometimes, we just need a good contemporary romance or rom-com. You know? When nothing else is hitting, that's my go-to for a palate cleanser. TL Swan, Meghan Quinn, and Elle Kennedy always hit the mark for me.

Q: Can you name a few of your favorite books?

A: This is like asking me to pick a favorite child! So let's do a couple from each genre that I find myself rereading from time to time.

Fantasy/Romantasy- *Daughter of the Drowned Empire* by Frankie Diane Mallis and *Broken Souls and Bones* by LJ Andrews.

Dark/Gritty- *Don't You Dare* by CE Ricci and *Lords of Pain* by Angel Lawson/Samantha Rue

Contemporary- *The Risk* by Elle Kennedy and *Not Safe for Work* by Nisha J. Tuli

Q: Are there any authors or famous people that you have been influenced by?

A: Before I started writing seriously, I was flying through books left and right as an escape. I had picked up Jennifer L. Armentrout's *From Blood and Ash* series when only the first book was out, and while checking out her website, I stumbled upon some of her bio information. I learned she had a degree in psychology and left the profession to pursue writing. In her thirties. I was also in my thirties and looking for a drastic change. I looked at her career, a mix of traditional and indie published titles. I looked at what she had accomplished over the years, and that was the first time I truly believed I could pursue my own dreams of writing. In an odd way, seeing that success made me realize it was okay to "start over" in my career choice in my thirties. Now I say I was 36 when I figured out what I wanted to be when I grew up.

Q: Had you ever tried to write before putting pen to paper for *Lady of Darkness*?

A: I have always loved writing. I was the over-achiever in school who was done with her assignments well before deadlines. In class, when everyone else was working on those assignments, I was writing stories in notebooks. But then life happens, right? You do the things you're "supposed to do," and those dreams fall to the side. You convince yourself it would never be anything serious anyway. It wasn't until we were facing our own grief and trauma that I realized no one else was going to chase those dreams for me. It was something I'd always loved doing, and there was nothing really stopping me from pursuing it at this point. Even if no one ever read it, at least I could say I wrote and published a book. Nearly four years later, and here we are.

Q: What would you say is the best part of writing a novel?

A: Finishing it. Haha! But truly, I love writing the angst. It's my absolute favorite. The stakes are high. Emotions are intense. You know it's going to affect everything to come. Delicious!

Q: Were there points in the series where you felt that the characters were steering you to write something differently to what you'd planned?

A: Oh my gosh! All the time. The characters are the reasons I'm a "pantser" writer*. Every time I tried to plot out more than ten chapters at a time, it always changed because the characters do what they want. We might fight about it for a while, but they always win. (Spoiler alert: it always turns out better when I follow their plan.) One of the biggest examples of this is Sorin's death at the end of *Lady of Ashes*. That was NOT planned, and I will never forget sitting back after writing it, with tears streaming down my face, and thinking 'what the fuck just happened?' But it allowed us to explore that magic can't fix everything, and when it can, the cost is steep.

* Authors who write by the seat of their pants.

Q: How did you become inspired to write dark fantasy?

A: Frankly I was in a dark part of my life and that can be isolating and lonely, even with the best support surrounding you. Writing became an outlet to process those feelings and then it became something more. I wanted others to know they weren't alone in their darkness, and that it was okay to take the time to process. Mental health became something *so* important for me to include in my books, and navigating the hard things is part of that.

Q: If you could go back in time to when you first started writing the *Lady of Darkness* series, what advice would you give yourself?

A: I did *a lot* of research before publishing. Nearly two years of it, and even with all that, there are some things you can't learn until you just do the darn thing. I wouldn't change much of my journey, to be honest. But I would remind myself to keep writing the stories that are demanding to be told. Not the tropes or trends that are hot right now, but the stories I *want* to write. They'll find the right readers at the right time.

Q: Did you ever consider a different ending for Scarlett?

A: Nope. When I write a series, I always know how it's going to start and how it's going to end. It's all the in-between stuff I don't know until I start actually writing. Specifically in regards to Scarlett though, I knew she'd be powerful and keep that power, and I knew she'd become a World-Walker.

Q: Did you ever consider different love stories for the other characters?

A: Not necessarily different love stories, but there were stories I didn't have planned from the very beginning. Eliza and Razik, for example. While I always knew Cassius was gay, I didn't have his story with Cyrus drop into my head until I was writing *Ashes*. Some of them just naturally came together like Callan and Tava.

Q: What is your writing day like? Are you an early starter and get 1000 words out before breakfast?

A: It took me a while to figure out what worked best for me, but I've learned over the years that I write best right away in the morning and at night. Now, to be clear, I am *not* a morning person. But I am usually the first one up in my house, and that quiet hour or two, when I'm still in sweatpants with coffee by my side, tend to be pretty productive. I've also learned my ADHD does not let me focus on writing in the afternoon, so afternoons are reserved for back office things: answering emails, signing shop orders, etc. When I'm deep in a writing project, my family also knows that I retreat upstairs around 8pm for "nesting time." (Yes, that is really what they call it.) I usually get a few more hours of writing in while snuggled under a heated blanket, and many times, one (or all three) of my boys end up lying in there reading while I write.

Q: Are there any characters or scenes that were lost in the process as you were writing the series?

A: No characters lost, but definitely characters added. I also have a folder of deleted scenes. Some became bonus content down the road. Others are still there.

Q: What was your favorite book when you were a child?

A: *Where the Red Fern Grows* by Wilson Rawls. I read that book so many times, pages were falling out!

Q: Is there a book you've faked reading?

A: I can honestly say no to this question. I'm a pretty open book, and have no problem saying if I've read or not read a book.

Q: Do you ever buy books just for the cover? If so, can you name some covers that have inspired you to do this?

A: Um . . . *stares at nine bookshelves of pretty books*. I collect special editions, so a lot of those are on my shelf because of that. I recently grabbed Helen Scheuerer's *Iron and Embers* when I was in Australia because of the stunning edge design.

Q: Is there a book that changed your life?

A: I can't pinpoint any one book that I can say changed my life, but I can think of several that resonated with me. Bits and pieces from various books that shaped me, challenged me, or made me feel seen.

Q: Did you ever consider writing under a pseudonym?

A: I never did. I always said if I was putting in the blood, sweat, and tears, I wanted to see my name on the cover of that book. I also never expected my career to become what it has. There have been a few times I've questioned the choice, but I'm fairly certain I would still make the same choice if I had the opportunity to go back in time and change it.

Q: Can you name a book for which you are an evangelist and you think everyone should read?

A: This was actually kind of hard because everyone has different tastes, so to say *everyone* should read it is tough. But I will say *1984* by George Orwell is up there. I wrote a few papers on this book in college, and with history and the current state of the world, I think books like this are important ones that should never be lost.

Q: Which half of the reading world do you fall into: persevere and finish reading every book you've started or give up if it's not compelling enough?

A: I wouldn't necessarily call it giving up. I do set books aside if they're just not for me right now. As I said, I'm a huge mood reader, and I'm likely just not in the mindset for that book at the time. More than once, I've set a book aside for a few months and come back to it. However, there are also books I've simply never picked back up.

Q: What is the last piece of art (music, movies, TV, or more traditional art) that you've experienced that impacted you?

A: *Hamilton*. That whole production is simply phenomenal. We were studying the American Revolution at the time (we homeschool our boys), and we all watched it together. We were all entranced, and it allows for excellent discussion still to this day.

Q: What is your idea of THE perfect day, where you could go anywhere and meet anyone?

A: My perfect day involves NOT leaving or going anywhere. Haha! I am a complete introvert who loves to travel. But when I don't have to leave my house for a week? That is the dream! We live on a small hobby farm, and we're slowly turning it into an oasis. We added a hot tub last year, and this year we just put on a new deck. If we're not traveling, home is exactly where I want to be.

Q: If you had a spirit animal from the series which would it be and why?

A: This was a hard one! I'd like to say Ranvir because, well, he's a dragon, but honestly, I'm guessing it would be Maliq. Why? I have no idea. Probably because I *love* dogs, and snuggling our border collies is my favorite pastime. I'm pretty sure Maliq would let me snuggle him . . . maybe.

Q: You've written a lot of bonus material on the series for your fans online. When do the ideas for these come to you? Did you make a note of them when writing the series or much later?

A: Those are always written later. Bonus chapters for books are usually the new POV that is being added or a specific scene from another POV. Other bonus chapters are usually centered around a theme for a merch box we are putting together. I miss the characters just as much as readers do and getting to hop back into their world for a bit makes my soul happy.

Q: Will you do the unthinkable and tell us your favorite character from the series?

A: There is nothing unthinkable about this. It is 100% Razik. He's mine and inked on my skin.

Q: Do you believe that writer's block is a real thing?

A: I think it can be, but I learned that for me, writer's block comes when I don't know where I'm going. This is when I realized that while I'm a pantser writer, I do need to have a little direction. Through trial and error, I learned that if I have the next 5–10 chapters laid out, it keeps me on track when I get "stuck." This isn't extensive plotting. I have two marker boards, and I lie on the floor and list out POVs, along with two or three things that need to happen in that chapter. Then I number them in the order I need to write them so that when I get "stuck," I can look and see where we're going. That gives me a little direction of "we're here and need to get there. How are we doing that?" That little bit of a focal point usually helps me keep going.

Q: If you could be any character in the series, who would you be and why?

A: Eliza. See answer to favorite character above. Haha! But in all seriousness, Eliza just wants to read books, be left alone, and occasionally stab things. She's tenacious and blunt, but she also has the kindest heart if you can get through her layers. She's not afraid to stand up for herself and injustice, and her self-confidence is something I envy.

Q: Do you feel your writing process has changed over time?

A: Absolutely, but I think that's to be expected when it becomes your career. Writing started as an outlet for me. Something I did in my free time. Now, it's my job. Deadlines aren't just guidelines. More than that, I didn't have alpha readers or beta readers or an arc team when I started. As my books grew, I grew with them. It's been a lot of trial and error and learning as I go.

Q: If you could have any superpower, what would it be and why?

A: I thought about this long and hard, and I have to say fire. Mainly because I am always cold, and this way it wouldn't be an issue. Plus my coffee would always be hot.

Q: Has any book ever made you cry? If so, can you name the one that stands out?

A: Oh man. I am a crier. It doesn't take much. I will cry happy tears or sad tears. It doesn't really matter. But the last book I remember crying while reading was *Till Death* by Miranda Lyn.

Q: If you didn't write, what would you do for work?

A: When I first started writing, I was tutoring part time at the local dyslexia center. I would likely still be there. I loved that job so much, and my students were like my own kids. As my books have grown and my travels have increased, I had to step away from that. I still think about them nearly every day.

Q: In the *Lady of Darkness* series, what was the hardest scene to write?

A: Easily Sawyer's sacrifice for Ashtine and the twins. I was sobbing while writing that scene. I would write a sentence, then have to take a moment to get myself under control.

Q: How long on average does it take you to write a book?

A: I am a pretty fast writer once I get going. The plot and story simmers for a long time, usually months, if not years, while I'm working on other projects. By the time I sit down to write, I'm ready to go. My average time for writing a book from start to finish is three to four months, especially if we're within a series. The first book in a series takes me a little longer because I'm getting to know the characters.

Q: What is your deepest joy about writing?

A: When readers tell me that they felt seen in one of my characters. When I get the messages from a reader telling me that my books helped them through one of the darkest parts of their lives. When a reader messages me telling me they just lost a pregnancy because they know I understand and don't want to feel alone. When a reader tells me they decided to pursue their own dream of writing because of something I did or said. When a reader tells me that my books gave them the courage to face their own darkness.

When I published *Lady of Darkness*, I told myself if only one person reads it and realizes they are not alone in their grief and trauma, that it was all worth it. I've gotten *hundreds* of messages. I've cried with and hugged people at events. And this is my deepest joy about writing. My books aren't for everyone, but the ones they are for? The books find them at the perfect moment, and that is worth all the hard days.

I save all those messages in a special folder on my phone for those hard days. For the days when I stumble upon something not great on social media. For the days I'm struggling to get the words on paper. For the days I'm wondering if it's something I want to keep doing. Those messages and memories save me on the days I'm drowning. They pull me from the river, and I'm forever grateful.

Q: What are one or two of your favorite scenes from the books?

A: I LOVE the hedge maze scene in *Embers*. It was a little break from all the intensity of the book, and we got to see a little bit of all the characters. The banter and the competition was so fun to write. I also love anything that leans into Razik's dragon tendencies. The bowl was never meant to be a thing, but it definitely became one!

THE REAPER: A NOTE FROM THE AUTHOR

Oh man! Keeping *The Reaper* secret while I was writing it was SO HARD! Not even my alpha readers got sneak peeks until it was done (much to their dismay. Haha!) But I think it was worth the wait.

I knew there was no way I could ever fully tell Rayner's story within the *Darkness* books themselves, so when I first started to entertain some novella ideas, I immediately knew Rayner would have one. Our quiet, brutal, vengeful Ash Rider who has a soft spot for a little girl named Tula. One of the biggest questions I've gotten is: why is Rayner so attached to her? I hope by understanding his past, you understand his actions a little more. And how about those throwbacks to the Inner Court before they were even a thing? Writing about Cyrus, Sorin, and Rayner when they were first getting to know each other was some much-needed delight in the middle of Rayner's tragic past, because let me tell you, I was *sobbing* writing that last chapter when Aravis died!

Wishing you a day full of caffeine and dragons ~ Melissa

UNRELENTING WINDS: A NOTE FROM THE AUTHOR

This novella was born out of a love for two of our favorite royals, and it would not exist if you, the reader, hadn't fallen for them so dang hard. From Briar's gentle and patient ways to Ashtine's quirks and oddities, writing their story was a beautiful reprieve from the dark and grittiness of my usual books.

Remember you are more than your titles and duties, expectations and responsibilities. You deserve joy and happiness, even if it's in something you keep just for you.

XO ~ Melissa

* * *

Let's Stay Connected!

I'd love to keep in touch! You can find me in several places, but I'm most active in my Facebook reader group (Melissa's Dragon Cave), my Patreon (The Chaos Archives), and my Discord (The Chaos Cavern). To stay up-to-date on release dates, new series, and more, be sure and sign up for my newsletter, too!

WHERE TO FIND ME!

Website: www.melissakroehrich.com
Signed Books & Merch: www.mkrtreasureshop.com
facebook.com/melissakroehrich
instagram.com/melissa_k_roehrich
tiktok.com/@authormelissakroehrich

CAPTIVATED?
JOIN SCARLETT
FOR THE ENTIRE SERIES

Book 1: Lady of Darkness
Owned by a ruthless Assassin Lord, Scarlett Monrhoe and her two sisters have been trained since they were children to torture and take life. They are the most feared trio on the continent, but they are also wild and unpredictable.

Book 2: Lady of Shadows
Whisked away to the Fire Court, Scarlett Monrhoe finds herself in the hands of the man who killed her mother. The Prince of Fire. Thrust amongst the Fae Court she loathes, she is at their mercy. She doesn't know what plans he has for her, but she has plans of her own. She just hasn't decided how thoroughly she wants to break him yet.

Book 3: Lady of Ashes
Scarlett Semiria knew the cost of her actions the day she sacrificed everything to keep her family, her Courts, and her twin flame safe. At least she thought she did. When she discovers the cost was more than she could have ever anticipated, she finds herself once again forced to choose between saving innocents or saving the ones she loves. But this choice might just leave her so broken, even the stars won't be able to bring her back.

Book 4: Lady of Embers
When they met her, she was a whirlwind of shadows and darkness. Standing among the ashes of betrayal and grief, now she is a tempest of rage and malice. Queen Scarlett Aditya will hunt them all down, one by one, and make them pay. Starting with the one who took her brightest star from her.

Book 5: Lady of Starfire
Scarlett Sutara Aditya has finally learned the full cost to save her world and correct mistakes that are not hers, but she refuses to accept the fate that has been decided for her. Making demands of her own, she fights for her twin flame, her family, and the realm that balances on her destiny. She has always played games by her own rules, but this time, winning might cost her everything.

Book 6: Winds of Darkness
Two spellbinding novellas brought together and featuring some of the most loved characters from the Lady of Darkness series. In **The Reaper** we meet Rayner before he became involved with the Fire Court, when he was the center of a curse as punishment for his rebellion. In **Unrelenting Winds** the Wind Princess, Ashtine, requests the help of the Water Court Prince Briar. He must decide if helping her is worth risking the anger of the Fae Courts, the realms and the gods.

ONE PLACE. MANY STORIES

Bold, innovative and empowering publishing.

FOLLOW US ON:

@HQStories